Night
Blade

J.C. Daniels

Night Blade

By

J.C. Daniels

Copyright © 2012 Shiloh Walker

2013 Edition

Cover Art by Angela Waters

Editorial Work Sara Reinke

NIGHT BLADE

DEDICATION

Thanks to everybody who encouraged me to continue with Kit's story. Be warned…she's got a rocky road ahead of her. But I hope it's worth it in the end.

With love, always, to my husband and kids. You're my everything…thank God for you.

CHAPTER ONE

I am aneira.
My blade is strong.
Strong enough to handle a lot of things but not enough
to handle the four shifters who had been trailing me all day.
Cutting through the streets of East Orlando, I checked them
out again and sighed.

Wolves.

That was what was my gut said, although it was hard to
be one-hundred percent positive, considering I had to watch
them from my rear-view mirror and they were tucked away
inside their nice, shiny little luxury sedans.

East Orlando was lousy with weres. We had the wolf
pack, the cat clan, and over the past few months, rats had
been trickling back in. They'd been scarce in these parts for a
good six years, ever since the last nest had been wiped out.

I didn't know why the rats had decided to start moving
back in now, but that was a puzzle to solve later. Right now, I
had to get to my office. Once I was there, I'd feel better
about facing these guys and seeing just what in the hell they
wanted.

Whatever it was, they had to want it pretty damn bad,
because they had been tailing me since shortly before
lunchtime and it was nearly four now.

1

The office for Colbana Investigations, Inc. is officially Assembly of Non-Humans—or ANH—neutral ground and if the wolves got testy there, things would go bad for them. The ANH frowned when their members got involved in bloodshed on neutral territory. That was why we had it. So we could carry on business like civilized people.

Not that we were. Well, some of us were more civilized than others. I tried to be. Civility proved useful in my case, since I wasn't strong enough to separate a body from its body parts unless I used a sword.

Still, if those were the wolves, I was probably being paranoid for nothing. Wolves were nice and orderly and all about following rules. They drove BMWs and Audis. They kept to the speed limit; they used their turning signal and they let other people in when the traffic was tight.

Yeah, the wolves were all about courtesy.

If it had been the rats, the cars would be clean but simpler—none of them had been around long enough to drive cars that nice. Plus, they wouldn't be so damned patient, they wouldn't be following the speed limit and they for damn sure wouldn't have waited all day like this while I led them on a merry chase.

And they weren't cats. The cat clan had a better way of getting my attention.

I was probably worrying about nothing. Still, I had ended up on the wrong side of the shifters before. I believed in better safe than sorry.

Just in case, I had already thought through my options. The best one was out. His name was Damon, and he was…well, my boyfriend, I guess, although nobody who ever looked at Damon Lee would think *boy*.

He was Alpha of the cat clan and there had been a time when he had terrified me. Now, he alternately dazzled, delighted and pissed me off. On occasion, he dismayed me, too.

I couldn't rely on him. For a couple of reasons. He was out of town. That happened a lot lately. I also had problems

2

with turning to him every time a situation got dicey. It didn't matter if there were four shifters and just one of me. I'd been handling myself for a long time and I'd prefer to keep it that way, even if *that* pissed him off.

Best option: get to the office, activate the new wards I had paid for recently. Hope for the best.

* * * * *

It all turned out to be in vain.

I had just come off one fairly lucrative courier job. Having another fall into my lap was unexpected but here it was.

Staring at the soft-sided cooling unit for a long minute, I debated. Five thousand and expenses to take that thing and its contents to a pack in the Smokies and deliver a message. It was too easy.

There had to be a catch.

Lifting my head, I looked from one wolf to another. All of them were staring at me with variations of polite, bored smiles. All but the Alpha. His name was Alisdair MacDonald. A few select people were allowed to call him Dair.

I wasn't on that list.

MacDonald didn't look bored at all. He looked very interested in my answer. And although there was nothing threatening about his demeanor, I suspected he really, really wanted me to say yes.

I hated when alpha were-anything showed up in my office and expected me to say yes. Well, except for Damon. Some of the things *he* asked for, I was more than happy to say *yes* to.

"Before I even agree to discuss this, I have a question," I said, pulling out one of my knives and tossing it absently. I heard a grumble from one of the suits and I shot a look in his direction. "Calm down, beefcake. I think better when my hands are busy."

MacDonald chuckled. "Beefcake…really?"

3

"Well, he isn't wearing a nametag." I shrugged and shifted my attention back to MacDonald. "If I say no, or even if I do this job or *try* to do it and I screw up, you're not going to threaten to eat my kidneys or my heart or anything, are you?"

"Good heavens, no," he said, scowling. A look of utter distaste crossed his face. He narrowed his eyes as he moved forward a few more steps. I had the impression of a dog—maybe a wolf—sniffing at something it had discovered on the ground. "Why on earth would you ask that?"

"The last time I had an Alpha asking me to do a high-paying job, I ended up being told if I failed, I was dead." The job had ended up leading me down the road to Damon so all in all, I couldn't complain, but I was trying to learn more caution.

"I give you word as Alpha that the only thing I plan to do if you fail to complete the job is just not *pay* you."

"Fair enough." I put my knife away and leaned forward, staring at the red cooling unit that sat on the ground by the suit's feet. "So...what's in there?"

MacDonald nodded to Beefcake.

Beefcake was a less-impressive version of what Damon had sold the world. Lots of muscle, power and loyalty. Beefcake would kill me in a blink if his Alpha told him to. Or... unseal the unit and lift out two plastic-wrapped heads.

All without changing his expression or showing any sign of emotion.

Dead eyes stared at me from behind the sturdy wrap of plastic.

"Please tell me that isn't your idea of lunch for my roadtrip."

The muscle in the suit gave me a hard stare.

But MacDonald laughed. "No. That's your delivery. I want you to deliver those...and a message."

Suddenly, that big pile of money made a little more sense.

"What is the message?"

4

* * * * *

Five thousand wasn't enough. I pushed for ten. We settled on seven-five. I suspected that was what he had been willing to pay anyway.

Contracts signed, I agreed to head out immediately. He informed me that he had a rental car already waiting. I appreciated the courtesy. My car didn't need the extra miles, nor did I want to run the risk of those heads stinking it up.

"One final detail," MacDonald said as he rounded up his men. The only one not moving for the door was the pretty, dark-eyed woman seated in the corner. She wore a dove gray suit and had legs that made me wanna cry.

"Yeah?"

"I am aware of your relationship with the cat clan. While I don't foresee you encountering much difficulty on this job, I would be remiss in not taking into account your human...nature."

That was a polite way of telling me, *you're human and while nothing bad should happen, if it does, your ass is toast and I'll be in big trouble so I better make sure there's somebody here to take care of you.*

Ah, no, thanks.

I didn't bother telling him I wasn't human; I was half. He would see it as splitting hairs. Leaning back against the desk, I stroked the black leather bracer I wore on my left wrist as I studied him. "I'm handling a courier job. ANH law covers me fairly well and I'm pretty good at handling myself."

"Nevertheless, you'll have an escort." MacDonald smiled politely. "It's covered by the contract—the pack will see to any precautions deemed necessary. I consider this necessary."

I clenched a hand into a fist, glad it was covered by my desk. It wasn't my human *nature* that had him worried. It was my *cat* boyfriend and the fact that the cats outnumbered the wolves two to one in East Orlando. MacDonald was worried that if something happened to me, Damon would take it personally and come after his ass.

It was possible.

And I didn't care.

"I've been doing my job with my human *nature* for quite a while, MacDonald. I don't need your bodyguard. It's a fucking *courier* job," I said quietly.

Behind MacDonald, Beefcake made a grumbling noise in his throat. It was an odd sound—I was used to hearing grumbling, all right. Damon did that at me a lot. But this wasn't quite the same. I shifted my gaze away from MacDonald and focused on the wolf, staring him down.

I hadn't played the territorial, kowtowing bullshit with Damon. I wasn't doing it *now*. And Damon had been so much scarier.

The woman sitting in the chair laughed. "You know, it takes balls to try and stare down a werewolf."

"No. It just takes common sense," I said, not looking away from the wolf. "I'm not were. I understand the ANH charter—I can quote more than a lot of people *know*. I haven't done a damn thing wrong and he's in my place of business. He's got no reason growling at me unless he's pissed off that I used the word *fucking*. Now, I could be wrong, but I'm pretty sure it hasn't been outlawed to say the word *fucking* in front of the wolf Alpha."

I slid MacDonald a look. "Has it?"

He smiled. "No. It hasn't." He glanced over his shoulder. "Eddy...wait outside."

Beefcake stiffened. "Sir?"

"Wait outside. Relax. Megan is with me, after all."

I glanced over at the pretty brunette...Megan, I assumed. She smiled at me.

A moment later, the door shut and some of the roiling energy in the room eased off. Beefcake could still listen in on us, I knew. Wolves, like all shifters, had the ability to hear things no human could. I could hear pretty damn well, better than any human, but nowhere near as well as a shifter, though I could hear him out there pacing in front of my door.

"He doesn't like me," I said solemnly. "That makes me

sad."

Megan snorted.

MacDonald gave me a curious look. "Why are you trying to piss him off?"

"I'm not trying." I shrugged. "He came in here pissed off. I might as well have fun with it." I didn't bother elaborating. Damon probably could have explained it rather well. When I'm nervous or scared, I poke fun, prod and tug a tiger…or in this case, a wolf's tail. But I was also irritated. The guy had come into my office growling at me. It just rubbed me the wrong way.

Sighing, I looked from Megan to MacDonald, trying to figure a way out of this. A bodyguard for a *courier* job. This was ridiculous. "Look, the bodyguard thing…I appreciate the concern, but it's unnecessary. I've never once had a courier job go downhill."

"It's nonnegotiable," MacDonald said. He shrugged and flicked a piece of lint on his suit. "And you already signed the contract, Ms. Colbana. If you don't wish to take Megan with you, I can always send Eddy. Maybe the time together will make him like you more and you won't…be sad."

My lip curled.

Then I glanced at Megan.

She looked like a soccer mom.

Appearances were deceptive, I knew. The previous Cat Alpha had looked like a damn Barbie doll.

"Well. How strong are you?" I asked. "If you're going with me, you…"

Weres could hide how powerful they were. It took practice and control, and the stronger they were, the better they could hide it. Weaker ones didn't hide well, but they didn't need to. High level shifters could appear more human than I could—it was actually a pretty impressive sight. Sometimes I wondered if that wasn't where the phrase *wolf in sheep's clothing* came from.

In the blink of an eye, Megan went from soccermom to Supergirl powerful and I gulped as my tongue glued itself to the roof of my mouth. The entire time, she sat there smiling. All she'd done was drop the human act. She hadn't shifted. Hadn't moved. Hadn't done a blessed thing.

And my hand burned, itched and in the back of my mind, I could hear the music of my blade...*Call me...I am here...*

That's my most powerful magic. I'm bonded to my blade and nothing separates us.

But I didn't need her just because the soccermom werewolf was super scary. My hand was steady as I reached for my cup of coffee. It was lukewarm by now—didn't matter. I needed something to do with my hands, because my right one wouldn't stop itching and I wanted my blade no matter how much I knew it wasn't necessary.

"Well, you hide pretty well," I drawled. "Does he even *need* that suit out there?"

Megan laughed. "Oh, sure. Eddy has no subtlety to him. Everybody is so focused on him, they never notice me." She smiled, a small, deadly little smile. Her eyes locked with mine. "I'm the knife in the dark. You can probably appreciate that."

I made them leave me alone for five minutes.

Any time I left town, I called.

Damon hadn't asked me to, but it just seemed...well, like the thing to do.

As his phone rang, I stood there, staring at the cooling unit and pondering the grisly contents inside. I was hauling two decapitated heads across Florida, Georgia, South Carolina and into Tennessee. I'd have to stop somewhere for the night, too...there was no way I was driving through South Carolina at night.

Too much vamp activity there.

Still, it was easier than some of the jobs I'd had to do.

And *this* one wouldn't involve giant snakes, alligators or humans who decided to make target practice out of non-humans.

"Baby girl."

It was stupid that just the sound of it made me smile. But something about the way he said it, that endearment—one that *should* have been sexist as all get-out—made my toes curl inside the solid, sturdy boots I had on. "Hey, Damon."

Over the phone, I heard a grunt. Then something that sounded like a hiss and a whine.

"You're busy."

"Cleaning house," he said.

His version of cleaning house usually involved bloody fights and sometimes death. Scratch that... it *often* included death. He'd killed the previous Alpha, a pretty, plastic-looking piece by the name of Annette. She had looked like a Barbie doll, all big blue eyes, big round boobs and blonde hair and she had been one of the most brutal bitches I'd ever encountered in my life. And I've encountered more than my share.

Annette had ruled over the cat clan in East Orlando and the entire southern region with a tiny, iron fist for more than a century, well before the non-human population had been forced to come out of the proverbial closet. She'd also been certifiably insane. A few months ago, she'd hired me to find her nephew after he'd gone missing. If I failed to find Doyle, she'd kill me—I found that out *after* the fact. One of the reasons I was trying to learn caution.

At the end of it all, I found Doyle. Annette ended up dead. And I ended up with Damon. It hadn't turned out badly, I guess, but he was still doing clean up—a necessity, according to Damon.

Annette had been *crazy*. Bat-shit crazy, and cruel with it. Like often attracted like, so he was going through and making sure the crazy and cruel that had been left behind were handled.

He wouldn't kill them unless he had to, but they would still need to be ousted from any positions of power in the clan, which tended to require thorough beatings to accomplish. Weres didn't back down willingly. It took physical force.

Sometimes he came to me so battered, I barely recognized him. It only lasted for a few hours, thanks to the amazing biology of a were. The virus in his genes healed wounds that would kill humans—or a half-human like me— only slowed him down and minor things like cuts or scratches disappeared in seconds.

I heard another grunt come across the line. "This is a bad time. I'll be quick."

"Nah. Chang and Doyle are with me. We're mostly done. This is the last of it and I'm letting Doyle handle it. He needs to get the shine off him." There was another grunt, followed by a roar that hurt my ears even through the phone. "We're just about done here. Only a few hours away. Have dinner with me tonight?"

"Can't." As I passed around the desk, I grabbed my sword and nudged the cooling unit with my foot. "I'm going to be out of town for a few days—courier thing to the Smokies. MacDonald with the wolves is paying me to deliver some heads."

"Ah, gimme a second."

I heard a roar—I recognized that one, a deep, barking sort of roar, unlike anything a lion or tiger would make. Damon's creature was a leopard, a rare one, although very few realized just how rare he was. I knew. I had no idea if anybody else did. Chang might. But for all I knew, that was it.

A few seconds and one scream later, and he was back on the phone. "Did you just say you were delivering some *heads?*"

"Yes. Literally. Seventy-five hundred dollars to deliver two decapitated heads to a small pack in the Smokies."

Silence stretched out, sharp as a blade and even over the phone line, I could feel his tension. Finally, he blew out a rough breath. "Don't leave yet. I can't go with you—I'm supposed to attend the next Assembly session, but I'm sending Chang with you. He can be there in two hours."

Sighing, I glanced out the window. All the wolves were

standing in line, waiting. Well, everybody but Megan. She was hauling a bag from the trunk of the Audi nearest my car. "I can't wait. I told them I'd hit the road immediately."

Another one of those taut, heavy silences. It grated on my nerves and I pushed my hand through my hair. The pale blonde mess fell back into my face and I made a mental note to get it cut. Not that I'd remember. "Damon, look…this is my *job*. I was doing it a long time before I met you, remember?" Then I made a face and shot a look out the window at Megan. "Besides, I'm not even going on my own. That son-of-a-bitch is sending a babysitter with me. One of his lieutenants is tagging along."

"That isn't precisely settling my mind," he said, a growl edging into his voice.

I stroked my hand down the grip of my blade and turned away from the window. "I don't have time for this. They're out in the parking lot and my-shadow-cum-baby-sitter is smirking like this is all very amusing to her."

"Her?"

Making a face at the phone, I said, "Yes. Her."

"He's sending Megan."

"Yes." Some of the tension had faded from his voice. I knew him well enough to figure out just what had caused at least some of the tension. My inner child lurks very close to the surface at times and she escaped my grasp before I could stop her. "I tried to get him to send that big piece of meat in a suit, but I don't think he likes me."

"Piece of meat?"

"Yeah." Rocking back on my heels, I stared at the wolf in question and smiled. "I think he'd like to be you, but he's not doing a good job of it. Still, I thought he'd make interesting conversation—"

"Kit. Are you trying to make me kill somebody?"

I laughed. "No. If I wanted to do that, I'd discuss something other than his conversation skills." I glanced around my office one more time. There were still weapons on the wall I'd love to take with me, but I wasn't exactly going to face an army. It was just one small pack. "Damon, try to remember...*I can handle myself.* I've got a job to do, okay?"

"I know you can handle yourself," he said, and that growl was back in his voice. "There's just a very fucked-up pack in the mountains there. Didn't he bother to inform you of that fact?"

I kicked the unit again. "I've lived in East Orlando for years. How much worse can that wolf pack be?" I asked. I didn't bother mentioning the reason he was cleaning up was because of the crazy bitch *he* had killed. "Damon...I was taking care of myself for a long time before you came into my life, remember? My job isn't exactly one where I teach school kids all day or work in a factory line. I deal with your kind on a regular basis. I haven't died yet."

"Damn it." He bit the words off like he was trying to tear them apart. Then, finally, after another terse, heavy silence, he said, "Stay safe, baby girl."

Ten seconds after I disconnected, there was a polite knock at the door. Polite...these wolves did everything so politely.

"Come on in."

Megan came inside, duffel bag in hand. "May I use your restroom? I need to change."

* * * * *

Well...one thing about this job, the *extras* were posh.

The rental car was a sleek, sexy little Roadster, a classic made back sometime around 2015 or so. It clung to the road like a lover and I kind of wanted to cry when I thought about giving her up. The cooling unit was tucked away out of sight and I could almost pretend I was just out for a nice, long, solo drive.

As long as I didn't look in the rearview mirror.

Megan was trailing behind me, perched on a wicked-ass motorcycle, clad in leathers from head to toe.

She hadn't been more than twenty feet away from me

this entire trip, not when we stopped to eat, not when we decided to stop for the night. If I'd gotten out of Orlando earlier in the day, we could have made it through South Carolina sooner, but it wasn't going to happen.

Once it got close to twilight, I decided to stop because of the threat of vamps.

Megan had deemed that a wise move.

I was so happy to have impressed her.

Seriously, everybody seemed to think I was completely reckless but I'm *not*.

I wasn't exactly familiar with the problems going on in the mountains in Tennessee, and I'd even taken some time to check, making some calls as I drove. I didn't get a whole lot of solid information—that was weird. I put in a call to Banner—Bureau of American Non-Human Affairs. Banner is the government's answer to dealing with NH affairs when they weren't happy with how things were going.

If anybody should have info on the Smoky Mountain pack, it was Banner.

But my normal contact wasn't available and my other one wasn't particularly forthcoming.

Weird. Okay, so I left a message with the one man I knew would get back to me and tried to piece things around in my head, but there was only so much you could do with next to no pieces.

One thing I was familiar with...South Carolina. Vamp infestation from *hell*. The US government had a mandatory curfew, one that had been in place and would remain in place indefinitely since nobody was having luck curbing the vamp problem. I'd heard rumors the government was considering a tactical strike that would wipe out most of the state if they couldn't clean the area up soon.

It was safe enough during daylight hours and many of the humans had already left, but it was still not the most ideal place to be. Getting inside the state border wasn't much more difficult than it would be to go to oh...say...Canada. ID, explanation of business and other assorted shit.

The older vamps claimed they were doing what they could to bring the problem under control but there was no way I was driving through South Carolina at night to deliver a couple of heads. The damn things could stay on ice for a little while longer. They weren't getting any deader, right?

The plan was to be up early and on the road as soon I had my brain alert enough to drive. Although she hadn't said anything, I was pretty damn aware of the fact that my escort, and her pack, wanted this job *done*. So by all means...I was going to get it done.

If I'd gotten an earlier start, I could have finished the job yesterday.

Still, we made good time, even with the stop to sleep. The hotel was fortified, protected by magic and expensive as hell. Everything in South Carolina was these days. In a few years, I figured the state would be a wasteland, home only to the vampires and surrounded by a magicked gate—assuming that tactical strike didn't happen.

According to a witch I knew, there were already noises being made about the gate thing. It was a scary thought, though. Most of the vampires were civilized enough creatures because it benefited them, and because they'd been around long enough to learn control.

New ones were a different story.

The infestation in South Carolina had started after a few of the newer vamps had managed to slip away from their masters and then they'd gone on a rampage.

What would happen if a bunch of them got out? The thing about gates, and magic...sooner or later, everything could fail.

Thoughts like that kept me awake half the damned night and I was cranky as hell when I woke to smell coffee drifting through the air. Cranky, tired, hungry. A quick meal and two cups of coffee helped with the tired and the hungry, but I'd stay cranky until we were out of South Carolina.

Megan took care of the bill for the meal and the hotel. Good thing, because the price made me cringe.

As South Carolina slowly became a distant memory, the weight on my shoulders eased and I felt like I could breathe. I hated that state. Pitied the poor fools who persistently refused to leave and I wanted to smack the government officials who insisted they were getting a handle on the problem.

They *weren't*. The feel of so many vamps still crowded my mind, but it wasn't a problem I could solve.

* * * * *

A little past ten in the morning, we found ourselves deep in the trees. The GPS had the coordinates for the pack programmed into it, but I didn't need it anymore.

My skin was crawling, all but buzzing from the energy I could feel dancing in the air. As the road narrowed down to nothing, I glanced at the woman on the bike behind me. She pointed to the narrow shoulder of the road.

Well. I guess we were walking.

Autumn was a cool whisper in the air as I climbed out and the bright red and yellow of the leaves made a colorful backdrop. We'd have a picturesque hike as I hauled around my grisly little delivery. I hefted it, put the strap over my shoulder and shifted around to make sure I could drop it fast if need be. I could. With the strap over my left shoulder and my hand resting near the grip of my sword, I met Megan's eyes. "Ready?"

"They won't like you bringing a sword." Megan eyed the blade critically.

"I'm on the job. I'm allowed to bring the weapons I normally carry." I shrugged. "And I'm not a shifter so they can't expect me to follow by their rules."

I could have left the sword.

But I get damn tired of people telling me what they *like* and *don't like*.

She sighed and settled herself at my side. "Just don't draw it."

"Gee, and here I was planning on attacking the first person I saw. But if you think I should keep my cool..." I smirked a little as we started to walk.

I could feel them.

Something was *seriously* wrong here. My Banner contact hadn't gotten back in touch with me, but I didn't need any information to figure out that something was wrong. I smelled death and decay and madness. It clung to the air like a disease, lining the inside of my nasal passages. A quick glance at Megan showed that she was catching the same thing, and probably ten times worse, but other than a faint crease between her brows, she gave no sign of being affected.

Hell, she had a *smile* on her face.

Not a *wow-this-is-fun* smile, but she was smiling, nonetheless. Like she was out shopping instead of clomping through the trees while I hauled around a couple of heads.

Off to the side, I saw a furred hide dart behind a tree. Too tall to be a wolf, unless they grew them six feet at the shoulder here, which wasn't likely. Wonderful. Even on their own turf, none of the packs I'd ever dealt with would be running around in that form with a human around, at least not right off the bat. I had no doubt they'd assume I was human. Almost everybody did, at first.

Something fucked up going on here, huh, Damon?

I should have called Banner again.

Even as that thought echoed through my mind, I heard a howl drifting through the trees. The sound of it sent goose bumps breaking across my flesh. That, of course, only pissed me off. It had been a long, long time since the sound of a wolf's howl in the distance had freaked me out.

But then again, I wasn't sure I'd ever been surrounded by this much...death...before.

This much decay.

It was everywhere.

Still, my fear wasn't going to help me any and I knew it. Swallowing back the bitter taste of it, I reached for that mental place of calm and started to focus.

NIGHT BLADE

I am aneira.
My sword arm is mighty.
I will not falter.
I will not fail.
My aim is true.
My heart is strong...

CHAPTER TWO

My heart is strong…

I told myself that even as the damned thing kept trying to rabbit out of my chest.

Over the past four months, Damon's been trying to work with me on controlling it.

Baby girl, that fear might be the death of you. You spend too much time around shifters and they respond to fear the way a shark responds to blood. Even if you don't show *it, you smell of it.*

And right now, I knew I was throwing it off bad.

My heart is strong. My heart is strong.

I pictured myself with Damon.

Pictured him with me.

The strength of him.

Pictured my sword. I had *her* with me and even just thinking of her calmed me.

"Whatever you're doing, keep it up. Your heart rate is slowing and that's a good thing."

I tuned Megan's voice out, kept focusing.

Calming thoughts. Strengthening thoughts.

My heart is strong—

By the time I saw another furred hide appearing through the trees, I was steady again. Or as steady as I was going to be.

This one had fully shifted and was down on all four paws, watching me with distrustful yellow eyes. He was so damned skinny, his bones jutted out against his pelt and there was something about his eyes that bothered me. Even in their other state, when a were looked at me, I could usually see some sign of their human self. They weren't human, but they still possessed that part in some way. That intelligence. A comprehension. Something.

But looking into his gaze, it was like there was nothing there...except hunger, and a lot of fear.

The musk of fear filling the air all but choked me. Too much to be coming from just one wolf, I knew. Sliding my gaze to the right, I watched the trees until another one slipped forward. Followed by another and another. Fifteen in all.

They stood there, staring at me for a long moment and then they turned and started to walk.

Glancing at Megan, I said, "I guess that means they want us to follow."

"Yep. That's my take."

Shifting the cooling unit around, I sighed. Hopefully, it wouldn't be too much farther. The damn thing wasn't heavy but it was awkward as hell.

* * * * *

Twenty minutes. Up one majorly massive hill but I made it up easy enough. I'd done hikes like this back when I'd been a kid, although they weren't considered *hikes*—they were *training* exercises and I'd often been running and dodging attacks the entire time. It wasn't fun, but I made it and wasn't even winded when we reached the top.

And that was it.

The rest of the wolves were there. I was even pretty certain this was the entire pack.

Forty-six of them, I counted, including those already in wolf form gathered around us. MacDonald had told me the pack only had forty-eight members. The heads of two were in the cooling unit.

"I have a message for the pack leader," I said, dumping the unit at my feet. "My name is Kit Colbana. I'm on official business from the pack in East Orlando."

A skinny kid, just barely out of his spike if that edgy energy around him was any indication, stood. A smile slanted his lips. He might have been a good-looking kid at some point, but the cruelty and the crazy on him had eaten away at that. The only thing I saw on him now was *thug*. I looked at him and saw somebody I'd either stay the hell away from or kill.

As he came prowling toward me, my palm started to itch.

"We don't listen to human whores from that pack," he said. "But if you want to be *my* little whore..."

I looked away. "I'm on official business. I'm a registered member for the Assembly and this contract was also duly registered. I'm expected to check back in with them in..." I checked my watch and then smiled. "Roughly two hours. If I do not, a Banner unit will dispatched to check on me. If I'm not found, your mountain will be searched and any wolf on it will be exterminated. No questions asked."

He snorted. "Humans don't get registered...and stupid humans should know better than to come onto wolf land."

He took another step.

Sighing, I shifted my attention to him. "You don't want to come any closer, kid."

"Oh, yes I do..."

I drew my sword before he'd managed to take another step. As the silver kissed his flesh, he yelped.

All around, people shifted.

Megan lost her skin.

As she went from a lovely, graceful brunette to a monster, trapped between human and wolf, I twisted my sword, watched as the silver bit into his flesh. Smoke drifted up from it as he whined, frozen in place by the shock of it.

Never felt silver before, it seemed. Badly trained, stupid.

What were they were doing up here? He had to have seen the blade...what did he think I was carrying her for? Looks?

"Again. I'm here on official business and I'm a member of the Assembly. That means..."

"It means you ain't human." A voice spoke from the crowd. "It also means you're afforded certain protections, bitch, but if you harm my boy, those protections are rendered void."

Ahhh...there's the pack leader. From the corner of my eye, I watched as he came striding my way. "Please take note, I told him not to take another step and he did so anyway. I carried my sword in plain view and he ignored it. Now...I'll put the blade away when you tell him to step back."

Growls rose in the air around me.

Megan was the one who decided things. She cleared her throat and damn if that's not an odd thing to hear from a creature that's almost seven feet tall, covered in gray fur and looks like something out of a nightmare. And although her voice was a deep bass growl, her tone was still so very polite. "If I may...Kit. You're wearing a bracer. Please remove it."

I would have glared at her if I dared to look away from those in front of me. "Not the time, Megan." And how the hell *did* she know?

"Oh, it's exactly the time." And her clawed hand struck, slicing through the leather cord that held the bracer in place. I managed, barely, not to flinch as the bracer fell to the ground.

"I'd like to ask you all to look at Ms. Colbana's left wrist. What do you see?" Megan said, her voice calm and cool, despite the fact that she sounded like something out of a nightmare.

If I wasn't so busy staring down the idiot kid in front of me, I would have glared a hole through her hairy head. No. Forget *glared* a hole. I would have *put* a hole somewhere in her furry hide.

The boy's eyes shot to my wrist.

To the bite marks left there by Damon.

"I was sent as her…companion," Megan said. "Because my alpha doesn't wish to cause unrest between my pack and the cat clan should anything happen to Ms. Colbana. The Alpha would be so very pissed."

"Why would the cat Alpha give a fuck?" the kid demanded.

The pack leader swore. "Shit, boy. Who the fuck do you think marked her wrist?"

He summarily jerked his son away with enough force that the kid went flying across the small clearing. I turned my head and stared at Megan. She shrugged.

Nothing to be done for it now. After I snagged my bracer, I stepped back from the cooling unit. I was *not* opening that thing, nor was I touching the nasty presents inside. "You have something in there," I told him, nudging the grisly container with one foot.

He stared at me. "Well. Open it."

I just tugged a cloth from my back pocket and cleaned the small bit of blood from the tip of my blade. That done, I slid her back into the sheath. She went back with a disgruntled sigh. She'd wanted a fight—I could tell. My weapons liked a good bloody brawl, the bloodier the better and they didn't have much sense. It didn't *matter* that Megan and I wouldn't have been able to fight our way free of this many wolves.

He growled at me.

I just stood and waited.

Finally, he glanced at one of the women and she came scurrying. Literally, chin tucked to her chest, shoulders hunched, like she was trying to make herself seem as small as possible.

Once she had it open, she dashed away, like she couldn't stand to be any closer to him than she had to be.

I couldn't blame her.

I sensed the energy shifters carried. Actually, it wasn't just confined to shifters. I could peg a shifter, a witch, a vamp, a human…and just about anything else with just a look. It had to do with the energy that wrapped around them. Their souls. All of it.

And this guy's soul was dark and dirty, the energy of his beast a dirty, snarling thing like a rabid monster, crouching and ready to bite.

As he looked down, I braced myself.

A snarl escaped him as he bent over and hauled the heads out, one in each fist.

"You dare…?" he whispered, staring at me through near colorless lashes.

"I didn't kill them." I watched as he hurled the heads. One went flying into the trees. The other almost hit somebody. The unfortunate person barely managed to catch it and stood there looking at it in dismayed horror for long, long moments.

The pack leader took a step toward me.

My hand itched. Burned. *Call me*, the sword whispered in the back of my head. *I'm here…we can fight, we can fight…*

No. Not the time.

"I didn't kill them. I'm here on official business, as a member of the Assembly. I'm to deliver this, its contents within, and a message," I said quietly. My heart rate started to skip and immediately, I focused on Damon's voice. The low, growling rumble. His strength. *My* strength. *I am aneira. My sword arm is mighty—*

"Give me the fucking message, nugget, and get the hell out of my territory," the pack leader rasped.

"Alpha Alisdair MacDonald cordially requests that you cease and desist sending your men to his territory to hunt for 'bitches to take back to the mountain'." As MacDonald had indicated, I made little quotation marks in the air, keeping my voice flat and impersonal. "You may or may not be aware, but the 'two bitches' they tried to grab were his teenaged daughters. The oldest killed one of your men. He killed the other. The next time one of your pack members tries to abduct one of his people, he will lead his enforcers into your land and kill every last man among you. You will be the last and he will kill you slowly, strangling you with your own entrails."

The pack leader was red by the time I was done.

My heart was racing.

Megan placed her hand on my shoulder. "We have one hundred enforcers, pack leader. Our pack numbers at five hundred. My Alpha awaits my call and if he doesn't receive it, you will be exterminated. You've been warned."

"Get the fuck *out!*" he screamed.

* * * * *

"You do good work," Megan said cheerfully as we made a quick stop in Gatlinburg. "Hey, you wanna hang around here for the night? There's this bar on the strip—they don't have many of our kind around here thanks to that bastard, but the guy who runs the place keeps a stock of decent liquor. We can go get plastered and head back in the morning."

"No."

I stared at the bracer as I tried to figure out a way to get it back on. It wasn't going to happen. Screw it. New laces would fix it and I had plenty of those. Tossing it through the open window of the car, I eyed the marks on my wrist and debated.

I could let it go.

Maybe I should.

Megan turned away and that's when I moved. Yeah, it's a dirty trick, but when somebody is strong enough to rip you apart with their bare hands, *dirty* is the best way to fight. I drew a blade I'd kept sheathed at my thigh. As I turned, I palmed another blade and threw even before I turned. A pained scream ripped from her as the silver buried itself deep in her thigh. I was on her in the next second, kicking at her left knee and listening as it crunched.

Her body trembled under mine and power rolled through the air. "Don't shift," I warned, pressing the tip of my other blade to her neck. "You know what Night is?"

She stilled.

"I think that means you do. This is a spelled blade…it's coated in *Night*—" Night was a narcotic that had been formulated to hit shapeshifters hard enough to render them unconscious. It would kill humans…and probably me. That's why it was spelled. "All it takes to break the spell on it is shifter blood. So if you're up for a nice long nap, just keep moving around."

"Do you have any idea just how much pain I can put you in?"

"Yeah, yeah." I sighed and looked around. We were parked next to a small convenience store just outside the National Park. It wasn't exactly busy, but we wouldn't escape notice forever. "You know how often I hear this song and dance, Megan? Listen, sweetheart. The next time you pull a trick like that, I'm going to get pissy."

"A trick like what?"

Glaring at the back of her head, I said, "You know what. Who I'm sleeping with doesn't have a damn thing to do with my job. I've worked jobs for your Alpha *before* I hooked up with Damon. The next time you bring him up on a job is the last time I'll *ever* work one for the wolf pack again. Pass the message on."

I shoved back and immediately put distance between us.

She shifted with a roar of rage, reaching around pulling on the silver blade I'd buried in her thigh. I smelled her blood and saw it gush out as she flung the blade to the ground.

I left it lying there, still gripping the spelled blade, my stomach in knots as I watched her.

I really had to work on that fear thing more.

"You crazy little bitch," she growled. "It worked, didn't it? We got out of there, no harm, no foul, right?"

"Did it occur to you that if I wanted to tattoo *Damon's girl* on my forehead, I'd do that?" I held the knife ready, wondered if I was going to have to use it. "Do you go around parading the fact that you're screwing MacDonald and think that's going to open and close doors?'"

In the form she wore, it was hard to read facial expressions. But something in her alien eyes flickered. And then, I felt the blast of her power against my skin as she shifted back to her human form. The shift from human to were had healed her leg and she stood before me now unharmed...unharmed, but still pissed and looking confused. "You're *not* a shifter," she pointed out. "You're just barely something more than human and you're easier to hurt. I was doing what I could to avoid that."

"I was the one hired to do the job." Recognizing that the threat had passed, I slid the spelled knife away. "Was I supposed to do the job or just come along for the ride?"

She inclined her head. "Point taken."

I turned away and headed around to the front of the car.

I wanted to get home. I *needed* to get home.

"You..." She paused and blew out a breath. "Look, you didn't do bad. I'm sorry if I screwed things up."

I went to open the door but she came up and I paused, shifting around to meet her gaze. "You should put some clothes on. Even with the pack here, they probably aren't used to seeing a naked woman striding around town."

She watched me closely. "Are you okay?

No. I was pissed. And although I wouldn't admit it, I was still freaked out by the monstrous pack we'd just left. Curling my lip, I replied, "I'm just super. Although it might have been nice if somebody would have mentioned the pack leader was an evil son-of-a-bitch."

"No, it wouldn't." She stared at me coolly now. "You held it together and even when you got a little nervy there, you got it under control. Hell, you didn't even let on that I'd pissed you off like that. But if we'd told you that Dex Conrad is a wolf who is rumored to butcher his own people when they try to leave him, that he rapes his own young and is pretty much everything humans *think* we all are...you would have walked in there throwing off so much fear, we would have needed an army to get us out."

"Oh, fuck off—" I started to say. Then I stopped. *Butcher—*

The heat in my hand flared so bright, so painfully hot, it *hurt.*

"He butchers those who try to leave him?" I said quietly.

"That's what they say," she said tiredly. "Word went out after this latest mess. If he tries anything else, we'll hunt him down. But for now, he's keeping it to the idiots too stupid to stay—"

I hit her.

I heard bone crunch in my hand, felt the pain flare up my arm.

"What the *fuck*—?" Megan snarled.

TJ. That was all I could think. There had been a time in my life when I had been scared and on the run, and a woman had taken me in. Given me a place to hide, a home. The very first bed I could call my own.

Her name had been TJ and she was a werewolf who would live the rest of her life unable to walk or run the way another shapeshifter could…all because her Alpha had amputated her legs when *she* had tried to run.

Shapeshifters can heal almost anything, but if the wound is healed through magic first…he had the wounds cauterized and closed and now her legs ended in stumps at her knees.

My fury almost blinded me as I stared at the woman in front of me. "You *fucking* coward. Too stupid to stay?"

I turned away from her before I did something that would put me in more hot water than I could handle.

Right then I was so pissed I didn't care.

But I knew what would happen if the two of us went head to head.

I'd get hurt.

And the man who shared my bed would take it personally. Personally enough to cause major hell and while part of me wanted that, it wasn't right. The cats outnumbered wolves two to one.

And as pissed off as I was, I had to keep my cool.

For now, at least.

I heard her coming behind me and I turned, drawing the spelled knife from my thigh. My palm itched, yearned for my sword, but unless I managed to cut her head off, the only thing I'd do with that was piss her off and this needed to stop and I could hear people drawing closer—we'd just been noticed.

This needed to stop. Now.

Gatlinburg was mostly human turf and if this didn't stop, our asses were in major trouble.

"If you take one more step toward me, I'm using this," I warned her. "And I'm feeling mean enough that maybe I'll deliver you tied and bound to that pack up in the mountains."

She sneered at me. "You wouldn't."

No. She was right. I wouldn't. Lifting a brow, I shrugged and said, "Probably not, but imagine what it might be like…if you were one of their young…a kid, sixteen, seventeen. Going through your spike, scared to death of your alpha and desperate to run. So you try. And you fail. What do you think happens?"

Her lids flickered.

"Still think all those people are *stupid enough* to stay?"

Her gaze slid away from mine. Her shoulder slumped and she turned away, using her hand to wipe away the blood running down her face.

"You all *leave* them there. You bunch of fucking *cowards*," I whispered, throwing the words out between us. Shaking my head, I climbed into the car, still gripping my knife.

NIGHT BLADE

CHAPTER THREE

I hadn't gotten home until almost eleven. The good thing about Florida, it's not overrun with feuding, hostile, hungry vamps the way South Carolina is, so I'd felt safe enough making the drive home. Colleen had been waiting for me.

Very unhappy.

I had called her from the road and told her I thought I had broken a bone in my hand and she might have to fix it.

She had.

By way of re-breaking it.

It sounds terrible and feels much worse, something I'm actually familiar with, since I've had it done several times. The first two times happened when I was a kid. My grandmother wasn't the loving sort and when I didn't perform well in training, my punishment wasn't extra training. It was lashes with a whip or broken bones or other forms of torture.

Colleen was a much kinder healer. Instead of forcing me to remain awake as my grandmother had, she gave me something to put me under.

I didn't come out of it until sometime near dawn and she was curled up in the chair, watching over me.

I stumbled to the bathroom to empty my bladder and when I came out, she was holding a mug.

The smell alone was enough to make me want to run back into the bathroom. I could hide in there. I'd be safe. Safe from whatever vile nastiness she'd put inside that mug. I almost did it.

Apparently the look on my face told her what I was thinking. "Don't try it, Kit," she warned me. "I helped build the damned wards for that room and I can break them. You need the damned tonic or you'll be dragging for a week."

I hated healing tonics.

They tasted like piss and vinegar and death.

"No," I said, glaring at her.

"Take it." She glared right back. Then she smiled evilly at me. "I can always call your sweetie and tell him you're hurt…he can come play nursemaid and you can take the medicine for *him*."

"You know…I'm sick and tired of people forgetting I'm an adult who took care of herself *before* I met Damon." Sourly, I eyed the nasty mess in the mug. It was the color of rancid milk and vomit mixed together and smelled about as pleasant. Taking a deep breath, I tossed it back as quick as I could and then concentrated on not puking it back up. After about sixty seconds, I thought I *might* be able to keep it down.

It was a full five minutes before I was certain it was all going to stay down. After another glare at Colleen, I stormed into the kitchen. I needed chocolate or something to get that taste out of my mouth and I needed it fast. Once that hit my system, I was going to crash. Hard.

"Hell, you don't need Damon to care of you. Who thinks that?"

Rooting through the cabinet, I pulled out a package of *Tim Tams*. "Everybody?" I said. I gave her the condensed version of the job I'd just finished as I ate two cookies and washed them down with milk. Already my brain felt logy. Bed. Needed bed.

I stumbled on the way to the bedroom and Colleen steadied me with her shoulder under my arms. "Bed, Kit," she said firmly.

"Brush my teeth," I mumbled.

"You have a fetish with this clean thing." But she helped me to the bathroom and kept me from falling over while I hurriedly brushed my teeth. "You know, it's not a bad thing the wolf was with you, right? It's not like you haven't worked with back-up before."

I made a face at her. Then, despite my thick tongue, I said, "The pack leader needs to die. He's the one..."

"What one?" she asked, guiding me to the bed.

I whispered, "TJ."

Colleen's face went tight.

That was the last thing I remembered before darkness grabbed me.

* * * * *

Sunlight greeted me. But that wasn't what woke me. I was so tired I could have slept if somebody had been shining floodlights in my face. No, what woke me was the fact that somebody was trying beat the door to my home down. Hard, hammering blows.

Blows hard enough to rattle the reinforced door in its frame and have my head begging for mercy.

Emerging from the stupor of a healing tonic left one feeling a little hung-over for a few minutes.

I just needed some coffee and I'd be fine.

But the idiot at my door wasn't going to give me five minutes.

Grumbling, I climbed out of bed. I had on yoga pants and a tank top. I used to sleep in a lot less, but my life has been...interesting lately and I'm dragged out of my bed too often. Better to just have something on already.

As I headed to the door, I flexed my hand and smiled. Good as new.

A glance out the peephole wiped the smile from my face.

Not somebody I wanted to see.

Sighing, I tipped my head back to the sky. *Why me?*

"Open the damn door," Doyle Channing snapped.

Doyle. The reason Damon and I were together. Four months ago, Damon had come to me to help find the kid after he'd run away. The kid had ended up caught in an awful mess—humans had decided to make up their own hunting game, with non-human kids as the prey.

I'd tracked him down, with Damon an ever-present shadow.

Doyle had been the previous Alpha's nephew, but Damon was the one who raised him. Damon was the one who loved him. Because of that, I tried to tolerate the kid.

Even though he hated me.

I wasn't entirely fond of him myself. He'd freaked me out from the moment I met him. He reminded me of somebody from my past, and he looked at me like I was food. I could handle that. But each time he saw me, he made it clear that he loathed the very air I breathed and it's hard to live with that kind of apathy without letting it affect you.

Pasting a bright smile on myself, I opened the door. "Hiya, Doyle. Lovely morning, yes?"

"Sure. Some of us actually have a *job*, though, and can't spend it sleeping." He glared at me, making it clear that he'd rather be doing said job—whatever it was he did for Damon. "Why in the hell aren't you answering your phone? He's been calling."

I scowled and looked around, not even sure where the damn thing was.

Doyle made a move to come inside but the wards pricked at him.

He hissed under his breath and I smiled at him. "Felt that, did you? I'd think you'd remember after last time."

Wards were expensive as hell but they helped. After I'd helped bring Doyle home, I'd used ten thousand dollars to bolster up the protections around my house and office. The one pricking at him now would feel like ants eating at his skin. It wouldn't *stop* him. The stronger ones were laid on my bedroom, with the strongest in my bathroom. This was just a warning.

One he ignored. His eyes gleamed a wild blue as he pushed through. I saw stripes dancing just under his skin before fading away. The mantle of his energy hovered above him like a giant cat stalking in a circle before settling back down.

Sighing, I planted my hands on my hips. "Why did you do that?"

"That won't keep anything out."

"It's not *supposed* to," I said. "It's just a warning. And a distraction. And I didn't invite you in, jackass."

He smirked. "I'm not a vampire. I don't *need* an invite."

Sometimes I really disliked this kid.

"Why haven't you called him? He's worried. Didn't you hear me?"

"Yes, I heard you," I said, turning away from him and searching the living room. Colleen had been in here when I got home, so…ah-ha. There was my vest. I grabbed it and found my phone in the front pocket. "Dead battery."

I plugged it in and then went over to my landline. It was an old-fashioned thing, but I sort of liked old-fashioned things. They didn't fail you when hurricanes came blasting or when you forgot to charge your phone. Old-fashioned was *good*. Reliable.

Numerous calls had gone to voicemail. I hit the button and listened to the first few. I felt the smile spreading across my face and kept my head tucked so the pain-in-the-ass kid wouldn't see it while I listened to Damon's voice.

By the fifth message, though, my man was getting a little cranky.

"Call me, damn it," he snarled.

"Good grief." I grabbed the phone and punched in his number, waited.

I didn't wait more than three seconds.

"Where in the hell have you been?"

"Sleeping." I flexed my hand again and studied it. It wasn't sore. That was good. The headache was fading, too.

"You couldn't answer the damn phone?"

Sighing, I pinched the bridge of my nose. "I did something sort of stupid and Colleen had to give me a healing tonic. I didn't hear the phone."

Silence.

Complete silence.

Finally, in a low, flat voice, Damon said, "What did you do?"

"I hit that wolf bitch Megan in the face and broke my hand. The bones were knitting together by the time I got here and I need my hands. Colleen had to re-break the bones."

I heard something thud. I think he might have been hitting his head on something.

"Are you banging your head on the wall?"

"No. My fist. Why did you hit Megan?"

I picked up a pen and absently started to sketch on the notepad I kept by the phone. "You ever met any of the wolves that live around Gatlinburg?"

"No. I recall telling you they were fucked up. I'd rather not meet the sick bastards...unless I need to kill them."

"They are sick, but no. You don't need to kill them," I said quietly. "Remember my friend, TJ?"

The thudding on the other end of the line stopped. "Yes."

"I think I met her Alpha. Megan, precious little sweetheart that she is, told me that none of the other wolf packs are going to do anything about him as long as he stays on his mountain. He can keep on torturing the people under his care...after all, they *are* stupid enough to stay," I said flatly. The sword I'd doodled on the piece of paper didn't look quite right. I wanted a new one. Not to replace mine, but a shorter blade, an extra one. Scratching it out, I started over. "She tells me this, so I hit her. End of story."

"One question."

I tried a different guard. "And that question is...?"

"Did she touch you?"

I narrowed my eyes as the design of the blade started to

settle in my head. "That's not entirely fair, you know. I *did* hit her."

"I don't give a fuck if it's fair. Did she touch you?"

"No. I think she was thinking about it. I pulled a blade, told her we could go a round, but we had an audience and I guess she saw the wisdom of not doing that." There was no reason for him to know anything more, really. I'd handled it. "She walked away. It's done."

He was quiet for a moment and then said, "Dinner tonight. I'm cooking."

I ran my tongue over my teeth. "How about we go out instead?" If he came over, we'd just end up in bed within five minutes and I'd probably have to listen to him snarl at me for thirty minutes afterward. At least if we went out, maybe we could actually *talk* and he'd calm down a little first.

"Kit…"

"Come on." I gave the blade a critical study. I usually went for more of a rapier-style than the leaf-blade, but that wasn't fitting what I had in mind this time. It was finally starting to take form—I could almost see it coming together, too. Might see if somebody could do the sword for me, if I could get it right. "We haven't gone out in a while."

"Fine," he muttered. "Just at Drake's, though. Got it?"

"That works." Drake's was the only place that *would* work, really. It was a local shapeshifter hangout, a place that served good food, and lots of it. Plus, Drake let me keep my sword. Everybody else made me take it off. I hated that.

"Eight o'clock," Damon told me.

"Yes, sir, Cap-i-tan."

"See you, baby girl." His voice dropped to a smoky drawl and I found myself grinning again. I didn't notice that Doyle was watching me until I went to hang up the phone.

"You know, if she'd hit you, Damon would be cleaning up a mess *you* caused, all because you're a fucking idiot," Doyle snapped.

"Oh, bite me." I shoved away from the counter and then stopped, glaring at the sword he held. "Put my blade up."

It wasn't *my* sword.

It was one of the practice blades I'd picked up for Damon. He had said something about learning how and I'd thought he was teasing, but then he said it again and I realized he was serious. He'd never be a swordsman, but he had fun with it and it gave me an opponent.

Doyle swung the blade around, smirking at me. "Why...afraid I'll hurt you?"

"Kid, that's a practice blade. You're more likely to hurt yourself, but that doesn't mean I want you touching my weapons," I replied.

"I think you're scared." A light glinted in his eyes. "You still smell like meat to me. I think you're scared I can carve you up...just *like* meat."

Narrowing my eyes at him, I said, "Meat, huh?"

He continued to watch me, a hint of that arrogant laughter dancing in his eyes.

I nodded. "Tell you what. I'll give you a chance to do just that. Give me five minutes." I left him alone in my living room as I headed into my bedroom to change.

* * * * *

Shapeshifters are fast.

Sometimes it makes them stupid.

That's why I do okay with them.

They never think that sword of mine is going to help me out much, because they are bigger, stronger, and scarier.

But I'm trained and I spent the first fifteen years of my life being tortured by somebody just as scary as any shapeshifter.

After I'd changed into clothes more fitting for a dance across the mats, I led Doyle into my gym. "You think you can carve me up, do you, Doyle?"

"Oh, I know I can." He continued to spin the sword and I was a little surprised to see he had some grace with it.

But it wasn't skill.

He didn't hold the sword right. And he'd already made the worst mistake possible. He did the same thing everybody else did. He'd underestimated me.

"Alright. I'm going to give you a chance to prove it."

He laughed. "Nice try. But there's no way I'm going to," he said, shaking his head. "Damon's having too much fun fucking you for now and if I laid a hand on you, he'd kick my ass." He winked at me and then added, "I'll wait until he's done playing with you."

It stung.

I can't deny that.

Yeah, I know most people think he's just toying with me and I know I'm still not entirely certain what we have going on with us, but it's not *playing*. There's something between us that I can't describe and it's so exhausting having people ignore it, insult it...

Pushing it aside, I nodded. "Damon would definitely kick your ass if you harmed me. But this isn't about harm. I always need a good opponent. Not that you will be, but I'll give you a chance. Tell you what...if you can get in a shot, I'll owe you a favor."

"A favor?" His lip curled. "What in the hell can *you* do for me?"

I stared at him. "Kid, did you forget who *found* you?"

"No." His eyes flashed. "Damon did."

I started my warm-up, watching him steadily. "Did he? He tell you that or did you just guess?"

"You sure as hell couldn't."

"If you say so. Okay. Maybe you don't want a favor from me. But look at this way. You hate my guts...you'll have the memory of humiliating me. A trained swordswoman, beaten down by an idiot kid just barely out of puberty." I smirked at him.

That goaded him into it.

He came at me with a snarl.

I waited until the last second and glided out of his way, tripping him so he hit the floor with a thud.

I was already on the other side of the room when he regained his feet.

"Never let your opponent get you angry," I warned him. "First lesson."

* * * * *

I would give him credit.

He had a rough, natural talent that was unexpected.

But he had absolutely no training.

Twenty minutes later, I'd disarmed him four times and he was bloodied in more than a dozen places.

But to my surprise, he was smiling when I finally said, "That's enough."

"Hey, I'm just now getting warmed up."

As he circled around, I shook my head. "That's lovely, Doyle, but I'm done. I have to get to the office."

He lunged.

There was an odd look in his eyes, one that almost looked like pleasure and I don't think it was just because he came *that* close to disarming me.

I grunted under the impact of his attack and just barely managed to get around him that time. He really wasn't half bad. Too bad he hated my guts. I could get him up to speed and have a decent opponent for the first time in forever, but it was dangerous to teach what I knew to somebody who despised me.

When he came for me again, I threw the practice blade down and called my real blade.

Light danced off the silver of her surface as I said quietly, "Doyle. I have to go to work. We went for twenty minutes and I'm done."

He stopped, staring at the silver between us for a long moment and then glared at me. "What the fuck? We were having fun!"

Fun? Well. Yeah. It sort of had been. And it didn't matter. "I have a job to get to."

He acted like he was going to hurl the practice blade down and then he stopped, sighed. Held it out to me, hilt first. "I…" he snapped his jaw shut in a manner so like Damon I almost smiled. "Would you maybe letting me do this again?"

"I don't think so."

He stared at me, anger so clearly written on that young face. "Why not?"

"Because you hate me, kid. You learn fast and you hate me. Why should I let you learn from me when I worry one day you'll decide to take one of those skills and stick a blade in me?" I didn't see the point in lying about it.

He growled a little, taking a step toward me. "I know what Damon would do to me."

"That's not enough. I wouldn't teach anybody who doesn't have some modicum of respect for *me*." I gathered up the practice blades and stowed them away. "See yourself out, if you would."

* * * * *

The workout had done a damn good job of clearing the fog from my head. What little lingered was dealt with by a hot shower and a meal…and coffee. Lots of coffee could cure almost anything.

As I finished my second cup, I went to start sketching on the blade I'd been thinking about.

Except the paper was gone.

I stopped and swore, staring at the note scrawled on the blank page.

Thanks for the match.

I didn't recognize the handwriting but there wasn't anybody it could be other than Doyle. I flipped the notepad over, searching for the sketch of my blade, but it wasn't on the other sheets, either.

The little jerk had taken off with it. My next blade.

I should have made him bleed.

* * * * *

It was too late in the day to get much done by the time I got in. A sealed envelope had been pushed under the door.

It bore the mark of the local wolf pack.

Inside was a lovely check for the agreed-upon amount, as well as a nice little flowery note of thanks that I didn't bother to read. I was tempted to call MacDonald and tell him he owed me double, but I didn't. After stowing the check in my bag, I dealt with all the calls I'd had come in, some paperwork and made sure I took care finalizing this last task with the Assembly.

I'd bluffed a little when I told them they were expecting me to check in.

Yeah, if somebody noticed I was missing, they might go looking for me, but they didn't operate on a timetable.

The people who'd come looking for me would be Damon and Colleen. I thought of TJ and my heart ached. She wouldn't look for me, not in the Smokies, but if she knew, she'd send some of her people out.

A mean smile curved my lips as I thought of Goliath tearing up that mountain if he knew who hid there.

I thought maybe I'd pay him a visit. The two of us had spent many, many nights wondering just who had done that to TJ. Now I knew. Maybe we should go after him together.

It was a thought to ponder.

I didn't want the helpless people who wanted to escape to be slaughtered. But the monsters needed to go. Goliath was a very good monster killer. I'd seen him do it.

Sighing, I brushed the thoughts aside. They were something I'd have to consider long and hard before I committed to them.

Focusing on the next message, I tried to will my mind blank.

A familiar voice rolled out of the machine and my heart stopped for one very brief second. It was only a second.

Really.

"Hey, Kitty-kitty."

Justin.

I closed my eyes.

Justin Greaves. He was the one partner—in *this* life—who could make me sweat when it came to swordplay—actual swords.

And…until Damon, there wasn't a man alive who had ever made my heart race but Justin had come close. He'd been the one who made me realize sex wasn't a bad thing and that had taken some doing.

I heard something crack and I looked down, realized I'd broken my pencil.

"Dunno where you are or when you'll get this message, but I need to talk to you. I have a job for you and you kind of have to take it."

I made a face. Justin was a Banner cop now. He was the Banner contact I'd reached out to the other day…apparently we'd been trading calls. I kept meaning to get the upgrade that would connect the line here to my cell, but I hadn't done it yet. I'd think about it when I didn't have the money, and when I did…well. Other things came up.

Why was a Banner cop calling *me*? Why was *Justin* calling me?

Banner had seduced him with the promises of *You get to kill things* and *we'll give you lots of weapons*. He liked weapons almost as much as I did. And he liked killing things…well, when they needed killing. Justin was like a loaded gun, a good weapon and he was most efficient when he had a target.

"Call me, set up a time, Kitty-kitty. Don't make me track you down, okay? You really do have to take this job…trust me."

I sighed and rubbed the back of my neck.

Trust him. That wasn't a problem. I did trust Justin. There weren't a lot of people I was willing to say that about but he was definitely one of them.

The message ended and I sat there, staring at nothing.

I trusted him, but I sure as hell didn't want to take any job that he might have to offer.

Jobs and Justin meant one thing: a connection to the Banner unit. The Banner units were exterminators. Non-human exterminators. Banner cops, slang for the Bureau of American Non-Human Affairs—were basically men and women like Justin, highly skilled, very deadly people who went out and eliminated the NHs who had been deemed too deadly to live. Generally, they didn't get to play much because us non-humans patrolled our own. That was the job of the packs, the clans, the order of witches and the Assembly in general. But sometimes there were those who slipped past the ever-watchful eyes of the Assembly.

Sometimes there were those the Assembly turned a blind eye *to* and the Banner cops stepped up to the plate.

If Justin was calling me, it was entirely likely that he wanted my help in tracking somebody down.

Damn it all to hell.

CHAPTER FOUR

I excel at ignoring certain things.

Justin wouldn't be ignored for long, but I could damn well put him off for one day and that was exactly what I did.

I had to get to the bank. Two checks from two different jobs, just waiting to be cashed.

And besides…I had a *date*. Since I had some money that didn't immediately have to be poured into fixing or strengthening my wards, I did something I never did. I went and bought a new outfit.

Nothing fancy because I still needed to be able to move, especially since I was meeting Damon at Drake's. Walking into a shapeshifter hangout looking like a sex kitten wasn't going to do me any good, because then I'd be nervous and I'd freak myself out…yeah, not going there.

But a new top, the same shade of gray as Damon's eyes, new jeans. I could do that. I saw a pair boots that I found myself coveting, but I wasn't about to do that today. New boots required breaking in. No, thanks. I did give in and buy a shiny, sparkling pair of earrings that fell in silvery threads almost to my shoulders. Not real silver. It wouldn't bother Damon unless it got jabbed into his flesh, but it was the thought that counted.

I would have liked to have gone home and changed,

showered, but I was in avoidance mode. That meant no going home. Justin knew where I lived. Instead, I changed in one of the ladies' changing rooms after I'd bought the clothes.

I managed to kill time until a little after seven and then I headed out, doing a quick glance around the parking lot on my way to the car. No sign of Justin, his bike, or one of the infamous Banner cars.

So far, so good.

The drive to Drake's took thirty minutes and I was twenty minutes early. Didn't matter. I'd go inside and wait for Damon in there, because I figure the last thing Justin was going to do was walk into that bar looking for me, even if he did track me down.

I'd just pushed the door open when I heard the roar of a motorcycle engine. I grimaced but didn't look back. Justin. He'd tracked me down, alright. I felt the weight of his gaze slam into my back but I just kept walking.

I'd call him in the morning.

If it was *that* important, he would have called again, right?

He hadn't. So it could wait.

* * * * *

I went from the frying pan into the fire, it seemed, as I crossed over that threshold. Justin Greaves looking for me and now a good forty shifters staring at me.

Almost immediately, they all looked away.

The only exception was a slim man of almost ridiculous beauty.

He had black hair done in a queue, pulled back from his face. His skin was pale gold, his eyes liquid black and he was even more insanely polite than the wolves.

In the past few months, I'd also learned that Chang was one of Damon's friends. A close one, too.

Sometimes I liked him.

I never trusted him.

"Hello, Kit."

"Chang." I shifted my grip on my sword. I wasn't wearing her. The sheath would look damned weird considering I'd attempted to look somewhat girly tonight. If Damon wasn't coming…

A faint smile tugged at Chang's lips. "He's on his way. He just asked if I would come in case you arrived early."

"Great." I sighed and rubbed my brow. "Because we all know I can't handle myself, right?"

"Nobody said that," Chang said. He gestured toward the back, courteously reaching for my elbow. My left one, of course, keeping away from my sword arm. Chang was all about being nice. "Would you like to sit?"

I shrugged away from him. "No. I want a drink."

Ever wise, Chang didn't offer to get it for me and returned to his seat.

After I'd gotten a beer, I made my way through the crowd and settled down in the one open booth, keeping my sword on the table. Nobody spoke to me. Nobody looked at me.

The noise level in the bar was conspicuously much quieter than it had been earlier, too. *Way to kill people's fun, Kit,* I thought sourly.

I was five seconds away from sending Damon a message, calling the thing off when the door blew open and two rednecks came stumbling in.

Stumbling against each other, snorting and laughing. One of them was almost as big as Goliath, a friend of mine from way, way back. Goliath didn't come by his name lightly. This guy, though, unlike Goliath, had a vague look in his eyes.

Some village has misplaced their idiot.

Big, strong, dumb. And a shapeshifter. Something isn't right with the world when you put that much strength and power in a body that wouldn't have the sense to control it.

But the other one was worse.

His gaze bounced around the bar and immediately locked on me.

Great.

I studied them as they made their way over to me. They weren't wolf or cat. And the nervous energy hovering over them made my skin crawl in a way I recognized too well. Rats.

I hated rats. Hated them with a passion.

The big guy's eyes were getting beady every now and then, too. Going to lose it in here?

Oh, yes. This wasn't good.

They came to a stumbling halt in front of me.

Behind them, I saw Chang rising from his chair.

I narrowed my eyes at him.

He cocked a slim black brow and folded his arms over his chest.

"Since when does a shifter bar serve meat...you're supposed to be *on* the menu," the skinny one said. "Not having food served to you."

"Oh, trust me. Nobody here wants to take a bite out of me." I tapped my nails on the table, keeping my hand away from my blade. "I'm too stringy."

"You'd be good enough for me." He bent down and peered at me. "Get up. Get out. You're in shifter territory which means if you get fucked over, it's your own damned fault."

When I didn't move, he did. I don't know if he was going to grab me or hit me nor did I really care.

Shoving the booth back from the table, I jumped into a crouch and landed on the seat, hand gripping my sword. Three men had eased forward, surrounding him. The man seemed to think they wanted to play. "There's not enough for everybody, boys," he said, laughing.

"Chang?" one of them said.

"She can have him if she wants him."

One gaped at Chang.

The second just shoved the skinny rat at me.

Others took the big bastard down.

I wasn't paying too much attention, though, because the

fucker coming at me had decided to change his skin and there was nothing less attractive than a wererat in the nude.

Muscles bulged in places they shouldn't and his legs were all out of proportion. He shouldn't be able to move well, if life and science were fair, but he could. As he came at me with a screaming sort of hiss, I held steady until the very last second and then moved, using his momentum against him as I spun and moved. I buried my sword deep, deep into the cavity of his chest.

I shoved forward with all the strength I had in me as I did so, riding him down.

He wasn't strong and his body had frozen as he took the silver of my blade into him. Now I was crouched on top of that misshapen body, smelling the way the silver burnt him, the stink of it in my nostrils while his body trembled and writhed under mine.

"Now. Who were you calling meat?"

The other one was roaring pitifully. From the corner of my eye, I saw him, struggling under the weight of four bodies and staring at us.

"Get the fuck off of me!" the rat beneath me wailed.

I was pondering just how to answer that when the door opened and I felt the blast of heat rolling over me.

"You know, here's the problem," I said, leaning on my blade and staring down into his eyes. "One...you're on neutral ground. Drake's is very, very neutral and you attacked me for no reason. Two...I'm not human."

I smiled at him. "My dad was...but my mother wasn't."

I could feel that heat spreading over me now and despite the insanity of the situation, my body was ready to jump up and down, all but giddy with pleasure. Damon was just a few feet away. I couldn't hear him, I hadn't seen him, but I could *feel* him.

"Since my mom wasn't *human*, that means under the ANH charter, I'm not recognized as such." I continued to watch the nerves bleeding into the man's eyes. "Never mind the fact that if you hunt humans on neutral ground in East

Orlando, you're fucked. We hunt your kind down and eat you for breakfast here."

"I want the fucking Alpha," he snarled. "Where's the Lady?"

I laughed. "Oh, that's funny. You're a fucking rat and you want to throw yourself on the mercy of the cat's Alpha?"

"There's no pack here! We have to align with somebody and you can't deny me that right. That's in the fucking charter," he said and then he whimpered as I twisted my blade.

"Well, that brings us to the third problem...and really, it's your biggest. If you're smart, you'll just move around until the silver in my sword shreds your heart," I said.

Damon took a step closer.

"I want the fucking Alpha!"

"Kit. Introduce him to the third problem," Damon said, crouching down by me.

"Sure." I twisted the blade again. "You sure you don't want to just kill yourself, rat?"

He spat in my face.

"Oh. That was stupid. But hey, it's your funeral..." I stood up and wiped the saliva from my chin, jerking my blade out of his skinny chest. I watched his injured form melt back into his human one. "Meet your biggest problem."

As Damon moved forward, I smiled. "This is the new Alpha. He's also...mine."

* * * * *

The body of the dead rat was carried out of the bar a few minutes later. I guess maybe I could have done the kind thing and killed him while I had my blade buried in him.

But he was a shapeshifter, he'd come onto shifter land and fucked with shifter rules. That was Damon's territory, not mine. Especially since he was still settling in here as Alpha.

The big guy was howling and crying like somebody had taken his toy away. Damon eyed him narrowly but I think we both realized the same thing. Something wasn't completely right with that one. Whether or not Damon had to do anything about him was yet to be seen.

Chang and the others muscled him out the door as Damon turned to stare at me.

"That wasn't my fault," I said, lifting my hands.

"Did I say it was, baby girl?" A faint smile tugged at his lips.

And me, stupid, idiot hormonal me? I stood there and felt my heart jump up to dance around in my throat like it had wings.

"You do realize I had this entire problem handled, right?"

"Oh, I can tell that. Believe me. I'm still fucking pissed off." His hand cupped the back of my neck for a moment before stroking it down the back of my shirt. "You've got a pretty new shirt on...and there's blood on it."

I sighed and glanced down. "Blood on me, too. So much for a date, huh?"

He nuzzled my neck. "Go wash up. I'll have some food put together and we'll just eat at your place."

I wanted to argue.

But I had blood on me. I was dirty...I couldn't stand to be dirty.

* * * * *

Five minutes in the restroom at Drake's wasn't enough to make me feel clean, but it helped.

I had the blood off my arms, off my hands. I'd washed my face and inspected my pretty new shirt...Damon had liked it, noticed it was new...I could get the blood out. The surplice styled neckline kind of hid the fact that I wasn't exactly generously endowed and it softened the lean lines of my body, so I was pretty damned glad the shirt wasn't going to have go in the garbage.

I lingered a few more minutes to try and calm my

spinning brain. Mentally, I was in knots and I even knew why, but I had to get it under wraps or I wasn't going to have a very good date night. It was already screwed-up considering my boyfriend had just killed a rat.

Rats. I grimaced. I swear, rats in my life were never good omens. The last time one had showed up my life, the relatively calm existence I'd created for myself had been disrupted and I'd never gotten it back.

Of course, if I'd been living *that* life, I wouldn't have found Damon.

Or rather, Damon wouldn't have found me.

Oddly enough, that thought managed to undo a few of those knots in my brain and I was able to smile a little as I left the bathroom.

As I was crossing the floor, I noticed the tables had been pushed back into place. One of the girls cleaning up the floor glanced up at me and I was startled to see a faint grin on her face as she saw me.

Startled enough that I stopped and just stared at her.

None of these people smiled at me.

They *ignored* me. On occasion, when they did look at me, it was usually with a faint sense of bemusement like they couldn't figure me out. Every once in a while, one of them was stupid enough to look at me with outright dislike, but that hadn't happened in a while, or if it had, they'd gotten better about hiding it, because *those* looks pissed Damon off. I just ignored them.

But they didn't *smile* at me.

Well, Chang did, sometimes.

Damon smiled at me. Even before we'd gotten together, he'd smiled at me. When I wasn't frustrating him or pissing him off, I'd amused him. Actually, I still do that.

But the rest of the shifters, I know they don't have much use for me and if it wasn't for Damon, I doubt they'd tolerate having me in here if I wasn't on business.

Still, that was definitely a smile on her face.

Okay.

I was about ready to smile back at her when Damon appeared at my side and stroked a hand down my back. "Food will be ready in another five minutes."

"That's quick," I said, looking away from the girl.

Forget the confusion of her smile.

I had the pleasure of his now.

He flicked one of my earrings. "Were you here long?"

"Nope. Not very. Five, maybe ten minutes."

He glanced over to where Chang was sitting. "And Chang was here."

I sighed. "We can talk about this later, right?"

"Nothing to talk about, Kit," he said.

But he wasn't being entirely truthful.

I knew it as well as he did.

One of the shifter cats—I think his name was Grayson—approached and I was glad. I didn't have to find something else to talk about, or try and act like I wasn't aggravated with him if he suggested that I should have let his good buddy Chang handle things.

"Alpha."

I squeezed Damon's hand. "I'll wait at the bar."

He didn't let go. "I'm rather engaged at the moment." He was staring at Grayson, an unyielding look in his eyes.

"It won't take long," Grayson said quietly, ducking his head respectfully. "I could buy the girl a drink and—"

"The girl has a name." Damon's eyes were gleaming now, and I knew that gleam meant dangerous things.

I tried to tug my hand away again, discreetly. When he didn't let go this time, I gave up.

"I came here to have dinner and couple hours away with my lady," Damon said, not bothering to keep his voice low or even polite. He awarded the entire bar a dark look. "It's kind of been shot to hell, as you all can see, but that doesn't mean I don't plan on salvaging it. If anybody has business with me, they can see to it in the normal way. *Not* when I'm trying to have a fucking meal."

He paused and looked back at Grayson.

The man had gone pale, the skin around his eyes all tight and he was twisted a ragged old baseball cap in his hands in a way that made me think he was going to shred it if he wasn't careful.

"Is that understood?" Damon asked, this time directing the question at the man in front of us.

"Yes, Alpha." He nodded, the gesture jerky, nervous. I started to feel bad for him but as Damon went to guide me away, I caught the look he sent me from under his lashes.

Yeah, the resentment I saw simmering in his eyes was enough to smash any sympathy I might have had. I would have been fine giving him a few damn minutes. If he wanted to get his tail in a twist, he could get mad at Damon.

Like *that* would happen.

"Got your food ready, Alpha," Drake said from behind the bar.

As the two of us crossed the floor, I noticed that hardly anybody was looking at him, at either of us, really.

"Does anybody call you by your name anymore, Damon?" I asked as he pulled some money from his pocket and tossed it on the bar.

"Sure. Smart-assed little hired killers do." He slid me a sidelong smile as he grabbed the bags from the counter. "Thanks, Drake."

"Well, *I'm* not going to call you Alpha."

"Yeah. Hell would freeze over. I'm aware." He glanced around and caught Chang's gaze, nodded shortly.

Chang inclined his head.

It seemed the two of them could carry on entire conversations with just a look. Sometimes it weirded me out. Like now. And when I was already nervous and edgy from what had happened earlier.

When I was nervous, I tended to run my mouth.

Falling into step alongside Damon, I glanced over at him. "By the way, I'll have you know, I hardly ever take on contract killings."

He paused in his tracks and then looked at me.

"Contract killings. Shit." Then he shook his head. "I don't want to think about that."

"Hell, how did you *think* a hired killer did it?" I shrugged. "It's not like I can just stand on the side of the road and hold up a sign... *Will kill for food.*"

I thought I heard somebody snicker somewhere out in the bar.

Damon skimmed a look around and that snicker died a strangled death in the person's throat.

I acted like I hadn't noticed as I slid my hands into my back pockets. The weird glint in his eye almost had me confessing a small truth. In the past six years since I'd opened up Colbana Investigations, I'd actually only taken on *three* cases that involved contracted killings. The men had deserved it, one I'd done kind of pro-bono, and the other two had been team jobs.

I did come from a long line of assassins, but it had never been the best fit for me. Too much human blood in me, I guess. I could do it—and do it well, but I never *liked* doing it.

I didn't see any reason to explain that to him right then. I gave him my most charming smile as he opened the door for me. "So you see, I'm not really *that* much of a hired killer."

"Well, calling you a hired-pain-in-the-ass just doesn't have the same effect, does it?"

Judging by the look on his face, he didn't know if he wanted to shake me or laugh.

I think I had that effect on him, a lot.

As we stepped out into the hot, humid air of the Orlando evening, a band I hadn't even been aware of slowly released from around my chest.

"Well," I said brightly. "That was fun. We should do this more often."

"Sure." Damon slung an arm around my neck and hauled me close. The feel of his lips on my temple caused this odd little lurch, right square in the center of my chest. "Maybe next time you can start an interspecies riot, baby girl. You up for it?"

The bad thing was…knowing me? I could probably do it, without even trying.

"Now…just out of curiosity, how *many* contract killings have you done?"

I slid him a look. "Why do you sound so aggravated? You're the one always popping off with the hired killer bit."

His arm fell away and we headed to the car.

It wasn't until we were inside that he said, "I knew vaguely what you were, that it had something to do with assassins and shit and that's what Annette had always called you." He shrugged and slid me a look. "There wasn't ever really any confirmation or anything that you *took* such jobs. But you have to admit, *hired killer* sounds better than plain old *investigator*."

"Yes." I slumped in the seat and started to root around the bag for some French fries. I could smell them and my mouth was watering. "It does. And since it's not off base, it's not an issue, either."

He started the car. "It's not off base."

"No."

"Nobody has ever said anything about this…and I would have *heard*," he said, his voice oddly flat.

I nipped a bite of French fry and smiled. "No, you wouldn't have. In order for you to *hear*, somebody would have to *talk*. And Damon…this is going to come as a surprise to you, but there are some things that I'm just that good at."

I paled in comparison to my family, there was no denying that.

But when it came to sneaky little killers, well…it was what I'd been made for, trained for.

His hand came over and curved around my neck. "Kit, it doesn't surprise me. Worries me, maybe. But very little about you surprises me anymore."

CHAPTER FIVE

The date hadn't been a total bust.

The meal was still mostly hot when we got home and even though I had to take a quick shower before I could touch the food, it still tasted pretty good. The mostly hot meal was followed by sex that had been totally hot, and Damon spent the night curled around me with his hand spread over my belly and the warmth of him heating my back.

It was sheer bliss, really.

But then the nightmares started.

It wasn't one of the bad ones.

Some of the bad ones were just...hell.

I was an orphan.

I don't know who my father was, only that he was human. My mother had raised me until I was five, but then she died. I don't know what happened to her—they never told me. I just knew she was dead and I was left alone, left to be raised by my grandmother and aunts. It wasn't a happy thing...for any of us. They hated me. I feared them.

To this day, I still have nightmares and the bad ones are lessons in pain, in humiliation, in fear. Up until a couple of years ago, I'd wake to find myself hiding in my bathroom. I was finally over that, but the nightmares still came.

Nightmares where I'd find myself tied to the whipping

post again, as the lash tore into my naked back, over and over again.

Sometimes I dreamed about when my grandmother had broken my arm. An aneira warrior *never* lowers her guard. And I might be a useless waste, a paltry excuse for a warrior, but I had her blood in me and she'd make me stronger if it killed her.

It had almost killed *me*, more often than I could count.

But it wasn't one of those times.

I was just...trapped.

Down in the hellish hole where she'd thrown me when I was fifteen. Trapped, huddling against the cold stone wall, scratching at my filthy skin and praying, crying, desperate for it all to end.

I was just trapped.

Cold—

So cold.

I cried and somebody wiped my tears away even as I heard her voice, Fanis, my grandmother.

Such a weakling...crying because you're cold. If I had any sense, I would have strangled you the moment I saw you.

"Kit."

I shivered, cringed away from her voice.

"Kit..."

That wasn't my grandmother's voice...

"Come on, baby girl..."

Now *she* was in my head, her voice all but shrieking. *He will not* stay *with you. How can he? He needs somebody to match his own strength...*

I sobbed.

All but dying inside.

A snarl echoed through the air. Loud, intense.

This time, her voice was fainter.

I felt a hand at my wrist. Squeezing. Tight, too tight, until I could feel the bones grinding together.

"Wake up, baby," he whispered. "Come back to me."

Damon. It was Damon's voice.

I clung to it. Flexed my wrist and focused on the heat centered there. He was there. He was there.

And I could damn well wake up.

I am aneira...

And I damn well wasn't going to let that evil bitch beat me. Not in a dream.

"Come on, Kit. That's it..."

I came awake to feel his hands stroking up and down my back. Strong and steady.

Raggedly, I gulped in air, trying to breathe.

"Shit."

His arms tightened. "Yeah. Tell me about it." One hand cradled the back of my head. "You wouldn't wake up, Kit. Thirty minutes. I've been trying to wake you up for thirty minutes."

I pressed my face against his neck and breathed in the scent of him. "I'm sorry."

"Don't." He pulled my head back and the sight of the fury in his eyes was like a fire on my skin. "You don't spend thirty minutes trapped in a nightmare where I can't help you and then tell *me* you're sorry. Damn it, Kit. Of all the things I can kill for you...I can't kill your past."

"No." I leaned in, snuggling against him. I was so damned cold and the heat of him was like heaven. "You can't do that."

His hand tangled in my hair, absently kneading at my scalp for a moment while his other arm wrapped around my waist. "I don't care if I can do it or not...it's what I *want* to do.

Closing my eyes, I sighed and just breathed him in.

Yeah. I wished he could, too. I wished we *both* could. There was no exorcising these ghosts, though. No killing the memories. You can't kill memories or ghosts like this—all you can do is deal with them.

Long moments passed before the shaking stopped. Eventually, the cold knot of fear inside me eased and I could breathe. I lifted my head enough to glance at the clock and then I dropped my head down on his shoulder with a groan. If I managed to get anymore sleep tonight, it would be a miracle. It was almost four. I guess I ought to be glad I got the four or five hours I'd managed.

Lifting my head, I peered at Damon through my lashes. He was ridiculously alert, but that wasn't a surprise. Shifters didn't need sleep the way humans did. And although I wasn't completely human, I did have some of the more basic human needs. Including the need for a little more sleep. Okay, maybe I just *liked* a little more sleep.

Lifting my head, I braced an elbow on his shoulder and shifted around until I was settled with one thigh on either side of his hips. In the dim light, his dark gray eyes were almost black. I stroked a finger across his lips and trailed it down his neck, along the line of his shoulder until I hit the dense, heavy lines of his tattoos.

They had been laid on his skin in his youth, before he'd spiked. Before a shifter hit their first shift, they healed just a little faster than humans. If it had been done after, his body would have just absorbed it.

The dense, heavy ink had always mesmerized me and tonight, I focused on it like a drowning man needed a preserver. "What's all of this mean?" I asked him, splaying my hand out over it.

He covered my hand with his. "What makes you think it means anything?"

"Tattoos hurt," I said pointedly. "And this took a while." All that heavy inking would have taken hours, I suspected. "Somehow, I don't think you did it just to impress the ladies or to look tough."

He snorted. "If you'd seen me when I had it done, you might change your mind. I needed all the help I could get when it comes to looking tough. Not that a tattoo would have done it."

"You didn't look tough, huh?"

"Scrawniest, most pathetic runt around." He lifted my

hand and kissed it, before lowering it back to his chest. "Remember how Doyle looked in the pictures I showed you?"

"Yeah." Skinny. Rail-thin skinny, too. Like he wouldn't have stood up had a stiff wind come along.

"I made *him* look tough." He skimmed a thumb along one area of the tattoo and said, "I had her use charm-infused ink. Wanted to make sure it would hold, although she still couldn't promise it would."

"So it means something."

"Yeah." He rolled his head over and stared at me from under his lashes. "It's the story of me...what put me on the road that made me what I am. I wanted it written someplace so I'd never forget. I knew it was going to be a long, long walk...I had a goal, things I had to do, and I still have to get them done. I can't let myself forget. But I can't talk about it yet."

Studying his face, I stroked my thumb over the hard line of his mouth. "I don't think I'm the only one with nightmares."

"Nobody ever did the things to me that were done to you," he said quietly.

"Nightmares come in a lot of different forms." I leaned back in, curled against him. It was early. Too early to get up, too late to really go back to sleep. Seemed to make sense that I just stay right there for a while, wrapped around him.

"We've both had enough nightmares maybe." He stroked a hand down my side and cuddled me close. "It's time for something different, I think. Why don't we focus on that?"

"Hmmm." Closing my eyes, I snuggled in closer. "Yeah. We can focus on simple stuff. Nice stuff. Normal stuff."

The rumble of his chuckle echoed under my ear and he swatted my butt. "Don't go getting all carried away. We wouldn't know normal if it bit us. But it might be nice to have something...well, nice."

"Yeah." Sleep was actually closer than I thought, I

realized, but I forced my eyes opened, stared outside. "Nice... what's nice and normal?"

"Christmas...you ever do Christmas, Kit?" His hand stroked my nape.

I snorted. "Hell, no. The aunts and Grandmother celebrated the solstice and I'd helped in the house, but I don't think that's the same as doing Christmas." I rolled my head to peer up at him through my lashes. "What about you?"

"Yeah." He stroked a finger along my cheek. "We always did it, just me and the kid." His hand slid into my hair and tangled. "You're going to do Christmas this year. With me."

I lifted up a little to look at him. "I am, huh?"

"Yeah." He lifted up onto one elbow and pressed his mouth to mine. "Nice, normal...it doesn't get much more nice and normal than that."

"Christmas, huh?" I lay my head back on his chest, smiling a little. "Are we going to get a tree?"

"Damn straight...a tree. I'll buy you presents. You can buy something, too. I think something red and slinky, like all those lingerie things you look at and never buy."

Sleep tugged at me harder but I found myself smiling. "You'd look funny in a red lace teddy, Damon."

"Ha, ha."

I think he might have kissed me.

I know I heard him whisper something. But I don't know what he said. I'd already tumbled back down into sleep.

This time, there were no dreams.

* * * * *

"Doyle was in here."

I was down in my gym. Damon hadn't made a sound, but I'd known he was coming. I'd felt the burn of him on my skin. He could lash that energy down, but lately, even when he was playing at being human, I knew when he was near me.

I lowered my blade and turned, staring at him as he stood in the doorway, a frown on his face. "You're the one who sent him over here to check up on me. Of course, he was here."

"I wanted him to make sure you were okay," Damon snapped. "I didn't tell him to..."

He trailed off, glaring at me.

"Check up on me?" I swiped my forearm across my brow before the sweat could get into my eyes. "Damon, I really wish the lot of you could get one thing through your heads...I've been taking care of myself for a damn long time. I don't need babysitters."

A muscle jerked in his jaw.

I sighed and turned away, staring at the mirrors as I lifted my blade again.

"Why was he down here?" Damon asked.

I smirked as I lifted the blade again.

"Kit..."

"Want an answer?"

"If I didn't want one, I wouldn't ask."

I met his eyes in the mirror as I drew the blade down in a diagonal cut. "Maybe I should make you fight me for it."

He gave me a pained look.

I laughed. Sparring with Damon was fun. He had to keep the brakes on, something we both knew but when he was keeping the brakes on, he couldn't keep up with me. Meaning I kicked his ass.

Damon was a decent sparring partner but he'd never be a swordsman.

"I'll tell you what...I'll answer the question, if you'll agree to do me a favor." I finished the attack pattern and then turned to him, smiling a little.

He wasn't looking at my face.

Clearing my throat, I waited until his gaze shifted from my breasts upward. "You are such a man," I muttered.

A faint grin tugged at his lips and he shrugged. Then he crossed his arms over his chest. "You know, I could just make Doyle tell me."

"But you asked me. And I can tell you. Right

now…exactly what you want to know, for a favor. All you have to do is something that's completely within your power to give," I said. I banished my blade. Her sheath was on one of the weapons tables and she settled there, quiet and quiescent as I strolled over to stand a few feet in front of Damon.

"What?"

"Stop." I studied his face, wondering if he'd understand what I was asking when I didn't fully *grasp* all of it myself. "Just…stop, Damon."

A muscle pulsed in his cheek.

"You're standing there worrying because you're thinking Doyle could hurt me," I said softly. "He's still young and new enough in his skin that I can handle him…and you know it."

Lashes drooped over his eyes.

"It would take blood and pain on both our parts, but I could do it. Plus…" I shrugged restlessly. "The kid hates me, but he trusts and loves you, so you need to trust him and stop worrying he's going to hurt me. Trust both of us."

"Fine," he bit off.

"That's not all."

Gray eyes narrowed.

"It's a bulk sort of favor."

"I only asked one fucking question."

I grinned at him. "Maybe I'll work out naked next time."

"Shit." He turned around. "What the hell."

"You need to quit worrying about me so much. I saw you looking at Chang last night and I already know what you were thinking. You wanted to know why in the hell he hadn't been the one to handle the rats," I said.

"He was the strongest one in there. It was his responsibility," Damon argued.

"But I was the one they decided to take exception with." I shoved a hand through my hair, staring at the weapons that decorated my walls. Because I felt better when I was touching something, I moved to the wall and took down one of the knives. I started to toss it, up and down, watching until it was a blur above my hand. "If it had been anybody else in there, would you have *cared?*"

The silence was enough of an answer.

"And you knew, from the second you walked in, that I had it handled, right?"

"I think I made it clear that I knew you did."

"Then why was it a problem that I *did* handle it?"

As he turned to look at me, I caught the blade by the handle and met his gaze.

"It's not *your* problem," he said quietly. "It's mine. And we both know that."

"I'm just asking you to let me be who I am. What I am...without worrying so much."

My heart raced so hard, so fast.

He stared at me.

Finally, he looked away. "I can't stop worrying. But I won't change who you are, either, baby girl. I'll work on it. Like I said...it's my problem."

It might not sound like a lot, but I knew Damon. He didn't make concessions easily. If he said he'd work on it, then that was exactly what he'd do.

"Your kid has a fascination with sharp, shiny objects," I said, returning the knife to the wall. "It almost seems to match mine. I suffered a temporary break from sanity and asked him if he wanted to spar."

Damon turned around, storms gathering in those amazing eyes of his. "You *what?*"

"Watch the tone, cat," I warned him. "I can take that kid, blindfolded."

"Not if he loses it."

"Yes. I can...and this isn't working on it. Remember that?"

He stared at me, the heat of his anger pounding against my skin.

But he said nothing.

Ahhh...maybe this was the start of a change? I could hope. "The kid is good for somebody who's never been trained at all. Natural talent. If he didn't hate my guts…"

I finished with a shrug.

"Anyway, he asked if he could come by again, but I told him no. Contrary to what so many think, I'm not a fool. He learns fast and I'm not going to give him the training to learn something he could maybe use against me."

"I thought you said he'd control that," Damon said, his voice flat.

"And I think he will…but even I know when to exercise caution."

* * * * *

I know when to exercise caution.

That was why I went straight to the office. I hadn't forgotten about yesterday and Justin's message and his promise to track me down. My lip curled as I thought about it. Track me down, huh? Did he really think it'd be *that* easy?

Still, I wasn't going to jerk him around. As much fun as *that* could be, I'd be better off to see what he wanted during business hours, so I could just shut him up and move him along while I could.

Somehow, I didn't think it would go over well with Damon if I took a job with Justin. Under normal circumstances, I wouldn't worry about it, but having a boyfriend who happened to be a shifter…well, those weren't normal circumstances. Actually, nothing in my life is normal so this isn't much of an issue, really.

Damon isn't human. I wasn't going to expect him to have human reactions.

And hell, even though I am *mostly* human, I know I wouldn't react well if I found out Damon was hanging out with one of his former lovers. I'd react badly. Probably with bloodshed. Grimacing to myself, I figured it would be best if we just didn't find out.

Not how *I* would react…not how *he* would react. So it was a good thing Damon left before I did. And a good thing that the dark-clad figure I glimpsed in the parking lot had waited until Damon left before he made his appearance.

Justin had never lacked for brains, I could give him that.

Somehow I didn't think my current lover would be overly happy if he saw my ex-lover loitering at my door, in the parking lot.

Especially in the uniform he wore.

Justin's Banner uniform was standard black, although in my rearview mirror, I saw odd flashes of silver that I couldn't quite figure out.

The dark mass of his hair was pulled back and shades shielded his eyes as he stuck very, very close to my bumper. Wasn't taking a chance that I'd lose him this time.

As I slowed down at a red light, I waved at him.

A slow grin curved his lips but he didn't wave back.

Well, the grin wasn't a bad omen, I decided.

If Justin was mad, he would have been glaring at me. Hell, I wouldn't put it past him to use his magic to stop my car in the middle of the road. He could do it. Justin was a witch. Up until he'd signed on with Banner, he'd been unaffiliated, not linked up with any of the witch houses but that was because he couldn't stand the rules and the structure that went with the few of them he would have been suited to.

Justin and I were a lot alike in some ways...problem children, to the core.

My office wasn't close to my home. It was on the far side of East Orlando, close to the main offices of the Assembly but also very, very close to the border. A few miles either way and I'd be in cat territory, wolf territory and just a little north of here was Orlando. Human ground.

I liked being accessible.

Not that many humans came looking for me these days.

They stayed holed up in Orlando. The tourists came for the parks, enjoyed their vacations and left. The rest of them stayed for the jobs and lived in spelled, gated communities because they didn't think it was safe with all the monsters around anymore.

Hell, *we* were safer than they were.

Their gangs killed more humans than we did.

We might kill our own, but we rarely killed humans.

Amending that—under *normal* circumstances, we rarely killed humans. I'd killed a few of them several months back. I'd gone after those monsters who'd been hunting NH kids. Anybody who does that doesn't deserve to live. I'd been careful. I'd covered my tracks. I was a born assassin and I knew how to kill, and do it without being caught. I hadn't been bragging when I'd told Damon there were some things that I was just good at. I was good at killing. Fortunately, the skills that made me a good killer were also useful for other things.

The humans...an uncomfortable itch settled on my spine as I slid Justin another look. Banner stepped in when NHs went over the line, and I knew I had. I'd do it again, but in the eyes of the law, I'd fucked up and if they found out, I was dead.

There was no way he could be here because of *that*...could he?

I was still mulling that over when I finally reached my office thirty minutes later. Mulling it over, considering my options...trying to figure out the best way to get the hell away from Justin, because there was no *way* I was going down over what I'd done. Not easily, at least.

As I climbed out of my car, I watched as Justin swung a leg over his bike. He didn't wear a helmet. Probably worried about messing up that pretty hair. He'd started growing the dreads out not long before we'd started dating and I had to admit...they looked very nice on him. But a cloth sack and bald head would look nice on Justin Greaves.

Sunlight danced off the silver worked into his sleeves and I studied it. Even up close, I couldn't quite make it out. It didn't look like decoration, exactly and while Justin was a vain piece of work, decoration didn't suit him, either. Justin *was* decoration.

"You decide to stop avoiding me?" he asked, grinning at

me.

"Hey, I wasn't avoiding you." I shrugged and shoved away from my car. "I was going to call you this morning."

"Yeah. Sure."

I shot him a dark look. "Since when do I lie?"

He didn't answer. He probably knew better.

"I finished two jobs back to back, hadn't been to the bank, I was tired and I had a date. If it was that important, you could have come inside to the bar to talk to me last night." I raked him over from head to toe and grinned. "Trust me, nobody would have gotten in your way."

"No chance of that happening, Kitty-kitty." He waited at the door, one hand raised as he sensed the wards. "These are new."

"Yes." I had to deactivate them using a series of charms at my desk and he waited patiently while I did it. Would be easier if I was a witch, but oh well. If I was a witch, I wouldn't be running a jack-of-all-trades investigation service and somehow, I didn't think Justin would be at my door. Hell, if I was a witch, I wouldn't be living the life I was living.

"Why so much firepower, Kitty-kitty?"

"Quit calling me that," I said as the wards shuddered, sighed, and faded away. I could come and go without them doing anything, but I wasn't the problem. They responded to the presence of others, not me. Staring at the charms, I tried to decide if I wanted to go into detail about Jude.

He was the reason I had so much firepower. Local vampire, big on the power level, low on the humanity level, and we had a complicated relationship.

Once, he'd saved my ass. Then he'd started annoying me...I can't exactly explain when he'd started to worry me, but it had happened.

Turns out, I'd had good reason to worry. A few months ago, he tried to hurt me. Actually, he *had* hurt me. Badly. But the really shitty thing was that he hadn't planned on stopping with that. So it was safer just to err on the side of caution when it came to him.

The wards were designed with him in mind, but they had lots of bells and whistles thrown in. The more power one had, the harder it would be to come through those wards unless I deactivated them.

Anything of the midlevel power range could come through easily enough but anything on that level, I could handle.

Jude and his fine ass would be stuck outside.

Even if he tried to bust the wards, it would also warn their makers: my friends, Colleen and other witches of the Green Road, one of the local houses. I had something of a singular honor with them—kinship. They wouldn't die for me...well, Colleen might, but they'd come if I needed them. If they sensed the wards being disrupted, they'd be there and Orlando was one of their strongholds, with one of their smaller houses a few miles away. In a matter of minutes, they would have people here.

If they knew I needed them, they'd come.

It was a reassurance.

Still, I wasn't about to get into it with my ex just then.

"You don't really need to know, Justin."

He studied me, green eyes watchful. "If you got that much trouble, you know I'll help if I can."

"Well...you're not here much," I pointed out. Then I shrugged. "Besides, it's not trouble, really. It's caution."

I tossed the charms down on my desk and dropped down into the seat.

I didn't bother letting him know the wards were down. He felt it and came inside, rambling around the office, pausing to study the spare weapons I kept mounted to the wall. One of them was a compound bow. I liked that bow. Damon had bought it for me and I'd used it to help track down some of the scum who'd gone hunting kids for recreation.

"I didn't think you liked modern weapons."

"I don't usually. But that one is pretty nice." Then I shrugged and added, "Besides, I don't have to like them to appreciate their value. You probably know all sorts of magic that you don't like. Doesn't mean you can't use it."

"Good point." Justin came over to sit down in the chair across from me. He stretched his long legs out in front of him and fixed his vivid green eyes on my face. Our gazes locked. Held. My heart slammed once against my ribs and somewhere in the back of my head, I heard a distant voice whisper, *Oh, shit.*

This was going to be bad.

I already knew it.

Something glinted in his eyes. It might have been regret. Then it was gone and he said softly, "You're going to take a job, Kit."

Oh, really…?

I wanted more than anything to tell him to get the hell out. Just kick his excellent ass out of my office and maybe use some force if I had to. But even as I glared at him, my instincts were screaming. His face was grim, his mouth set in unsmiling lines and his green eyes were dark and unreadable. That wasn't like him at all.

So as much as I wanted to tell him to fuck off and go away, those instincts of mine were telling me to shut up and listen. Still, I wasn't about to let him think he could tell me what to do.

Slouching in my chair, I watched him with a faint smirk.

Justin leaned forward, elbows braced on his knees. "I can see what you're thinking," he mused. "It's written in your eyes. You never have learned how to control that, Kitty-kitty."

"If you keep on calling me that, I'm going to punch you," I said, smiling at him.

He snorted. "Won't be the first time."

"Probably won't be the last. Now, why don't you finish spouting whatever crap you have to spout, so I can tell you no and kick you out?"

"You can't," he said and the gravity of his voice served to ratchet up the tension building in my chest. "And I think you already know something is fucked up. Because I can see that, too. I know you too well."

"If you know me, Justin, then you know I don't like games. Tell me what the hell is going on and quit screwing around."

He nodded, a slow dip of his head. "You don't want to tell me no, Kit. You can't. You have to do this job…and you can't fuck it up, because if you do, it's very, very possible an extermination squad is going to be sent after your man, Kit. And I don't think you want that."

CHAPTER SIX

He had my attention.

My hand heated, so hot and so painful, I could feel the hilt of my sword in my hand, even as I sat there staring at him.

Justin had never been a threat to me.

He'd been a friend.

A lover.

A pain in my ass.

And when he left, briefly, he'd been a pain in the heart.

But he'd never been a threat and I'd never once felt the need to draw on him.

I felt it now.

"Are you ready to listen to what I have to say?" he asked quietly.

"I'm ready to kick your ass," I whispered as I fought the urge to call the sword.

One thing stopped me.

Justin wasn't here because he wanted to give me a heads-up about the order.

He was here because he wanted to stop it and he thought I could help.

At least, that had *better* be the reason.

The muscles in my neck, shoulders and arms were tight,

so fucking tight, it was agony just to move but I had to move before I lunged over the desk at him. Shoving backward, I started to pace, well aware that he was watching me with a close, wary gaze. We were a match, he and I. We'd fought before, trained together. If we ever had to fight for real, I didn't know which one of us would win.

Right now, I was mad enough to find out.

"Talk," I said quietly, standing in front of the wall and staring at the bow. I chose that one because it was the only weapon that I wouldn't be tempted to grab. Bows weren't good weapons for close combat. Anything else and I'd be tempted to go after him.

"You need to be aware that you can't discuss this with anybody. You're now bound to that," he said.

"I'm not agreeing to that," I snorted.

But even as I said it, I felt something simmer in the air, simmer...then drop down and wrap around me, settling inside me. Realizing what he'd just done, I whirled around and glared at him.

"You son of a bitch—you don't get to use that Banner shit on me!"

Justin just stared at his hands. "Normally, I wouldn't. And if it was anybody but your cat, I wouldn't have bothered, because I know you'd understand the importance of this. But I can't have you warning him. Since I don't expect you to give me your word, I had to take the precaution."

"By stealing an oath from me?" I rubbed a hand over my chest, feeling the sizzle of the magic he'd laid on me settle deep, deep inside.

Nobody looking at him would realize what he was.

I hadn't, the first time I'd seen him.

He was one of the very few who'd surprised me, but that was one of his abilities. He hid what he was and he hid it well. It was one of the reasons Banner had wanted him so bad.

One of the strongest witches in the United States sat in front of me. He was, like me, a born killer, a fighter, a thief...whatever he needed to be. But he worked for the U.S.

government and he hunted his own kind.

And the son of a bitch had just laid a spell on me.

Screw this.

I lunged for him.

I had the blade at his throat before it hit me that he hadn't tried to fight, hadn't bothered to try and defend himself.

Hell, he was *lying* there under me with his hands held up, passive as could be.

"You can do it and maybe get away with it," he said calmly. "I slapped a spell on you and you can always claim you reacted out of self-defense. I'm in your office, I haven't claimed that I'm on official business and you know I'm not human. One of the Green Road witches would probably back you up…it's very likely you could just get fined, a light sentence and you'd walk."

I glared at him. He was giving me an easy way out if I decided to attack.

"I won't dispute it if you go that way," he said, his voice still soft and easy.

I pressed harder with my knife, watching as the iron tip pierced his flesh. Witches weren't sensitive to silver but iron weakened them, interfered with their ability to throw spells, to heal.

"But if you do it, you don't stand a chance in hell of saving him, Kit. I'm one of few who thinks this whole mess is fucked up and that we're being led around by our noses. Now are you going to let me help you or not?"

Swearing, I hurled the knife away.

It buried itself in the wall with a thunk.

I smashed my fist into Justin's perfect nose. I heard bone crunch, smelled his blood on the air and it did nothing to satisfy me. Standing up, I shoved myself away from him.

Fury, hot and potent, held me in its grasp.

What in the hell had I gotten into *now*?

* * * * *

The board in front of me held the images of five men and women. Four of them were vaguely familiar, but the fifth man, I was fairly certain I'd never seen him before.

I was almost certain he was—or had been—a vampire.

I was absolutely certain that these people were all dead.

After all, Justin had just informed me of that and I figured he'd be in the position to know. Banner was good at knowing details of that nature and Justin was one of their best cops. Justin was pretty fond at excelling in everything he did.

"Why am I staring at a bunch of dead Assembly members?"

"You recognize them?"

"No. I'm just very good at guessing," I snapped. I was still pissed and not in the mood for chitchat. "Look, don't beat around the bush, okay, Justin? Just out with it."

"I need the answer."

"Oh, bite me," I muttered, shoving a hand through my hair and storming up to the board. Tapping my one finger against the picture of the pretty woman up in the corner, I said, "This is Maxine Maguire. Better known as Max. She was a witch out of Blue Sky. One of their preeminent seers—I'm assuming she's dead, right? She was talented, but also something of a shark. She'd sell her skills to anybody who was willing to pay. Grew up broke and she was pretty determined to never go back there. It didn't matter if she sold her visions to somebody who was willing to slaughter thousands, or if she just sold an old woman information on where she left her car keys."

Justin crossed his arms over his chest and waited.

I moved to the next picture. "Silas MacDonald. Cousin to Alisdair, current Alpha of the wolf pack. Old Silas, I think he would have liked to have been the Alpha but he has a bit of a problem with Torque. Being an addict sort of causes control problems, you know. Any time he's ever tried to challenge Alisdair, he's come up short. I'm not sure why

Alisdair hasn't killed him, unless it's out of loyalty to his family or whatever. Nor am I entirely sure why he still serves on the Council. You'd think they'd have better wolves to choose from."

"Silas has a Torque problem but he's also damn good at ferreting out information. That's why he still served on the Council. Any time they try to get rid of him, he unearths something that would work as bribe or blackmail material." Justin slid me a look. "Plenty of people breathed a sigh of relief when he finally bit the big one."

I grunted and flicked my hair out of my face. It must have been recent. I hadn't heard a damn thing about his death. I'd heard about Max's, yes, and whispers of a couple others, but Silas…hadn't heard a damn thing. And I would have. I was good at hearing things.

The third one was another shifter, but a cat. It bothered me to look at that one. By law, he should have owed loyalty to Damon, but I knew Robert Moriarty. He owed loyalty to nobody but himself and he had a fondness for gambling. He was a rich jackass so he could cover things. He also had a problem with…cruelty. That was a problem the Council had worked hard to hide, a problem that Annette, the previous Alpha hadn't worried about.

And a problem that Damon would have killed him for.

I'd heard about his death just a couple of days before I took the courier jobs and I had to admit, I'd breathed a sigh of relief. Moriarty had been known for fighting hard and dirty. Damon could take him but I didn't want him coming home bloodied and battered any more often than he had to.

Still…it didn't fit.

"This one doesn't make sense." I looked at Justin and said, "It just doesn't. Damon was cleaning house, which is his right as Alpha. He was going through and making sure everybody was loyal to him, making sure they'd fall in line— he wouldn't tolerate the shit that Annette had tolerated."

Justin winged up a brow. "Annette?"

I snorted. "Don't act like you don't know her name.

Banner knows everything." I went back to staring at Moriarty's face. "He had every right to face Moriarty, call him out and if the bastard didn't fall in line, kill him. I've met Moriarty. He's strong. But he wouldn't stand a chance against Damon. If Damon wanted him dead, he wouldn't have to do it quietly or in the dark."

"Unless there was a reason," Justin said amiably. "Keep going."

I studied him for a long moment and then looked back at the board. "The brunette is another witch and she was an ugly piece of work. One of the independents and if you looked up *evil* in the human's dictionary, you'd probably find a picture of her. Complete with broomstick. I don't think the independent witches elected her to speak for them because they liked her—Veronica Ewing was *strong*. I'm talking Category Five Hurricane strong. She had power and connections."

"Yes." Justin nodded and stroked a hand down his jaw. "She had them. Not anymore, unless she's making them in hell."

I blew out a breath and studied their faces again. Five dead. If I remembered right, the first dead Assembly member had shown up dead about two months ago. The rest, scattered over the weeks that followed. I'd looked into it, because that's what I did. I hadn't seen a connection, but I hadn't paid that much attention.

It didn't mean there wasn't one, but what was it?

All of them were strong, I thought. And Veronica, in particular had been a piece of work. It would take somebody with either a lot of power, skill, or determination—or all three—to take her down. Storm-cloud grey eyes danced through my mind.

Damon had all of that. In spades. Plus the cunning to see through just about any plan.

"Which brings us the vampire," I said, staring at his picture. "I've heard about everybody but him and Silas…and I don't even know this guy's face."

"Not surprising. Reclusive bastard. Not local. Has territory here and since this is where he's registered, this is where he acts as speaker when he has to."

The speakers for the Assembly were those who would represent their correlating factions. They weren't on the ruling Council, but they had considerable influence. A friend of mine, Es, was one of the speakers for the House of Witches.

So this one had been a speaker for the vampires.

"Name?"

"Samuel." Justin's eyes glittered hot and bright. "He was a vampire who didn't like the changes that came out when humans found out about us. If he had his way, he would have made enough vampires to turn humans into slaves. That's what some of the old ones wanted anyway."

"A lot of the ones like that are gone."

Thanks to the Assembly, thanks to Banner. The past five decades had been bloody and brutal; it had settled down and the past ten years had been calmer but there were still reports of NHs, the young and the old who died. Brutal and harsh. Most of them were taken down by the Assembly. Some were taken down by Banner.

Except the latest five.

Taken out in silence. By a knife in the dark.

"Why are you so sure it was Damon?" I asked quietly.

Justin's gaze shifted my way.

"Questions, Kit. Too many questions asked." He shrugged again, the light in the room dancing off the silver worked into the sleeves of his uniform. "Rumblings, really. Whispers. Would have to be a high-level NH to do this. Not just the strength, but the skill, the brains. Not enough new players on the scene."

"Why a new player?"

Justin made a weird little clicking sound and skimmed a hand back over his dreads. "Because I'm the investigator...and I don't recognize the player." He shot me a look before turning back to the board. "You know me, Kit. I don't lose a signature once I've had it and in the past ten years, I've come across almost everybody in the Florida region who'd be strong enough to do this. I've either met them or tasted their magic, their power...something."

His gaze moved back to mine as he added softly, "All except your boy."

"Damon's not a boy."

I turned away and started to pace.

"No. He's not." Justin continued to talk. "He's a cat who showed up out of nowhere twelve years ago."

Not out of nowhere. Came from Borneo, thank you very much.

"Worked his way up through the clan. Strong enough to take a position as an enforcer for the previous Alpha—and from what I've heard, would have been strong enough to serve as her second, but he doesn't do that."

I stared at the wall.

"Not only is he a strong-ass bastard—and I know he is because he took her down—he's controlled. Almost all of the shifters she surrounded herself with were messed up. They kept it all contained within the clan, but I still heard the stories. Nobody ever heard anything about him, unless he was dispatched to kill." Justin went quiet and I tensed as I heard him coming up behind me. "You know when he first caught my attention?"

Studying my neatly trimmed nails, I tried to pretend like I had no idea.

But I already suspected I knew.

"Rumor went out that he was going to take down the investigator hired to find the Alpha's ward, if she failed," Justin said, his voice taking on an edge. "Now *that* caught my attention...and I started watching."

"Don't see why."

Justin ignored me. "The next thing I hear is a report that the new Alpha and Jude Whittier are battling it out while you're injured. I'm suiting up to head down there and then the word goes out across the wire that it's done and the new

Alpha is roaring and snarling at anybody who comes close."

"I'm a little disturbed you know so much about my life, Justin." Under the protection of the table, I rubbed the marks on my wrist—marks Damon had given me. Was he going to mention those? Had he seen them? The long sleeves of the shirt I wore would cover them, but still… "Stalker, much?"

"Ha, ha."

I tensed and turned. He'd gotten quieter—standing just two feet away.

"Don't come up on me like that," I warned him.

"Don't stand with your back to me." His gaze narrowed on my face. "You're getting in pretty deep with the cat. You're serious about him. Right?"

I just stared at him.

Justin nodded. "I'll take that as a yes. Here's the problem, Kit. Damon was *seen* with a few people recently before they died. It's not just that I caught a trace. But he was seen."

"Why is Banner interested in this?" I looked back at the board, shaking my head. "It doesn't make sense. Those are Assembly members and if anybody should be investigating, it should be them."

"Two reasons. The first—we were asked." He studied at the board. "Apparently, they feel they have a snake in their ranks and that just means they are idiots for not realizing that earlier. The second—a few people in Banner are worried it's somebody moving for a power play, which is why they are so damned worked up about an aggressive extermination." He shrugged, a restless uneasy gesture. "But they want an impartial party doing it…which is why *we* were approached. With the new Alpha is just settling in and a lot of the cats are pretty damned pleased with the new change of leadership…"

I stared at him. "None of the bastards in the Assembly want to dirty their hands. They are dumping it on you—they don't want to piss off the cats when this goes bad."

"Entirely possible." Justin looked about as troubled as I'd ever seen him. "The Assembly members who reached out are claiming that he's acting *out of control*...enough to warrant said aggressive extermination. All tied into that so-called power play, one they feel is a threat to the mortals in the area."

That would be enough to bring Banner on board.

NHs really didn't have the rights people would like us to think we had. They could pretty it up all they liked.

But if any of us were deemed too dangerous to live, they just killed us.

"Damon's not moving for a power play," I said as everything inside me went cold. "He didn't even want to take over the East Orlando clan."

He did it for me—

I kept that behind my teeth, but it was true nonetheless.

"You might well believe that, and I'm fine buying it," Justin said quietly. "But that doesn't mean I can make my superiors believe it. I need to convince them he had another reason for killing five speakers to the Assembly."

I met his gaze and my heart slammed hard against my ribs as I saw the seriousness in his eyes.

"If I don't get them a valid reason? He's dead, Kit."

"What's a valid reason?" I demanded.

Now he smiled a little. "Oh, come on, Kit...the charter was written for a reason. They know we're going to kill. Unlike humans, we even have *license* to do it." His green eyes glowed a little as he leaned in close. "Just find me a damn reason."

CHAPTER SEVEN

Justin left.

I had several files worth of information, which he conveniently spelled to open only at my touch, a list of names, a gut full of acid, a pounding head and an aching heart.

I couldn't talk about this to anybody.

That was what was killing me.

Not that I wanted to tell *everybody*.

But the one person I wanted to talk to, the one person who could explain every damn thing so I could just *fix* this?

I couldn't say anything to him.

I'd asked Justin why in the hell I couldn't just ask Damon, too.

Although I knew the answer.

Now, come on, Kit. I know you don't think he's making a power play or what the hell, but I can't just pass gut instinct to my superiors. I need justifiable action and proof. If you just ask him, he's got time to cover his trail. Proof, Kit. Give me proof…and if you fuck this up, you could be signing his death warrant.

Gee, way to ramp up the pressure.

So. First things first.

I had to start looking at all the various deaths, see if there were connections and look for more victims.

Because another thing Justin hadn't outright said—the Assembly was worried there would be more deaths.

I felt sick.

And when this job was done, I was changing my fucking business. I wasn't going to be *Colbana Investigations* anymore. I'd change my name to *Colbana Taxidermy*. *Colbana Interior Designers*. Anything. Shoot, I might even enroll in college courses and take some classes in accounting. Being an accountant would be less painful than this, had to be.

Colbana Accounting. At your service.

I could do that. I'd gotten away from the evil bitch that was my grandmother. I'd helped bring down the rat pack. I'd faced a son-of-a-bitch master vampire and lived to tell about it...barely. I could crunch numbers, right?

Anything would be better this.

How in the hell was I going to investigate Damon?

I adored him. Sometimes I thought I was in love with him, when I let myself think that way. It wasn't often because I was terrified of what might happen if I let myself actually be happy.

Things like *this* would happen.

The ache in my chest just wouldn't go away. It was still choking me four hours later as I finished going through the names and making a board of my own. I used string and pins. Sounded simple, but it worked for me. I liked looking for connections and sometimes there were connections where there didn't seem to be any.

Right now...there wasn't *any* connection to Damon.

His only connection to the Assembly was the fact that as Alpha, he was afforded the status as speaker, something he'd grudgingly acted on only twice, to my knowledge.

And I'd double-checked that, too, logging in using my Assembly code. As one of their registered investigators, I had clearance to access the public logs and I could even go a little deeper, but I didn't need to in order to see that Damon had attended all of two meetings in the four months since he'd killed Annette. The first one had been four days after that.

I clicked on the file that would let me view the meeting. As always, the sight of him made my heart lurch a little.

He was sitting in the front row where the speakers were allowed to sit and Chang stood at his back. I wasn't surprised by Chang's presence. Sometimes I wondered just what their connection was—they were friends, but it was more than that. I had a few casual friends, and I had a few closer friends. But I didn't have a bond with any of them that was quite like the bond Damon shared with Chang.

They'd bleed for each other, I knew. They'd bleed. They'd burn. They'd hurt. I somehow suspected they'd done all of that already and were prepared to do more.

Friendships like that alternately confused me and filled me with a wistful sort of yearning. I didn't let myself form those kinds of bonds, because I didn't trust them. Even the friends I had, I knew I could take off running tomorrow and leave it all behind if I had to. All except Damon that is…he'd be harder to leave.

The kind of friendship he and Chang had? It wouldn't allow for that, I didn't think.

I envied it. But I didn't understand it. Absently, I rubbed my finger over the scars on my wrists as I watched the vid play out. Once, Chang bent down to murmur in Damon's ear and I had to wonder at what was said. There was no telling, if I went by Damon's expression. He simply didn't make one. That hard face was impassive as all get out. So far, nothing that had taken place at the meeting had caused much of a reaction.

Somebody called his name and he canted his head to the side, stayed sprawled in his seat for a minute.

It wasn't until somebody said *Alpha Damon Lee* that he bothered to rise and he did it with all cagey, coiled grace.

The video image just didn't do him justice, I thought, crossing my arms over my chest.

When he spoke, there was an odd sort of power in his voice that I hadn't ever really noticed before. I knew he kept the brakes on around me, but he wasn't bothering with these guys.

Of course, the Assembly was all *about* power. The more you had, the more they respected you.

"I present myself as the new Alpha of the Cats in the Southern Region," Damon said. Despite the power rolling from him, from his voice, his tone was...bored. Very bored. Like he'd rather be anywhere but there.

"So noted," one of the Councilors said—I recognize that voice. One of the Green Road witches. Her name was Anice, I thought. Stern. Borderline mean, but fair. She didn't like me, but she wasn't cruel with it. All in all...fair.

"Why did you just now decide to take these actions?"

I studied the video screen, hands braced on the desk until I found the person speaking that time. A fairy's voice. *That* witch, I knew. Max. The dead witch. Seer abilities. She had her legs crossed, hands folded neatly and resting on her knees as she studied Damon.

And the look on her face was the kind of look you'd expect to see on a cat's face when it had a mouse corned.

Idiot.

You don't play cat and mouse games with another cat.

He flicked a look at her and went to sit back down. "To my knowledge, I'm not required to answer to the independents," he drawled.

"Perhaps not."

My lip curled when I heard *that* voice. I didn't even need to look for him. It was Jude. The son of a bitch who'd been behind the hunting games—the bastard who'd broken seven of my ribs not that long ago. I still hadn't made him pay for that.

"But the house of vampires is curious about it. Alpha Annette had long been our ally. We've yet to determine if you will be. Why was she taken out, Alpha Lee?"

A slow smile curled Damon's lips as he stretched his legs out in front of him. The indolent way he sat there, the look in his eyes, everything about him pretty much screamed *fuck you*. "I guess maybe I was tired of having a crazy bitch run my fellow cats into the ground when I could do better," he said easily, with no sign of anger.

Maybe nobody else saw it.

But it was there.

Damon hated Jude about as much as I did.

"There have never been formal complaints against her," Alisdair MacDonald said quietly. "Are you certain this was a legitimate action and nothing to do with…personal reasons?"

"Oh, it was entirely personal." Damon shrugged. "And it was entirely legitimate. It was a fair kill. I challenged her in view of witnesses and she lost. She tried to bring in three others at my back and I could have killed them. I chose not to. It's over and it's done—the pack is mine now."

MacDonald nodded. "I, for one, have no complaints."

"I'm curious how much this has to do with the assassin."

I didn't know that voice.

It was low and insidious. Deadly cold, iced poison dripping against my skin. Even though I was just watching a fucking *video*, I felt my heart jump into my throat and lodge there, swell up and choke me as a man moved into view.

Old. He was old. I could feel the punch of his power even though it wasn't him I was facing. It was just a digital recording.

He was pale, in that way the old vampires are—his skin hadn't seen the sun in centuries, and his hair was black as coal, pulled back to reveal a face that was harsh and blunt and unyielding.

I'd seen his picture just hours ago. Minutes ago, really, as I had finished stringing my web and looking for connections that didn't seem to exist.

This was the vampire Samuel and he had power that made my teeth hurt, even just watching him on a fucking *video*.

Damon kicked up his booted feet and rested them on the desk in front of him, arching his brows.

Lazy, arrogant cat.

Fear flooded me even as I wished I could be that cocky

in the face of something as terrifying as the monster moving across the screen. I could maybe fake it—sometimes—but Damon didn't fake it. He sat there, all but silently laughing at anybody and everybody who thought they could fuck with him.

"Tell me about the assassin, cat...what does this have to do with her?"

"Seeing as how she can't serve as Alpha or speak for us, I'm pretty sure it doesn't have anything to do with her," Damon said, shrugging.

"So your attack on Annette had nothing to do with the fact that she wouldn't give you leave to go chasing after your little whore? Is she really that good? I have to admit...I'm tempted to find out."

Damon's laziness disappeared in a blink.

He went from that lazy, feline sprawl to a springing attack, landing on the desk. The vampire, who'd stopped just in front of it, now had a shifted, clawed hand gripping his throat.

"What did you say, leech?"

"Ah, ah, ah...You can't attack me here," Samuel said, chuckling.

"Oh." Damon's eyes flashed. "I think I can. The charter gives me to leave to do what*ever* in the fuck I want on any ground except human territory if I feel a threat has been issued against one of mine." He leaned in. "She's mine, leech."

"Enough!"

Voices rang out through the grand room and Samuel fell back, laughing.

"Alpha, that wasn't a threat. When I make a threat against her, you'll know."

I swallowed the gorge rising up in my throat.

Well. There was one I could probably mark off Justin's list. Damon wouldn't have walked away from that.

The rest of the video was no help. Neither was the next

session. Damon neither spoke to anybody nor responded to any questions. Anything directed at him was handled by Chang.

Nothing had been put before the Assembly on his behalf, either.

A shitload of deaths had been filed under his name, though.

All deemed righteous.

When a new Alpha settled in, they had a period of six months to determine loyalties. During that period, anybody could request leave of the new Alpha and it was to be granted.

A handful had requested and Damon had accepted all requests.

More than a dozen new cats had requested to come into the clan, though and that was…interesting.

The numbers were still lower than they had been before Annette's death, though. He was taking the '*cleaning up*' seriously. We hadn't seen each other as much as either of us would have liked and a lot of the time was because he had his attention split between regular clan leader responsibilities and his new duties. Running the clan was like running a company with a thousand employees and he seemed to be taking it seriously.

Obviously. He'd killed more than seventy people in the past three months. I grimaced as I read through the death reports.

Seventy-five challenges.

Each report was concise and simple.

He explained why he'd called each member out.

Some had plainly said they'd been happy with Annette's rule and didn't plan to change how they lived.

Damon advised them that they *would* change or they'd leave. Or die.

In the end, a few left. Many had died, thinking they could handle the cat who'd previously held only the rank of enforcer in the clan.

In the past month, the reports had finally slowed down. Were they figuring things out?

I hoped so.

Finally, I logged out of the Assembly's website and stood up. I was in the middle of stretching out the kinks in my back when I felt the familiar warning prickle of heat dancing on my skin.

Shifter...

A moment later my senses whispered: *Cat.*

It wasn't Damon.

I knew that much.

I rested my hand on the grip of my sword. She rested against my desk, and the feel of her sent a warm rush running through me. Her music sounded in the back of my mind. *I am here—*

Yeah. I knew that. But I left her where she was, out of sight and hidden behind my desk as the door swung open.

The sight of Doyle standing there didn't do anything to improve my mood. His mood, his attitude would just have to wait. Until forever sounded good to me, I figured as I grabbed my blade. Sliding her into place, I leveled a flat look at Doyle. "Kid, I've got a huge job and I've got to do a deadline like a chopping block. Whatever it is...just go away."

"Ah...I need a minute, Kit. Just a minute."

If it hadn't been the nervous, erratic tone of his voice, I would have just ignored him as I gathered up the files. Ironically enough, I noticed those files were all blank.

They hadn't been thirty seconds ago.

Apparently just the presence of another was enough to activate whatever spell Justin had laid on them.

Frowning, I shoved them into my bag and then looked at Doyle's face. He was staring at his feet. His shoulders were slumped and he had his hands loosely linked together in front of him.

I'd seen that position before...every time Damon dressed him down over something.

"Doyle," I said tiredly. "I'm serious. If Damon's trying to

get you to babysit me or check up on me again, I'm going to kick his ass. I've got work."

Doyle jerked his head nervously. "No. He…ah. He's out of town for a few days again. Chang's covering. They don't know I'm here."

"He's gone? Again?" I scowled. The guy didn't even bother to tell me? Then I wanted to kick myself. Wasn't like he was required. But still…

"I asked Damon," Doyle said, the words spilling out of him in a rush.

"Asked what?" I glanced at him, distracted. I took one of the longer blades from the wall and swung it. It would work. I grabbed a bag from the floor and slid the blade inside. When hunting for bear…

"About…" His breathing hitched and I felt the crush of his power as his fear spiked.

Slowly, I turned, bracing myself.

But he wasn't staring at me with that panicked, focused gaze. He was still staring, docilely, at the floor. "I asked about the Glades," he whispered. "He said…"

Shoving a hand through my hair, I snagged a few of my throwing knives and then headed back to my desk and got my vest. I slid it on and zipped it halfway, tucking the blades into the concealed sheaths at the sides. "Doyle. You're fine. Go home."

"I can't," he snapped, jerking up his head and glaring at me. "Damon was going to head one way to look. He told me. *You* are the reason he went east. You made him go that way. *You* are the entire reason he was down there to begin with. The Everglades was your idea, all along. And *you*…" He stopped and swallowed. "It was you all along. Damon caught on our scent, but only because you put him on the right road to begin with."

I shrugged. "Look, if we hadn't found you that night, we would have found you the next day."

"But it would have been too late for me. Erin…" He licked his lips and looked away. "I was already so close to breaking with her and right before we heard you all coming, I was sitting there thinking: *We aren't going to get out of here. I can just go ahead...*"

His eyes flashed gold as he looked back at me. That soft blue bled away until the eyes of a tiger were staring at me from his human face. Stripes ghosted under his skin and I knew he was holding on by the skin of his teeth. It wasn't anger causing it. It was fear. He'd been through hell, the poor kid.

Sighing, I tried again. "Doyle... it's okay. Just go home."

But he didn't seem to hear me. "You know what I was telling myself?"

Okay. So he had to do this. Crossing my arms of my chest, I leaned back and waited.

"I had myself convinced that it would better if I just killed her, because at least I could make it quick and I wouldn't hurt her the way the hunters wanted to. And I was going to do it. That night. Once it was dark, I was going to kill her, and then the wolf girl. I was going to kill them both. I couldn't handle it anymore."

My gut twisted as I listened to him. I wasn't equipped for this. I didn't know how to handle this. Where in the *hell* was Damon? I dragged my hands over my face. "Have you talked to Damon, Doyle?"

"Yeah. He keeps telling me that I would have been fine, but I know better. I wasn't fine. And I didn't want to be...not anymore. I was going to turn into a monster, just like people think we are. You're the only reason I'm *not*," he said, his voice cracking. He sounded so terribly young.

It broke my heart that much more.

"If you were a monster, you could have broken at any time in the past four months, Doyle." I shoved away from the wall and grabbed my bag. I didn't have time for this hand-holding and I didn't know what he wanted from me. I wished I could give it to him, but I didn't know what he wanted. What he needed. "You wouldn't have bothered trying to control yourself as long as you did. You haven't broken. You held it together far longer than a lot of others could have."

Those golden eyes continued to stare at me.

I waited for a minute before I said, "They had fun, watching you all act like animals. Seeing you scared. Why let them win…even now?"

Then I headed for the door. "I have to go. Pesky little thing called work and all that."

He trailed along at my back and when I chanced a look at him, the golden tiger eyes had faded away, replaced by the tired, dull blue eyes of a kid who still looked more than a little lost.

I could relate.

I hadn't been able to find my footing ever since that bastard Banner cop had shown up in my office that morning.

* * * * *

One thing I needed to do.

Talk to the so-called witnesses who claimed they'd seen Damon around when the Assembly members had been killed.

This was where things would get dicey.

Two were cats.

They'd talk.

One was even dicier Jude had been on the grounds of the vampire Samuel's house and said he'd had an *unpleasant confrontation with Alpha Damon Lee.*

There was something messed up about that, because if Damon had come across Jude, I didn't see him just letting it end with an *unpleasant confrontation.* A battle nearly to the death? Yes. Had it happened on one of the nights when he'd come to me battered and bruised and bleeding?

I didn't know.

But one thing was clear; I had to talk to Jude.

It was entirely possible he'd get ugly when I talked to him.

It was entirely possible he'd get physical.

It was entirely possible he'd try to make another violent

move in my direction, so the first thing I had to do was log the visit with the Assembly.

The good thing—I was doing this at Banner's request which made it official as all...

Wait.

I grabbed my phone and dialed a number I hadn't called in years. Justin didn't answer. It rolled to voice mail and I was fine with that. I left him a variation of the message he'd left me: *Call me. It's important.*

He didn't want me cluing people in to the fact that I was investigating Damon, right?

Not too many ways to do that without people doing something terribly clever and using their brains. So he was going to help me with this. I'd backed Banner up a few times in the past few years. Wasn't my favorite way to earn a living, but I'd been contracted by them before and that's what this was.

He could figure out some way to make this look *other* than what it was. Shame punched through me as I acknowledged what I was doing.

Hiding it from Damon.

But I had to.

If he found out what I was doing, he'd get bumped up on the executioner's block and I'd lie, cheat, steal or kill before I let that happen.

I'd go back to my grandmother's before I'd let anything happen to him.

There wasn't anything I wouldn't do to help him.

CHAPTER EIGHT

I wasn't meeting Jude at his home.

I didn't want to meet him in person *if* I could avoid it.

The best thing to do was set up a meeting at my office, which was doable. Damon was going to go ballistic if he found out, but there wasn't any way around it. And the best time to do it was now.

I put the call in and got passed to his demented tormentor in training, Evangeline. She hated me. I hated her. It worked for both of us.

"Ms. Colbana," Evangeline said, her voice dripping with ice. "I do not believe Jude has attempted to make use of your…services recently."

The innuendo there was unmistakable. I suppose it was intended to affect me somehow. I'm not sure how. "Oh, I'm not calling about business…not his, anyway. It's Banner business." Even though I didn't feel at *all* cheerful, I could fake it with the best of them and my voice came all cheerful and chipper, so cheerful that I wanted to gag myself. "I need to speak with him…like *pronto*, or we'll send an escort for him."

Banner business tended to be taken seriously. Even though I was bullshitting about the *escort* thing. Evangeline probably didn't know that.

"Ms. Colbana, would you look out whatever window might be around you?"

I didn't need to.

"Oh, I know what time it is." I tapped a stylus against my thigh. "It's mid-afternoon and I know he's not required to attend to any…formal…business until after sunset. But if I don't hear from him *by* sunset, I'll put in a formal request for his presence at Banner HQ. Since I'm logging off thirty minutes *after* sunset? He'll spend the night on premises."

A long, taut silence passed and then, in a frigid voice, she informed me, "I'll pass the message along. I assume you'll be at your offices?"

"I'm not sure." That wasn't lying, either. I wasn't *entirely* certain it was safe to speak to Jude without a little more firepower on hand. I'd never gotten my hands on that rocket launcher, either. "For now, he can call me. I'm sure you can track down my info for him, right? If I need to make it a face-to-face meeting, I'll let you know."

"Very well."

Right before I could disconnect the call, she said, "Ms. Colbana. Jude is a busy man…when he does call, keep this short."

* * * * *

I wasn't on the premises when Jude decided to return my call.

And the son of a bitch *did* go by the office. I felt his presence ripple through the wards. The only reason I *could* feel it was because I'd had them made to respond to the presence of anything soulless.

Vampires aren't undead the way literature paints them to be. But they do lose their souls over time. Something like *that*? Magic can pick up, very well. And since Jude had placed his loathsome ass in my office before, it wasn't that hard to key my wards in so they reacted to his particular soulless self.

I felt the buzz of his presence echo through me while I

was talking to a couple of other *witnesses* and it wasn't long after that his beloved Angie gave me a call.

"Ms. Colbana. If you're going to request that he speak with you, *can't* you have the courtesy to be around when he tries to do just that?" she asked, his voice all tight and prissy.

Sometimes I thought about how much fun it would be to kill her. I could do that. She was almost as soulless, almost as evil as her master, and I don't say that just because I dislike her. I've seen her backhand people for so much as bumping into her as they walk down the street.

Needless to say, she doesn't leave NH territory much. She has to behave on human turf and she hates that.

"Angie, I think I told you I doubted I'd be *in* the office today." I glanced over my shoulder as I made tracks for my car. The two I'd just spoken with were watching me and they weren't really giving me warm, fuzzy feelings. Bottom-level witches—had worked with Max, mostly doing fetch and carry shit and serving as power sources when she did high-level spells, but I still didn't want to mess with them if they got testy.

It would take time, and time was something I didn't have.

"Why should he *bother* to speak with you if you can't be accessible?"

I rolled my eyes. "Oh, for fuck's sake. Put him on the phone or tell him I'll send the escort on down his way. His choice—and don't tell me that he isn't around. I know better."

Two seconds later, his voice came on the line and a shiver of cold raced down my spine, followed by the oh-so-unwelcome sensation of pleasure curling through me. Vampires could work their voices like a weapon...one of pain, or one of seduction. "Darling Kit," he murmured.

"I'm not your darling anything, Jude. I have questions."

"Come by. We'll discuss anything you want over dinner."

"No can do." As if I'd step foot in his house.

"If you can't come by for a few minutes, then I'm afraid

I can't answer your questions."

Curling my lip, I resisted the urge to hit something. Instead I climbed into my car and shut the door. "I'm on the other side of East Orlando and I'm finishing up with other business. Answer a few questions now and if it's necessary to speak in person, I'll arrange a meeting."

"I'd prefer to discuss all of this in public."

Yeah. I bet. Snakes didn't like phones—made it harder to attack their prey. As much as I hated it, when it came to vamps as old as Jude, I *felt* like prey. "Look, I'm busy as hell and don't have time to waste chasing down dead ends. I just need to know if you have any information about a Speaker...vampire by the name Samuel. He was killed and the Assembly asked Banner to look into it."

A taut silence stretched out between us.

When Jude spoke, his voice was sharp as a blade. "Since when do you care about the comings and goings of Banner, Kit?"

"Since I got dragged into it," I said, managing a very put-upon sigh. "They dump a case into my lap and leave me to work it blind. Since he's an old vampire—and so are you— I'm assuming you know each other. Or *knew*. Several Speakers bit the big one lately and I was asked to consult. Who knows why, but I've got this job on top of my other work. Now...Jude. Do you know anything about the Speaker's death?"

"I knew Samuel." Then, before I could ask him to expand on that, Evangeline was on the phone.

"If you want any more information, you'll have to speak to Jude in person. Threaten away, if you wish, but I'll just have one of the lawyers contact you. He's a Speaker of the Assembly and that grants him certain...protections."

I curled my lip as the call was disconnected.

Throwing the phone into the seat beside me, I tried to decide if that had been useful, at all.

It only took five seconds to decide.

No. It hadn't been helpful at all.

* * * * *

Justin still hadn't called.

I'd spent most of the day churning up absolutely nothing.

Jude was now expecting me to grace him with my presence—I'd have to figure out a way to suffer through that, and *survive* it, or just put him off until I solved this case on my own.

I *had*, however, figured out a few things…time and locations of death.

The Assembly was almost fanatical about tracking their speakers.

Two of the dead Assemblymen had been killed at one of their other homes. They might be registered in East Orlando, but some of these people had money out the ass and homes all over the damn world.

Veronica and Silas hadn't died here.

I shrugged my shoulders a little, twitching as I pondered that.

Jude claimed he had seen Damon, but Damon wasn't an idiot.

He was too smart to get seen outside of East Orlando right before he planned on killing somebody.

A fact I planned on pointing out to Justin, as soon as I talked to him.

This whole damn case had me cranky, and not being able to get answers *immediately* was making it even worse. Plus, I needed some information from Justin and he hadn't called. Jerk.

I could track his ass down easily enough, but I didn't even want to spare the time to sleep, much less go looking for him. Before I went home, I swung by the office. There was one more weapon I thought might come in handy. I tugged it off the wall as I made that next call to Justin.

This one wasn't so polite.

"If you don't call me, I'm going to hunt you down and use your bike for target practice. I've got a Desert Eagle .44 Magnum that I hardly ever get to practice with...it's getting kind of lonely."

As I disconnected the phone, I studied the Eagle.

It was like touching a stick. Guns had no music for me. No meaning. They didn't talk to me and they didn't whisper. Almost all of my other weapons did.

Still, even my firearms had their place.

And this mean son of a bitch would put nasty holes through the bike Justin loved so much. Especially since the ammo I used had been magic-charged. Colleen had given me a look of much pain when I'd asked her to find me a warrior in her house who'd do it.

Colleen, a healer out of the Green Road House of Witches, adored me, but she was a pacifist. Most witches were. But as I'd once been told, even a peace-loving house needed their warriors if they wanted to survive in our world. The witch she'd found to charge the ammo had been utterly delighted at the challenge.

And one touch to the jacketed, hollow-point beauties told me one thing...the charge was still there.

Yep. If he didn't call me, I had a date with that bike of his.

* * * * *

Useless waste—

The nightmares found me.

It wasn't a surprise.

I huddled against a wall, clutching my broken arm and staring at my grandmother.

She wasn't alone this time.

Samuel was with her. The vampire—the one who'd called me a whore. The one Damon had supposedly killed. He smiled at me and opened his mouth to reveal fangs that made me think of a snake's.

Deadly.

So deadly.

"You can't save him. You couldn't even save yourself," Samuel said, smiling at me. It wasn't a kind smile. It was the smile a madman would give his victim right before he ripped off her head.

"I did save myself," I said, trying to think past the pain in my head. I shifted my gaze to Fanis. How I hated her...her face was an elegant, more beautiful, older version of mine. Unlined, despite the fact that she was coming up on her third century. Lovely as the day was long. And so very cruel. "I got away from *you*."

"Did you?" She smiled and bent down to stroke my hair. She *tsk*ed as she drew her hand away and reached for a cloth to wipe it clean. "Filthy thing. And you didn't get away. I'm still *here*, aren't I?"

"No." I lurched upward, swallowing a scream as my broken arm smacked against the stone wall at my back. "I'm dreaming. Just a dream. You're nothing but a nightmare."

"Darling...I'm one of your worst," she whispered, still smiling. "But that doesn't mean I'm not *real*."

As she reached out to touch my cheek, I batted her hand away with my unbroken one. "Don't touch me, you twisted bitch."

She laughed and backhanded me. Men rushed up to grab me and I shuddered as pain danced through me. My arm...fuck, my arm.

"Does it hurt?" she asked, studying me. "Tell me it hurts, Granddaughter. Let me hear you scream..."

I came awake with the scream trapped in my throat.

No—

I didn't scream.

Not for her.

Not anymore, not even in dreams.

Not for a long, long time.

Huddling against the headboard of my bed, I flexed my

arm and all but sobbed as I could move it without pain. Three times, now, it had been broken. Twice by her.

The memory of the pain was awful, a sickening beast that lived in my belly and I wanted to curl up and hide away from the memory of it. Instead, I drew my knees to my chest and breathed.

Quietly.

Slowing my breaths down took practice. Focus.

But I wasn't going to let her win.

I *had* gotten away.

She wasn't in my head and those dreams were just that.

Dreams.

* * * * *

Morning took too long.

I spent the rest of the night huddled in my bed and fearing the darkness like some young child who lived in fear of the monsters under the bed. My monsters lived inside of me, and that made it all the more pathetic.

Part of me kept hoping the phone would ring.

Part of me wanted to reach for the damn thing and call Damon.

Hearing his voice would fix everything.

Instead, I waited in bed until dawn and then stumbled into the shower. Once I was in there, I scrubbed my skin until it glowed red, washing away the dirty stain of the dream, scrubbing my hair, then scrubbing my skin a second time.

I wasn't filthy.

I wasn't the weak, dirty child who'd run from her, broken and terrified years ago.

Lifting my face to the water, I whispered, "I am aneira. My sword arm is mighty. My aim is true. My heart is strong..."

And my grandmother hadn't broken me.

* * * * *

I was finishing my second cup of coffee and a donut so smothered in chocolate there might as well not *be* any donut when I felt the warm prickle on my skin.

A powerful male, that much I could tell without opening the door.

It also wasn't Damon.

And I knew my early morning visitor, too.

Sighing, I glanced down at my clothes and made a bypass by my laundry basket to grab a tank top. I tugged it on over the sport bra I usually practiced in and then I made another stop.

The Desert Eagle was sitting right on top of the duffle bag, all matte black and pretty. I loaded it with two bullets, though I figured I'd only need one to make my point.

I was at the door before Justin had managed to bang on it even the first time.

He had his fist raised.

Shoving the door open, I stepped back out of his reach and took aim over his shoulder. "Now it's *my* turn," I said flatly, narrowing my eyes as I aimed at the back tire.

"If you pull that trigger, I'm going to paddle your ass."

"Yeah, yeah." I narrowed my eyes. "You've seen what a Desert Eagle will do, right, Justin? I can put a bullet-hole in a man the size of a soft ball...or bigger."

"I've got wards around my bike," he snapped.

"And I've got magically charged ammo."

I shifted my gaze to him and smiled. "Iron. Hollow point. Charged by a warrior out of Green House. Wanna see who wins?"

"You're a bitch. Don't you have a fucking job to do?"

"Yes." I went back to staring at his bike.

"That gun is too heavy to hold for long," he said.

"Wanna bet?"

The Desert Eagle *did* feel heavy in my hand, but I could hold it. The beauty of not being entirely human...I could do things no human could, no matter how strong they were.

Seconds ticked away. Finally, he spun away with a snarl. "What the fuck, Kit?"

I lowered the gun and smiled. "You ready to come in and talk?"

* * * * *

"I *can't* help you," he said again. "This was made damn clear."

I stretched out my legs and folded my hands over my belly as I stared at the ceiling. "Here's the problem, Justin, and you can either explain it to the big shots at Banner or I'll go to Colleen and Green Road."

His eyes slitted. "You can't talk. I made sure of that."

"She's an empath. I won't have to…at first." Sitting up, I rested my elbows on my knees and stared at him. "Then she'll pick up on the fact that I had a binding laid on me without my consent. Dirty pool, there, you know it and so do I. She can break it and if she can't, somebody in her house can."

He started to pace.

"Once the oath is broken, I'm going to go to the Assembly. I've seen enough of their meetings in the past day to know one thing—some of them don't like Damon. He's a maverick. But even more of them *hated* Annette and they are glad he came in and took care of her."

"Nobody disputes that." He shot me a dirty look.

I smiled serenely at him. "Here's what *I* dispute. If I go to them and say a handful of people are trying to set him up and I don't like how it's playing out…there are going to be problems. And you know it."

He stopped pacing and turned to stare at me.

"Somebody is working this," I told him. "I don't know *why*. I don't get it and I don't see *how*, but somebody is working this to get him out of the way."

"It doesn't change the fact that he likely killed five Assemblymen for no reason."

I reached into my bag and pulled out the picture of

Samuel. "One of them made a perceived threat against me."

"Samuel." Justin's eyes narrowed. Then he shifted his gaze to me. "Perceived how?"

I gave him the brief version.

"He'd kill because somebody called his girlfriend a whore?"

Rubbing my hands over my face, I fought past the headache, past the pain in my chest and past the clinging dregs of the nightmare for some modicum of composure. When I thought I could speak clearly, I lowered my hands and then reached for the black leather brace I'd taken to wearing around my left wrist. I didn't *always* have it on.

But Damon worried that the marks would make me a target.

I didn't like him worrying any more than he had to.

So when I was out working the job, I kept it on.

Unlacing it, I stripped it off and dumped the leather on the table and then held out my hand, wrist turned up so the light shone down on the silvery marks there.

"It goes a little deeper than his girlfriend," I said quietly.

Justin hissed out a breath.

"I think you knew it was pretty damned serious, or you wouldn't have bothered approaching me." I reached for the bracer but before I could put it back on, Justin was there, holding my hand in his, staring at my wrist. I tugged on my hand, but he didn't let go. "Do you mind?"

"Yeah." He nodded slowly. "I knew it was serious, but shit, Kit. This is permanent for him. He warned you about that, right? Did he make sure you understood what this meant for him? When a shifter does this, it's…." his voice trailed off and he lifted his gaze to stare at me.

"I know what it means, Justin." It was a permanent thing, that mark. Not just because I scarred from it—if I was a shifter, it would have healed. It wasn't the mark, but the meaning behind it. Shifters don't bite like that unless there's something serious…something *permanent*. When Damon did it, it was his sign that he'd accepted what he felt for me.

When I *let* him, it was my way of telling him I was cool with it. Rubbing my thumb of the scar, I tugged my wrist and this time, Justin let go.

A heavy sigh drifted from him. "I'd heard rumors, but...well. I guess the cute leather bracer isn't just to make you look tougher than you already are," he said, moving away to stare out the window.

"If I wanted to look like a badass, I'd get a Banner cop uniform and stick pretty silver sparklies on the arms."

He didn't respond, just stared outside as if the answers to the universe and everything were written somewhere on the broken pavement. Long moments ticked away before he finally said, "Kit, you understand, regardless of what the Assembly is up to, Damon has Banner worried. If we can't show just cause, they want him dead."

"Then we find just cause. But you have to convince them that I'm working blind and I need help."

He turned around, staring at me with unreadable eyes. "And why do you need help?"

"You never used to be stupid, Justin." I finished lacing the bracer back on and climbed off the couch. I needed to do something with my hands. Since I was no longer planning on shooting up his bike, I decided to put the Desert Eagle up. "How easy do you think it's going to be for *me* to go up to anybody who has any connection to Damon and start asking questions without it getting back to him? Think that through. You want me to play this all hush-hush, but I'm involved with this guy."

"I've got that much figured out," he muttered, his voice dark.

I shot him a sidelong look. Had there been something there? Something in his voice.

"How am I supposed to accomplish this without him asking what I'm up to?"

He rested his hands on his hips, head cocked as he watched me. "And how am *I* supposed to help?"

"Oh, that's easy." I gave him a wide smile. "You can

make up some bullshit reason—you're a Banner cop and Banner often works through…intermediaries. I'll play your go-between, there to help out. *You* act like *you're* doing the investigation just long enough to ask the questions that need to be asked. If Damon says a damn thing, I can tell him I got dragged into it because I have a history with Banner and the local Assembly. It's the truth, on both sides. He won't like it, but it will pass."

"And if he asks what I'm investigating?"

"I'll say I'm not authorized to discuss that and you've placed a binding on my ass." I smiled serenely at him. "Then I'm going to tell him another truth—as soon as this job is done, I plan on kicking your ass over it, Justin. You never should have done that. I would have helped you anyway, and you know it."

The words Justin left me with weren't all complimentary. They involved: *I'll do what I can. Accompanied by if you touch my bike, I'm hexing your ass and you went crazy the past few years, Kit.*

But as he paused at my door, he reached up, touched my cheek.

"I'm sorry."

I backed away from his hand. "For what, fucking up my life?"

"I'm trying to help fix it," he said grimly. "If I'd known he was that important…"

Then he just shook his head and walked off. The wind kicked up, blowing a few of his dreads away from his face. Sunlight glinted off the silver worked into his sleeves and again, I wondered about it.

"Stay in touch, Justin," I called out. "I can only do so much more of this solo."

He gave me a short wave over his shoulder.

He'd work it out. Somehow.

He was good at that sort of thing.

I scrambled and skated by.

Justin always managed to rise above and glide.

Once he was gone, I locked up and reset the wards. I had one thing I thought I could maybe do today without a lot of trouble or grief.

One thing.

The two people who claimed they'd seen Damon around Silas MacDonald's place were wolves I knew. A couple of bottom feeders who hung out in Wolf Haven. It was a trip that would keep me busy for most of the day. I could get down there, question them. And the good news, if they had to die, nobody would miss them.

I was feeling violent enough that I almost looked forward to confronting them.

* * * * *

"You sure you wanna talk to them on your own?"

The massive man in front of me was Goliath. He didn't come by the name lightly. He was nearly seven feet. I'd once seen him crush a person's skull with one meaty fist and I'd also seen him rip off heads like he was just crunching his way through peanut shells.

His strength would be scary if he was human. But he was a werewolf and even for one of them, he was staggering. The sight of him tearing a person's head from his shoulders was still one that gave me bad moments, but the first time he'd done it, the man in question had been in the middle of trying to do terrible things to a woman, so I didn't hold it against him.

Still, it wasn't a sight that I'd ever forgotten.

In all honesty, I wouldn't *mind* taking Goliath with me.

I couldn't, though. For one, he'd tell TJ. And while I knew it wouldn't go anywhere but her, I wasn't exactly keeping things confidential if two other people knew what I was doing. Also, I didn't even know if the fucking oath-spell on me would *allow* for it.

TJ heard *everything* and if she heard about this, and somehow heard about what I was doing when I started questioning others…yeah. Not happening.

Besides, Goliath wouldn't go anywhere until his counterpart showed up to cover the door. That wouldn't happen until nightfall.

Since I wasn't waiting around, I was going solo.

Smiling, I patted his forearm. It was about as high as I could reach on him without stretching. "I'll be fine."

He bent down, staring into my face. "I don't like it, Kit. Dunstin and Rick ain't the problem, but they hooked up with a new piece of work and he's nasty. Name is Bonner and the three of them started dealing with new players that sell dirty Torque and any time somebody goes after them, they end up dead."

I grimaced. Torque was bad enough. Dirty Torque? Even worse. "What are they cutting it with?"

"Not sure." He straightened back up as a car came rumbling down the road. "Somebody said it might be strychnine and silver. The drug's so potent, it covers the stink of silver. And you know TJ, she don't let anybody deal in her place." A big hand curled over my shoulder. "Wait until dusk. I'll go with you."

"I can't." The worry in his eyes made me smile a little. "I'll be okay."

I patted his hand and eased away. "The wolf Alpha know about these bad wolves?"

A sneer curled his lips. "We handle our own here, Kit. You know that."

I waited.

He just smiled. "We're working it. Just taking care. Gotta make sure we get all the players."

"Huh." I had a feeling he'd be swinging those sledgehammer fists again soon. Technically, Wolf Haven fell under the territory of MacDonald, but TJ was a law unto herself. Wolf Haven was a law unto itself. No man's land. MacDonald would came in when and if he had to, but he'd come in force and there would be a lot of bloodshed before it was over. TJ and Goliath would probably be a lot more precise, and a lot more effective. "Have fun, then."

His big, moon-sized face was still sober, tight with worry as I headed back to my car. "Kit, anything happens to you, you know TJ is going to have my ass."

"Hey, I'll be okay." I shot him a quick look over my shoulder. "I managed here for a long time on my own, right?"

* * * * *

Famous last words.

Walking in on a drug deal gone wrong hadn't been the problem.

The problem, in the end, had been Dunstin. He knew I was friendly with TJ and Goliath; *that* had been the big problem. I'd planned on just paying them to answer a couple of questions and then I'd get the hell out. Unfortunately, Dunstin and Rick were already nervous—they had apparently figured out their days were numbered and they thought I had been sent after them.

For his troubles, Dunstin was dead.

For my troubles, I had a bloody ragged hole in my gut where he'd tried to take a chunk out of me. With his teeth.

I had my blade up as Rick and another wolf pressed closer. Was this Bonner? Maybe. There was still somebody else off in the shadows, too. Don't know who that was. Didn't care. Had to survive this, then worry about that one.

I really should have waited for Goliath.

"Who told you about the drop?" the one on the left growled. That one was a problem. He had a decent kick to him. Some power in him. Yes. A problem.

"Nobody," I said for the tenth time. "I came in here to ask a couple of questions about Silas and the day he died, fuckhead."

He snarled and snapped at me.

I got my blade up just in time, jabbing it into his neck and twisted. He yelped and fell back a few feet.

"You lie," Rick said. His eyes were yellow and angry. So

109

angry. "I know you. See you talking to TJ, Goliath. You're one of the fucking Banner bitches."

"I'm not with Banner. I'm an independent investigator, you dumb ass." I had about ten feet to get to the door. If I could get outside, I could scream loud enough that Goliath would hear. If it wasn't for the fact that too many shapeshifters like their homes and businesses nice and soundproofed, he would have already heard me.

But if I got outside, I could get his attention.

I knew that.

I just had to make it happen.

Had to—

I slipped in the pool of my own blood and it cost me precious seconds to keep from going down. Pain ripped through me and I felt another hot wash of blood running down my side.

Rick's nostrils flared and he smiled, lunging for me.

"You're bleeding bad, stupid bitch."

This time, I didn't get my blade up in time and blackness danced in front of me as my head slammed into a brick wall. The good news—I was closer to the door now.

The bad news: I was trapped between Rick's body and the wall and I was dizzy, barely able to move, plus I was bleeding. Couldn't move and there was a predatory creature who had me pinned up against a wall. I knew what the look in his eyes meant, even if my head was spinning round and round like a child's toy.

This was bad. Very, very bad.

"Fucking cunt," Rick muttered. "I ought to have some fun with you before we gut you. Leave you on that crippled bitch's door step—"

"Oh, that would be smart." I couldn't use my sword now. He was too close. I banished it and focused on getting my hand into my vest. I had blades there. Silver blades. The one nestled at my back was another charged blade—it had silver nitrate coating the blade, held in place by a thin veil of magic. Too bad it wasn't the one coated in Night, but it would do.

The only thing that would nullify that spell and let the silver seep free was shifter blood.

If I could just...

Blackness swirled closer as I pulled the knife free.

"Boys. You might want to step back." That voice...knew that voice.

Hot blood pumped out of me as I summoned the last of my strength to tear the knife from its sheath. Rick shot a look to the side. "Fuck...take care of that punk," he snarled. "Now or he'll–"

His words ending in a horrible, awful howl as I pulled my blade free and shoved it, deep, deep, deep inside him. His blood spilled out over both of us and I smelled the stink of it—his flesh burning as the silver nitrate began to work on him.

He shoved back from me and I slapped a hand over the bloody, ragged hole in my side, panting for air.

Something flashed between us—silver.

There was a scream.

"Burn, baby, burn," I heard somebody say.

But I didn't have the strength to look and see who it was. I just stared at Rick—as his flesh blackened, smoked. Damn...

Rick writhed on the ground, screaming and clawing at his side. Fur flowed across his skin, but melted away in the blink of an eye. Silver—blocking his shift. It was a nauseating, sickening sight. His eyes flashed gold as his head whipped around, his gaze locking on me. "Kill...you..." he snarled.

My hand was clumsy as I reached for the gun I strapped to my thigh. I hated guns, but yeah, sometimes they were handy. A few seconds later, his head exploded in a mess of blood and bone and I rolled my head around. There was another, wasn't there?

No.

Just a smoking pile of...something. A screaming something...and...was that Justin?

CHAPTER NINE

"Damn it, Kit. I told you I'd fucking see what I could do."

Yes. It was Justin.

That was the only clear thought circling through my mind when I came to. I didn't know how much time had passed, but I was still light-headed. I was still losing blood and that had to mean the hole in my side wasn't closing. Wonderful.

Also, I was still in Wolf Haven.

Justin wasn't an idiot. Banner cops weren't going to loiter around here for any longer than they had to so if he was still here it was because I wasn't safe to move.

"Just..." that was about as far as I got.

"No talking, Kit."

I cracked open an eye and saw Goliath staring down at me—no. Wait. I groaned. "Why are there two of you, Goliath?"

"Shit, she's got a fucking concussion," Justin muttered.

"She's alive. All that matters." Something cool and soothing was pressed against my side. "Come on, Kit. Be still. Let Goliath get the bandages on."

TJ. That was TJ. But what was she talking about? Bandages? I tried to focus, but vision was still wobbling in

112

and out of focus. "Two of you, TJ? Two Goliaths. Two TJs. The world can't handle that."

"Ha, ha, smart-ass," she said and her voice was so tired, even I heard it.

The dizziness intensified as the healing pulsed and spread through me and I closed my eyes to keep from seeing the room spinning in circles around me. That didn't block out the voices.

"She needs to get the fuck out of Haven until I clean up this mess; that will be a few days. And she can't be alone." TJ—as tired as she was, she was also pissed. I could hear it.

"She can stay with me," Justin said.

"No." I managed to think past the pain enough to know that was a capital bad idea.

"You need firepower if those wolves come gunning for you. Enough of them know who you are," Justin snapped. "You want to take this to Green Road? They don't need this mess because you were too stupid to wait."

"Lair." I swallowed the knot in my throat. "Take me to the Lair."

He swore.

The world spun around me as I forced my eyes to open. My head pounded but that was okay. I could handle an aching head. Now...I just had to sit up—*that* didn't go so well. Goliath stopped that nonsense by pressing down on my shoulder with one big finger. "Stay down, Kit." He smiled a little. "Don't want to make me hold you down, right?"

I reached up and gripped his wrist. Every word was a struggle, but I couldn't go with Justin. That would be *bad.* So very bad. "Lair, Goliath. Take me?"

"I can watch you for a few days, Kit," Justin said again.

"Boy...don't you know who she's with?" TJ said, her voice a low, amused chuckle.

"I'm just trying to help. He's gone half the time or still dealing with the fuck-ups from the old Alpha."

"And if she stays with you, you put her in a bad place...*and* you. She needs to be with him. Goliath, you head out. I'll be fine—"

"Screw it. I'll take you to the fucking Lair." Justin looked about as happy as I felt.

* * * * *

"Is he there?"

At least I think that was what Justin said. Hard to tell over the pounding in my head. The ache. The bandages plastered on my side were soaked through and I needed medical attention. Bad.

"Justin…don't let anybody do anything…about that order…" I mumbled.

"I'm working on it, Kit," he said quietly. "Where in the fuck is he?"

I forced my lids up and stared out my window.

We had cats gathered all around the busted-up excuse for a car I drove, but no Damon.

That most likely meant Damon wasn't here. Any time I drove up, it was like he heard me coming. And he probably did.

I didn't see him.

But I did see one person I recognized. Doyle was running toward me, a grim look on his face and he jerked on the door so hard, I thought I heard metal screech. "Kit, what the hell—?"

"Problems." I all but pitched out of the car and would have done a nose dive if he hadn't steadied me. If I hadn't been hurting so bad, the care he took might have surprised me. Doyle wasn't the best person to ask for help, though. *Damn* it. Where was Damon? "I need a place…"

That annoying black cloud swarmed up, swamping me again. It wasn't complete this time. I could hear Doyle and Justin. The words *drugs, Torque, outnumbered* and *Haven* came up.

The pounding in my head made it hard to think, made it hard to focus on anything. It was sheer will that kept me from curling up in a ball right there. "I just need to crash for a while, Doyle. I—"

"It's cool, Kit." Doyle's hands steadied me. Or maybe I was dreaming. Dead? Doyle couldn't be being *nice*, could he?

Then I stiffened as another voice cut through the pain of fog and nausea—concussions. Fuck, they sucked, but this one was *bad*.

"Doyle, what in the hell?" A woman's voice, unfamiliar.

I shuddered as gentle arms lifted me. Tried to get my mouth to work, but I couldn't.

"She's hurt. Had a run-in on her job and needs a place to stay. I'm taking her to Damon's quarters." Doyle eased me up against his chest.

I whimpered as my side came in contact with his body.

"Sorry, Kit. I know it hurts."

"The fuck you are!"

The woman's voice again. Angry and hard.

Doyle snorted. "You can't say she isn't allowed, Sam. You know better."

"I can damn well tell you that you aren't taking her to the Alpha's chambers," she growled. "Take her to the damn medical ward."

Dimly, I felt the power, the presence in her voice. It was an angry prickle on my skin. "Medical ward is fine," I mumbled. Or that was what I tried to say. I think I managed, *"Meh—"*

And Doyle was already moving. "Sam, you and I both know that you aren't going to stop me physically. You can snarl and growl at me, but you might as well know—that won't work."

"I out*rank* you, you snot-nose halfbreed," she said.

"You do." Doyle stopped and for the first time in months, I felt the full power of him rolling. It was hot and wild and if I had any sense, I'd be afraid. But I barely had the energy to stay conscious. "And if you want to take issue after I'm done here, I'm up for anything you want to dish out. But the old Alpha isn't in charge anymore. Remember that."

"Take her to the fucking medical ward."

That was the last thing I heard for a good long while. My body had already figured out one crucial detail—I was safe, so I needed to stop fighting nature and just *sleep*.

I slid under without even fully realizing it had happened.

* * * * *

When I woke up, it was to the sound of a roar.

It was bigger than anything I'd ever heard.

And there was a tiger crouched by the bed. A *giant* tiger.

Chang stood by my head, smiling down at me like he wasn't at all worried about the tiger. As he saw my eyes opened, he leaned over and studied me. "Kit…you look awful."

I actually felt a lot better than I had. The pain in my head had receded to an almost tolerable level and I was almost positive I was no longer losing copious amounts of blood.

I heard another roar and just couldn't stop myself; I tried to look. It didn't send unending streams of pain ripping through my torso. Startled, I touched a hand to my side and Chang eased the blankets down a bit. "We had our healer deal with some of the damage. Not all. But you should be feeling better…are you?"

"Yes." I dared on glance down and then froze. "Chang…?"

He touched my shoulder gently. "It's okay, Kit. You have my word."

His word. Okay. I trusted that. His word was pretty much Damon's. But I couldn't stay flat on my back considering what I'd just seen. No way. Swallowing my pride, I held his liquid black gaze. "Help me sit up?"

"Of course."

The room spun in awful, terrible spirals around me but there was no denying one very simple fact. There really was a tiger near the foot of the bed. Pacing and snarling. And it was nearly double the size of any normal tiger.

116

I stared at it for a long moment. "Why is that here?"

Somebody shoved the doors open and I winced, pressing a hand to my temple as the noise sent more pain chasing through my skull. It was a lot better than it had been. But not gone. Not by far.

At least there weren't two women standing there glaring at me.

One was enough, I was pretty sure.

She was tall, probably over six feet in height, beautiful and poured into tight leather with what looked like a corset for a shirt. Her dark hair was scooped back into a ponytail and she had high cheekbones, a mouth slicked blood red and her eyes stared at me with a gaze that made it clear...she found me very lacking.

"Wow. Are you doing your shopping at *Dungeons R Us*?" I asked. "That's an awesome look for you."

Her lips peeled back from her teeth and she snarled at me.

Chang rested a hand on my shoulder. "Sam. You should know better than to think you can storm in here," he said, his voice almost absurdly gentle.

"She doesn't belong here."

The tiger pacing between her and the bed roared and this time, it shook the very room.

"Doyle," she said quietly. "You are to report for security detail."

Doyle? That big-ass tiger was *Doyle?* Okay, I'd known, in theory, he shifted into a tiger. But *theory* and actually *seeing* that shape-shifter tiger—that *giant* shapeshifted tiger were two different things. He was *huge*.

As he roared again, I realized something else—he was also pissed.

Chang cleared his throat. "I've requested Doyle's reassignment." He smiled and flicked a speck of lint from his sleeve. "It was granted this morning."

Her eyes flashed and went green before bleeding back to brown. "You had no right."

"I disagree. I'm Damon's adviser, Sam. He leaves me in charge to handle day-to-day matters while he is gone and this is a day-to-day matter."

"She's a fucking security breech and under my domain."

At that, I started to laugh. I would have laughed harder, but it hurt too much. "Sister, do I *look* like a fucking security breech?"

"Call me sister again, nugget, and I'm going to hurt you," she warned.

I flexed my hands and wondered if I could steady my bow. I was pretty sure I could. Although I doubted it would be necessary.

As she took a step toward me, the tiger swiped at her with a massive paw.

She sprang backward, catlike in her speed, in her grace. Still, those claws just barely missed grazing her. "Doyle, I'm going to hurt you, too, if you try that again."

"And you'll face a reprimand," Chang said, his tone bored. "He's following orders."

Orders—?

"Whose fucking orders?" Sam demanded.

I was kind of curious about that myself.

Then I felt a prickling, familiar rush and I closed my eyes. Both dread and delight thudded in my veins and I sagged against the headboard. "Daddy's home."

Chang smiled. Doyle roared.

As the door opened, Sam turned and bowed her head.

I had to fight not to puke as my head started to spin and dance on my shoulders. I didn't want him to look at me and see me puking.

For a minute or two, Damon didn't even seem to notice me.

"Whose fucking orders, Sam?" he echoed back at her.

Thunderheads piled up his eyes as he stared at the woman.

Doyle sat down on his huge haunches and batted at the air with one paw. There was something almost mischievous about it, like he was pointing at the woman and laughing.

Damon came prowling forward, stopping just a few feet away. "*My* fucking orders," he whispered in her ear. "Now get the hell out of here."

She moved. Not quite running, but pretty damn close.

As the door swung shut behind her, Doyle let loose with another one of those deafening roars.

I groaned and covered my ears with my hands.

Not that I didn't appreciate the odd switch and the cute, overgrown tiger/protective bodyguard deal just then, but the roars..." Do you have to be so loud?" I grumbled.

The bed bounced and I whimpered, groaned and buried my head against my knees. It took forever for my skull to stop vibrating, or at least it seemed that way. Then I realized my *skull* wasn't vibrating. The bed was. Warily, I looked up. The tiger sprawled out, stretching that massive body over the foot of the bed and the bed was vibrating because the massive thing was *purring*...or something that sounded terribly close to it. Before I could figure out how to handle that, a hand curved over the back of my neck and then Damon was there.

Right at my side, staring at me.

I groaned and turned my head, staring at him. "Hi, honey. You're home." I went to move against him, but stopped with a gasp as my healing body protested.

He sighed and just moved in, settling into position behind me. "Remember how I told you I'd try harder, Kit?" He rested his head on my shoulder. "I'm trying hard now. Really, really hard."

"Hey. I made it out okay." I didn't need to go into detail about Justin. I would figure out something. Somehow. I always did.

"I know."

I closed my eyes. "Why is Doyle guarding my feet?"

Damon kissed my brow. "I think he's wanting to keep you in one piece so you'll teach him how to use those swords. He doesn't do much of anything but talk about it now. I may have to sweet talk you into it, just to shut him up."

"Doyle hates me."

Something nudged my foot.

I looked up at saw the tiger rubbing his head against my foot, the way a housecat might when he was looking for a cuddle.

"Doyle doesn't hate you. He's just an idiot kid who managed to get his head out of his ass. Cut him some slack." Damon nuzzled my neck.

I might have grumbled a little more.

I can't remember. The darkness came up again, but this time, it was gentle, easing me under. Rest. I needed to rest.

* * * * *

The dreams weren't unexpected.

Rick's hands, his voice—right before I'd plunged the silver-coated blade into him—so cold, so cruel. Full of malice and the need to hurt. I'd been at the mercy of that sort of man before. My body remembered it. Once I was lost in the dreams, those memories rushed out to taunt me.

The pit...back to the pit.

But this time, there was no rope for escape.

Rathi was there.

Not at first. There was a wolf at the mouth of the pit and he jumped down. I think I might have screamed, but I don't know for certain.

Any sound I *tried* to make was a waste of breath, though, because nobody would come for me here. I was trapped, drowning in my own filth and the wolf turned into Rathi before he attacked me and threw me against the wall.

Nobody is coming for you, bitch.

I stared at him, fumbling for the knife I had at my back.

He just laughed. *You think that will work against me? Don't you remember what I am?*

It would work. It was silver and he'd just turned into a wolf.

120

He smiled.

You really are stupid, Kit. You always have been.

I lunged at him and he knocked me down.

Before I could get back up, he was on me, one forearm against my throat so I couldn't scream, the other tearing at the pitiful rags that made up my clothes. And all the while he laughed.

* * * * *

Cold—

I choked on the water as it came raining down on me. Cold as ice and stinging my flesh.

"Come on, baby girl...wake up."

A familiar voice, that low, achingly-familiar rumbling in my ear.

And icy water pounding against my skin.

Sputtering, I shoved against Damon's chest. "Damn it, what in the hell is wrong with you?"

"Finally," he muttered.

He shifted in the massive shower and turned the water to hot.

"Put me down," I snapped, my head aching, buzzing, spinning—

The dream.

Not another one...

Damon pressed his face against my neck. "I'll put you down in a minute. Maybe sixty of them. Ninety tops."

"You can't stand here like this for an hour or an hour and a half, Damon," I mumbled even as my heart ached a little.

One hand stroked down my spine, tugged me closer. "Want to bet? You scared me, baby girl. Wouldn't wake up. And after yesterday...damn it, sometimes I just want to chain you to me and never let you out of my sight."

"Not going to happen," I said, sighing. I tucked my head against his chest and closed my eyes. As his arms came

121

around me, I decided maybe this wasn't a bad place to be for a few minutes. Sixty, maybe. Ninety minutes, tops.

The dream clung to me, nasty and thick, sticking in the back of my throat and turning my limbs to sludge. "How long was I down?"

"You started crying about an hour ago. I left it alone for a few minutes," he said against my temple. "Just made Doyle leave once you started getting restless. But you didn't wake up and I figured it was going to be a bad one so I tried to wake you up, but I couldn't."

I nodded. Under my cheek, I could feel the sodden material of his shirt and I lifted my head, frowning at him as I splayed my hand over his chest. "You're dressed…"

"I never got around to getting undressed." He covered my hand with his. "Once you fell asleep, I didn't want to risk moving around because you were hurting pretty bad. Then I fell asleep, too. Didn't seem worth the hassle."

"And then I wake you up with a nightmare." Dropping my head onto his chest, I groaned. "Sorry."

"Don't do that." He said it against my hair, voice flat and uncompromising. "You don't ask for that hell to come into your head, do you? No reason to be sorry for it."

I managed to bite back another apology. He was right. I knew that. I wouldn't want him apologizing for things he couldn't control, either, but the impulse was still there.

I lifted my head and tried for a game smile. "Well, if I have to wake up to a stinging shower of ice, this isn't a bad place to do it," I said, making myself take stock of the area. I'd used the shower a time or two, but up until a few weeks ago, it had been in the process of being redesigned. It was finished now and I had to admit, it was…wow.

Dark grayish-brown tile made up the walls and multiple showerheads, all of them placed at varying angles lined the walls. It was designed in a jagged Z and the bottom edge of the Z where we were held a bench. I turned my head and then did a double take. "Wow, Damon…you're not one for skimping on the little luxuries, huh?" I stared at the gas fireplace tucked into the wall in front of us.

"Well, I've got this lady in my life who sometimes complains about being cold. I wanted to make sure she never felt cold while she was in here." He stroked a hand down my back and rested it low on my spine.

"So that's all for my benefit?"

He snorted. "Well, maybe for both of ours. I like the heat."

Rubbing his chin over the top of my head, he murmured, "Can you talk about the dream?"

Rathi—

Screams echoed in my ears and I knew they were mine. Had I screamed while I slept? I hoped not. Even thinking about that made me cringe in shame.

"I'll tell you later," I whispered.

I needed something else then. Needed to not think.

Lifting my head, I grasped the wet material of his shirt and tugged at it. "You've always been really good at distracting me in the shower," I teased. I leaned in and flicked my tongue against his lips. "Why don't you do it again?"

He watched me, dark eyes hooded. "You need to not think, baby girl?"

"Badly."

He didn't give me the distraction in the shower.

Figures he wouldn't cooperate and nothing I said or did would change his mind.

He did take the time to stroke me down, head to toe, with some of the soap he knew I liked, although I don't know how he got his hands on it. I had it made for me and it wasn't anything you could buy at a store or online.

He washed my hair and tucked me back onto the bench while he dealt with his wet clothes and washed up, his gaze ever watchful...hungry. It was the look that turned my blood into lava and made me wish for crazy, needy things.

Crazy, needy things that he had the damnedest way of understanding.

123

I was about ready to self-combust by the time he turned off the shower. I went to stand up and he was already there, picking me up and carrying me out of the ridiculously lush enclosure, setting me down and drying me off with a towel that was even warmer than the water had been.

"You do realize if you try and do something nice and gentleman-like, I'm going to punch you," I told him.

He laughed a little.

"You do realize I can still see where something took a bite out of your side, Kit." He splayed a hand over the wound. It didn't ache nowhere near bad as it had earlier, although I could still feel the tug of healing flesh deep inside. "And there's still some swelling here..." He touched gentle fingers to the back of my scalp and I grimaced as pain emanated out, a little starburst radiation.

"I know. They didn't do a full healing. But I'm not fragile." I turned around and slid my arms around his neck, leaning against him and pressed my lips to his. "I'm bruised and battered—doesn't mean I'm broken."

"No...you're not. But I think I can take you in the bed instead against the damned wall," he muttered against my mouth.

Hot little shivers raced through my belly and I smiled as he trailed his lips down my neck, biting me right where it curved into my shoulder. "Oh, I can deal with that, I think."

He boosted me up and I wrapped my legs around his hips, sighing in pleasure as I felt the heat of him nudging me between my thighs. This...just this. This was what I needed, what I wanted.

I curled around him, my nails digging into skin as he went to lay me down and he shuddered. "Drives me nuts the way you do that." He nipped my lower lip.

"Do what?" Whatever it was, I needed to know so I could it a lot.

"Do everything." He trailed a path down my collarbone, caught the tip of my nipple in his mouth and tugged. "Everything you do drives me nuts. Either you make me want to beat my head against a wall, or I want to put *you* against a wall and do this…"

He slid a hand between us and I gasped as he pushed a finger inside me.

"That?" I managed to gasp out. "That's all I make you want to do?"

The laugh that escaped him was caught between a groan and a laugh. "This. And a hundred other things…Kit, shut the hell up." His mouth on mine made sure I did just that.

And as he settled between my thighs, I wasn't too interesting in talking anyway.

He came inside me and all the dark, awful shadows faded away.

There wasn't any room for them when he was here.

And when we were together, like this, there wasn't room for anything, or anybody but us.

* * * * *

Damon lay stretched out beside me, one hand on my belly. He had a leg flung over my thighs like he wanted to make sure I wasn't going to go anywhere.

"Tell me now?"

I closed my eyes.

"Just don't start growling at me," I warned him. "I'm already…"

The word *fragile* popped into my head and I wanted to stab it with my sword until it was dead, dead, dead. But how could I kill a word? "I'm already messed up and I don't need you growling at me, okay?"

"You've had enough shit happen," he said, even as his fingers started to flex on my skin, like a cat kneading its claws. In a way, I guessed that's exactly what was happening. When I was stressed or pissed, I popped my wrist and flexed my fingers, absently reaching for the sword that always whispered in the back of my brain.

When Damon was brooding, he had a habit of doing

things like this…*if* he felt comfortable letting his guard down.

I was about the only person I'd ever seen him doing it around.

"I was questioning a couple of wolves—the two of them on their own, I can handle. I know them, have had to deal with them before—even in ugly situations. But this time…well, things got dicey," I said stiltedly. "Confidential case and I can't discuss it, but I had to talk to them."

"I already heard things went down bad." He slid his hand up my torso until he could brush my hair back. "Chang said a Banner cop dropped you off here. Are you working with them?"

"I do sometimes," I said and guilt settled nasty little hooks in my heart. "The Assembly and Banner both see me as a fairly neutral faction so I'm a good bet. I don't have to do it often, but this was one of those jobs I pretty much had to take."

"Why?"

"Because nobody else can work it as well as I can." *Because if I don't, you're going to die and I won't trust your life to anybody else.* "I guess it's that bulldog mentality of mine."

"Aided by a streak of luck?" he said softly.

"That, too. You know me. I usually land on my feet."

"You ended up with a massive hole in your body this time."

"And worse." The hole that worried me was the one acid and guilt were chewing in my heart, even now. "Neither of them were high-level. I could take the two of them. Like I said, I knew them, which was why I went. But they were waiting on a drug drop and they panicked. I took them out almost right away, but their partner showed up and he was higher level. Had enough power in him to worry me so I focused on slowing him down while I tried to get out. All I had to do was get outside and I knew I could get Goliath's attention. I slipped—I was bleeding bad and…well, one of them got close enough to grab me. He threw me, but it was closer to the door. I could get out. I just needed to get my hands on one of my knives. It's one of the ones the Green Road did for me."

He grimaced. He knew those blades. The first time he'd looked at them, his eyes had flashed and gone dark. Then he'd smiled at me and said, *"You're a mean little bitch sometimes, baby girl. Well done."* I took that as approval.

"He had me pinned against the wall for a few seconds— he didn't do anything, but while I was getting at my knife, he...it just put me in a bad place." I didn't want to talk about that bad place. There were things that had happened to me and Damon *knew* things had happened, but I couldn't talk about them to him. Not yet. "Anyway. I got the knife in him and he shoved me away. That's when the Banner cop showed up. I guess he dealt with the other one. I just sat on the floor and watched the silver work on the one who'd had me against the wall."

I darted a look at Damon. "He didn't even do anything, but it still freaked me out. Put me in a bad place mentally. It set a nightmare off."

Silence swelled up, one of those deafening silences where you're painfully aware of the ticking of the clock, of every breath you take, of the slightest, smallest sound.

"I'm told one of them got away. Which one?"

I closed my eyes, tried to think. "I don't know...there was a third, weaker wolf in the background. Nobody I know. I think Bonner was the one Justin killed. Not sure of that guy's name, but he was strong."

Damon nodded. Then he sat up slowly, his eyes narrowing. "Justin. I know that name."

Oh. *Shit.*

"He's the Banner cop I'm working with."

"No. That's not why I know it, Kit."

I stared at his back. The black ink from his tattoo spilled over the top edge of his left shoulder and I could see it shifting, rippling. Muscles flexed under the smooth surface of his skin and I could see the wild heat of his energy hovering above him. Mad. He was mad. Oh, yes.

127

"Who is Justin, Kit?"

I leaned back against the headboard and drew my knees to my chest. "I used to see him for a while."

The muscles in his back knotted tighter. "Find another Banner cop to work with."

"Not an option, Damon." I blew out a careful breath and swallowed past the knot that had decided to lodge itself in my throat. "This *isn't* a thing for you to worry about—"

He went from sitting on the edge of the bed to crouched over my knees so fast, I never even saw it coming. I was good. I was fast. I *thought* I knew how fast he was…and I was wrong.

"Don't tell me what's a thing for me to worry about," he whispered, his voice just barely human now. "I told you that I'd try harder, but I never said I'd hold it together while you worked with some guy you used to fuck."

"Stop it," I warned him softly even as a forgotten fear tried to wing itself to life inside. I wasn't going to be afraid and I wasn't going to do this. Lifting a hand, I touched his cheek. He tensed like he might move away and if he had, I might have shattered. He didn't though and I managed to keep that part of me from dying. "If I had a choice in this, I wouldn't work with him. I don't *want* this job and if I had my way, I'd bury my blade so far up his ass, I'd see the end of it out his throat."

"Then do it," he snarled. "I'll help you bury the body."

"I *can't.*" *If I do, they're going to kill you, damn it…*I stared at him and even though I didn't say a damn thing, wasn't even really planning on it, I felt the edge of pain slicing through my brain, like some nasty little parasite had decided to settle down inside my skull and chew its way through me. *Thanks, Justin.* The fucking oath he'd put on me.

I couldn't even *think* the truth around Damon.

Only one thing kept me from showing the pain that was ripping through my skull and that was the fact that I was used to it. Far too used to living with pain and I was able to breathe through it, even calm myself down enough that my heart slowed and I was able to meet his eyes and say again, "I have to work this damned case, Damon. If I had any other choice, I'd walk away, but I don't."

Something had him worried, though. Whether he sensed the pain I was in or he saw something in my face, because that fury leeched away from his eyes, replaced by something that bothered me even more. It was that probing, insightful stare. His storm-cloud gray eyes locked on my face and he reached up, closing a hand around my wrist. "How much trouble are you in, baby girl?"

"It's not me." I closed my eyes so he wouldn't see the fear in them. "It's not me, Damon. I can swear to that." I formulated the words I wanted to say and even though the headache grew to nauseating proportions, I managed to force them out. "But I have to work this case. I need Justin's help and he's the only person who can back me up the way I need."

With my heart racing away like a Thoroughbred in the Derby, I made myself look at him, trying to focus through the pain. "I can't let people die because you don't want me working with an ex-boyfriend. That's all he is to me. Somebody who came into my life for a while."

"He's more than that. I can see it."

I sighed. Wiggling away from him, I shifted to my knees and draped my arms around his neck. "Yeah. For a while, he was. Damon, you don't know how broken I was. For a very long while. I just…" I traced my finger down the lines of his tattoo, searching for the words. "Remember the wolf girl who was with Doyle?"

She'd been one of the ones trapped in that pit, one the hunters had turned into a toy. One they'd chased, over and over again. She'd never reached her spike and now she was living with one of the healer schools while they tried to fix the damage that had been done to her, body and soul.

I'd seen her a month ago and even that had been like a slice to my heart. She wasn't even a shell of a person…and she'd reminded me too much of myself.

"For a very long while, I wasn't much better than her. I was creeping out of that shell when I met Justin. He helped me climb the rest of the way out. So yeah, he mattered…for a while.

"But he's not what you are to me." I leaned back and cupped his face in my hands. "He never could be. Nobody could."

His hands closed around my waist, kneading the flesh there as he pressed his head against my neck.

I held still, trying not to move, not to breathe, because I knew I was pushing this. Pushing him too far—

He sighed and shifted, rubbing his mouth along my neck. I shivered a little and relaxed. Everything was okay. Everything was just fine—*shit*—I hissed out a breath as he sank his teeth into my neck. My mind processed what he was doing but before I could decide if I was going to do a damn thing, his hand tangled in my hair, arching my head to the side as he pressed down harder, harder until his teeth broke through the skin.

He growled against me and I groaned.

It *hurt*—

There isn't anything remotely sexy or romantic about having a six-foot five, two-hundred fifty pound werecat sink a powerful set of teeth into your neck.

But it was over in seconds and I was still in processing mode as he grabbed something from the bed to press against my neck. "You're asking me to deal with something that I can't change and I hate it," he said, his voice hard and flat. "That's how I'm dealing. The next time *anybody* looks at you, they're going to see what I wanted everybody to know months ago."

He lifted his head and stared at me, the storm-clouds in his eyes darkened to near black.

"Well. I guess this means there's no point in worrying about whether or not I'm going to be a target anymore," I said. "We just deal with that as it comes now, right?"

He snorted and shifted his attention to the bite on my

neck. "Kit, you walk around with a target on your back. Sometimes I think you enjoy it."

CHAPTER TEN

Two things woke me.

Well, one thing...the phone rang and it forced me out of the exhausted well of sleep. I did my damnedest to escape the sound, burying my face in my pillow and trying to roll away.

That was what really cleared the cobwebs from my brain. The second I moved, pain flooded me. Pain from *everywhere*. Pain in my side. Pain in my neck. I groaned and reached up, trying to remember why my neck was hurting. I remembered the mess with my side—you don't forget when a werewolf takes a chunk out of you, trying to get to your spleen, your heart. Whatever his intended snack had been.

But at first, I didn't remember my neck—*oh, wait.*

Damon pressed a kiss to my shoulder. "How are you feeling?"

I jabbed my elbow into his gut. Since he was built like a tank, all it did was hurt my arm, but I felt better. "I feel like somebody bit a chunk out of my side and like a Neanderthal decided to mark his territory by chewing up my neck." I cracked open one eye to glare at him.

There was a large clock dominating the wall opposite us. He had pretty keen eyesight, so I had to assume he just liked the look of it. It was ornate, kind of old world style and I figured it was pretty. But I'd rather not know how early it

132

was. I just wanted to sleep.

The phone rang again. Once. Only once. Then it went silent. Hadn't it just done that?

"Why in the hell is it doing that?"

"They want my attention," Damon said. His hand rested on my hip. "They can have it in a minute."

I sat up, taking my time with it because I expected to hurt like a bitch...damn, I wasn't wrong about that. There wasn't a part of me that *didn't* hurt and that wasn't good. I might not be super tough shifter stock, able to heal massive holes in my body in the blink of an eye, but after a night of rest, I should have felt better than this.

The fact that I didn't told me one brutal fact: I'd been closer to dying than I'd been in a long, long while.

I didn't feel up to much of anything just yet, but I needed to get over that. Food would help. Coffee would help. A shower. But first, I had to sit up.

Pain lingered as I shifted upright into the bed. It wouldn't keep me from fighting, from moving, from working though, and that was all that mattered. A hot meal or two, slowing it down a bit and I'd be fine. There was an odd, residual ache in my side and I could feel the pull of healing muscles, but that was it.

In the end, I was alive so hey, I couldn't really complain. Considering the lingering weakness, it was probably nothing short of a miracle that I *was* alive, actually.

I slid a hand down and ran it over my side, grimacing as I felt the new array scars. "Who did the healing?" I asked. A full-fledged healing would have taken care of the pain, so I hadn't gotten that, but somebody had done something.

"There wasn't one. I was going to call Colleen once you woke up." He covered my hand with his. "This could have been bad, kitten."

I looked at him. "You know how many times I've seen you stumble through the door over the past few months, bones broken? Bleeding so bad sometimes I don't even recognize you?"

His eyes flashed and he opened his mouth.

But to his credit, he said nothing.

"If I was fully human and untrained, running around doing something I had no right to do, then maybe I'd understand," I said quietly. "But this is what I'm *made* for…and short of trying my hand at full-time contract killings, Damon? This is the one thing I'm good at."

"I told you I'd try." Then he looked back down and blew out a ragged breath as he bent down and pressed his lips to my side. "Although, fuck, Kit, if I'd known it was going to be this hard right out of the gate, I might have made you agree to start working out naked all the damned time."

A grin tugged at my lips as I curved my hand over the back of his neck. "You're a deviant."

"Hmmm. A little." Then he straightened up and probed the wound at my side.

I leaned back and let him. He'd taken enough beatings in his life to know what to look for, plus I suspected he'd helped with some of the minor injuries that had happened within the clan, back when he'd been serving as one of the enforcers.

"It's healing well," he said softly.

"I can tell. As bad as I feel, I ought to be flat on my back, so somebody either helped me or had something handy to speed things along."

He smoothed my shirt down over my ribs and glanced up to meet my eyes. "You can thank TJ for that. Apparently she had some high quality witches put together whatever she used on you before she sent you off with the Banner cop."

She did have some high-quality witches. Colleen was the only witch TJ trusted so it was Colleen's magic that had healed up the damage done to me. Sliding off the bed, I headed over to one of the mirrors and stared at my reflection. I don't look like much. My hair is pale and under the summer sun, it would lighten to near white. We were deep into autumn now and the sun sometimes played peek-a-boo with the clouds so my hair was darkening to its natural light blonde shot through with streaks of platinum.

I'd expected to look almost gray with exhaustion, but I didn't. Admittedly, I didn't look my best, but it could have been worse. A lot worse. A hot shower, a couple of meals and I'd be okay.

Dropping my gaze to my neck, I stared at the new mark there.

A shapeshifter wouldn't scar from such a bite, I knew. They bit each other when they acknowledged some sort of deep bond in a relationship. Damon had already done this to me once and I carried those marks on my wrist. At the time, he'd chosen my wrist to make a point—I'd fed Jude, the vampire I later realized was out to screw me over so very badly from the same wrist and Damon knew Jude would notice.

It wasn't long after he'd taken the position as Alpha that we'd decided to play it quiet.

He worried I'd be a target.

I didn't care. I didn't *enjoy* being a target, but I'd dealt with it for the first part of my life—I could handle it. If I had him? Hey, *that* made this better all around already.

I had him and that was more than I'd ever expected. Sometimes my head still spun when I thought about just *what* I had with him. It didn't always make sense, but he filled some empty space in my heart that I hadn't even realized was there until he came along.

Now there was a new empty space, one caused by this mess Justin had dumped in my lap, and it was worse because if I messed things up...*No*. I cut that thought off. I wouldn't mess it up. I knew how to do my job. It was one thing I was good at. I'd do my job and Damon would be fine.

I closed my eyes as I sensed him coming. I never heard him, but I always knew. I could feel the energy a shifter threw off and his in particular; it was warm, buzzing against my skin.

A living blanket.

As he moved to stand behind me, wrapping an arm around my upper body, I opened my eyes to look at him.

With hooded eyes, he stared at me. "How much trouble are you in, Kit?" he asked, his voice lower than normal, rougher. "You need to tell me so I can help. Nobody is going to hurt you again, but I need to know what the hell is going on."

He'd asked me that before.

"I already told you...I'm not." I heaved out a sigh as I hooked my hands over his forearm and met his eyes. *I want to tell you...*And even as the thought entered my head, the headache slammed back into me. I swallowed back a groan and let my head fall, staring down at the plush area rug. The floors were hardwood, but Damon had put some rugs down. I suspected he'd done it for me. The floors always felt cold to me and I hated being cold...

"Something's bothering you," he whispered, drawing my eyes back to him. "Don't tell me it's not. I know you too well."

"It's not *me* that's in trouble. I'm not lying."

The phone rang again. That annoying, insistent, polite little ring. I swore under my breath and drove my head back against Damon's chest.

"Hey...watch it. You had your head busted open, remember?"

"It's fine." I didn't even have a headache now. Well, except for the magically induced one. That phone, though...

Sure, enough. It did another ring. I glared at it. "If you don't answer that thing, I'm going to."

He laughed a little. "Before you do—or I do— whichever, we should talk. I've been out of touch for a bit and that means they have business to discuss. They'll come in here and see you–"

"I'll go into your library," I said sourly.

"No." He stroked a thumb under the mark on my neck, careful to stay away from the wound itself. "I put this there for a reason, Kit. I'm not hiding you away and *you* aren't hiding away. We're done with this."

"Damon...you just took your place here. They need to adjust to that before you throw *me* at them. For crying out loud, they'll look at me and see somebody—"

Anything else I might have said was smothered against his mouth.

When he lifted his head, it was just enough for him to whisper, "I don't care. I took you before I took this. *You* took me before all of this. I keep you. You keep me. It's done. And if they don't like it, they can try to remove me." As he straightened, a mean smile curved his lips. "Let them try."

Sighing, I eased away. None of the cats here who would even *want* him gone stood a chance. I knew that much, thanks to Chang and my own careful study of things over the past few months.

"So we do this now, huh?"

"We should have already done it." Gray eyes bored into mine as he cupped my cheek. "We should have never bothered to hide it. That was my fuck-up. Maybe if I hadn't tried to keep it quiet, something like yesterday wouldn't have happened."

"Not likely," I muttered. "Anybody with eyes, anybody who actually pays attention already knows."

I thought back to the confrontation back in Tennessee. Megan had known. Justin had mentioned there were rumors.

The word was out there. Some people listened to the rumors, some didn't.

I eased away from him and absently scratched at my arm. "I need a shower, big guy. I don't care what in the hell you have to do with whoever keeps calling." I glanced at the phone, waiting for another ring. It didn't happen. Maybe they'd gotten a clue. "Whatever you expect of me, it needs to be after I—"

The damn phone rang. *Again.*

I glared at it.

Damon moved away and answered it mid-ring.

"Ten minutes," he snapped.

As he lowered it, he looked over at me. "Shower. Come out when you feel up to it. They'll be in here a while. But *no* hiding…we do this, got it?"

I was tempted to do something really childish like say, *You can't make me.*

I settled for sticking my tongue out him.

* * * * *

My bag was waiting for me in the bathroom and I grabbed it with greedy hands. Clean…I could be clean, and dressed…

Then I deflated as I realized the only thing I could be *dressed* in were jeans, clean panties, one of the tanks I wore under T-shirts. Oh. A bra. I did have a clean bra.

But where the hell was my spare shirt? I went through the bag again, but it didn't magically appear. Even after I checked the pockets and dumped it upside down. Sighing, I gave up. For all I knew it had been used as one of the bandages on my side last night.

I saw the switch outside the shower and hit it, leaning in a little and smiling as I saw the fireplace come on. I could get used to that, I decided. A long hot shower. Maybe if I stalled long enough—

Then I scowled.

No more hiding.

So as much as I wished I could hide in the warmth of the shower forever, I made it short.

It took less than ten minutes; the heat of the water worked a miracle on my battered body. I stepped out of the shower feeling almost ready to face the day.

But then I heard the low murmur of voices outside and decided, no, I really wasn't ready to face the day. Or Damon's people. Pressing a hand to my neck, I closed my eyes. "We do this," I told myself.

Come out when you feel up to it—

"Not ready yet."

The room where we'd been sleeping wasn't *precisely* the main chamber. He had a series of rooms in front of it where his primary team stayed, and then his own private quarters behind those. Back here, there was a small kitchen, the ridiculous luxury of the bathrooms, his library and office. I could maybe grab one of his shirts, and clear my mind in the library or something. A couple of minutes. That was all I needed.

I paused by the massive walk-in closet adjacent to the bathroom and studied the clothes there. For a guy who mostly just wore T-shirt and jeans, he sure as hell had a lot of clothes. Reaching out, I touched my fingers to one of the shirts hanging closest to me. It was gray. I'd developed a mad love for gray it seemed, over the past few months. Tugging it off the hanger, I pulled it on and buttoned it up. It fell almost to my knees. That didn't work. I tucked it in and started rolling up the sleeves as I left the closet.

I stopped at the door to the library, but for reasons I can't really describe, I didn't go in. Something tugged me toward his office. The lights were off and I left them that way as I slipped inside. The desk was a state of organized chaos. I studied everything, taking it all in as I rounded it. What was I looking for? I didn't know, but there was something.

I knew this tug in my gut. It was the very same thing that had led me to Doyle. The very same thing that had helped me find Mandy all those years ago. The very same tug that had helped me solve I don't know how many cases. That damned streak of luck.

Careful not to touch anything, I stood there. If I lingered too long, I leave too much of a scent trail and I couldn't do that. If I touched anything, same problem. Blood roared in my ears as I stood there behind that desk, wrapped in his scent, listening to the voices out in the main chamber for far too long. A female voice, one that I didn't like even though I couldn't recall why.

Where are you, damn it? I wondered. *What am I looking for?*

I willed my mind to go blank and just stared.

And then, finally, I saw it.

I'd been staring at the neat little list for a full sixty seconds before my brain processed what it was I was staring, just *what* it was I needed to find.

This was Damon's most private area.

He'd allow *nobody* in here and by law, it would take a hell of a lot for it to get searched. He had the sort of immunity to things that a human foreign dignitary would have when it came to having to his private quarters, his belongings searched. He'd have to literally be caught red-handed, in the middle of something very bad, like killing a human, before the Assembly lawyers would even think of trying to acquire a warrant.

Now they might try to take him out. But search his private library?

Different story.

It made sense that he'd feel fine leaving things out in here, things that he would never let anybody see.

Anybody but me.

I swallowed as I stared at the list of names.

Seven names.

Five of them, I knew, were dead.

The other two...one was vaguely familiar. Cedric Marlowe. Old witch. I had an image in my head of a guy who wore black robes, spoke with one of those proper, upper-crust accents and hailed from an old, old family. Like touched-down–with-the-*Mayflower* old.

He had been one of the ones who'd resisted coming out to humans, even though there hadn't been a choice. It had been unavoidable after humans had caught a couple of werewolves going at it on video. There had been a few here and there before that, but this one...an outright sting, and it was decided by the old Assembly that the NHs could either step forward...or be hunted.

I wasn't surprised by how they'd handled it. It was better to control your own destiny than have it decided for you.

Marlowe had been of the mind that if enough witches banded together, then they could undo what had happened. It was entirely possible, but magic came with a price. It had been voted down by the world order of witches and many of the other NHs had spoken against it as well.

Marlowe had been an ass about it ever since.

He'd probably been an ass all along, but that wasn't the point.

But why was he on this list?

I didn't know.

The last name, I didn't recognize.

Delores Richards.

Sounded common and easy. Like a kindergarten teacher or a soccer mom...

But Damon wouldn't go after somebody like that.

My throat was tight, aching as I turned away from the list. Damon was a killer and this was something I had no problems with. *I* was a killer. But I only killed a certain target and I knew how to recognize my own kind. Damon was my own kind. He was stronger than I was, quicker...but he was like me. Probably more efficient and a hell of a lot more ruthless, but I understood him.

The people on this list were on it for a reason.

I needed, so badly, to understand what that was.

Vaguely, I heard his voice and I made myself walk away from the desk, from that damnable list, too aware of the voices out there, what was going on. As much as I'd like to hide in here, as much as I might like to *run*, to get away from the knowledge I had here, I couldn't.

I had to get to the bottom of this.

When I'd stepped out of the shower, I'd almost felt normal, just a little weaker and more tired than I'd liked. But now, every muscle in my body hurt. And my heart felt like a gaping, aching wound.

I had to get it together. If I went out there like this, Damon would see it in a heartbeat and I'd have deal with it on top of this. And *this* needed to come first. Had to fix this.

Taking a deep, slow breath, I closed my eyes. *I am aneira*—

By the time I made it to the door that opened into the main chamber, I could almost think. I could breathe. And

141

even though I felt like I was made of spun glass and threads of nothing, it was something that I'd never let show.

The knob of the door turned easily and I was so distracted that I didn't notice how quiet it had gotten out there. Not until half a dozen pair of eyes swung my way.

Damon was the only one not looking at me.

Everybody else was. Chang was there and he was smiling at me.

The rest of them were staring at me with what ranged from disgruntlement and confusion to outright hostility—hello, Sam...suddenly I knew why her voice had sounded so familiar. Memories of her over the past night leaped into mind. I'd almost forgotten about her. I rather wished I had.

Instead of looking at any of them, I focused on Damon. He was so much easier to look at, so much easier to focus on.

"I'm missing a shirt," I said, a little surprised when that came out. "I swiped one of yours."

Damon slanted a smile my way, his gaze lingering very briefly on my neck before skimming over the rest of me. Some of the uneasiness faded, leaving behind heat in its wake, although that wasn't much better, considering we had an audience. He quirked a brow at me and said, "You were bleeding. You had a compress on you, but there was a shirt covering it—one of yours, I think. I saw *Grateful Dead* on it."

I scowled. My *Grateful Dead* shirt? Seriously?

Sighing, I dumped my bag on the floor and glanced around the room. There was an old saying I'd heard humans use: *fifth wheel*. That's about how I felt. Damon was sitting on the couch, sprawled in front of the fire with his legs stretched out. Chang had the chair to his right and everybody else was standing in front of him, heads bowed.

No. Not everybody. As I stood there, the giant tiger from the previous night came pacing my way. He butted his massive head against my hip and I frowned as I looked down at him. "Ah...hey, Doyle." Unsure what else to say or do, I reached down and rubbed at his head. A sound oddly like a purr escaped him before he turned back and padded over to the sitting area.

"Sir, perhaps your...*friend* would like to move to the guest quarters adjoining your room," Sam said. Although she didn't spit it out through gritted teeth, she might as well have.

I snorted as I crossed the floor to drop down on the couch beside Damon. Nerves had been jangling inside me, but they were gone now. Maybe I should send her a *thank-you* gift. "Hear that, pal?" Kicking my legs up on the couch, I stared at Sam even though I was talking to Damon. "I'm your *friend*. Do we get play-dates now?"

"Didn't we just have one of those?" He closed a hand around my ankle.

Doyle sneezed and stretched his massive body out in front of us. Absently, I was aware of Chang moving to stand behind us. He touched my arm and I glanced up at him, frowning. He wasn't looking at me, though.

He was staring at the people in front of us.

And he wasn't smiling.

"Sir," Sam tried again. "We do have Clan business to discuss. She is not Clan."

Well, there was truth in that—

"She is." Damon smiled, that cagey grin of his lighting his face. "The problem is, none of you saw it."

Then he nudged the tiger down at his feet. "Except for this big fur rug. Doyle, why in the hell haven't you changed back?"

Doyle made an odd grunting sound, deep in his throat and focused his gaze on Sam.

"I've been telling him to change back all night," Sam said sourly. "I think he's still having control issues."

"Oh, like hell." Damon nudged the tiger again. "Change back, Doyle."

The change was slow, almost comically slow. If I didn't know a hell of a lot about shifters, I almost would have thought it was a struggle. But I knew better. Changing back in that way took a hell of a lot more control than doing it any other way. Damn.

I was impressed.

Doyle moved as he shifted and by the time he was done, he was sitting on his butt with his back against the couch where Damon and I were sitting. Light sweat gleamed on his skin but he wasn't breathing heavy and I could see the smile on his profile, too.

He was grinning at Sam, all but laughing in her face.

What are you up to, kid?

"That's better." Damon shifted on the couch and rubbed the ball of his thumb down my foot.

I shoot him a look. *Better? The kid's sitting naked just a few feet away and he's laughing at that nasty bitch—*

"If he wasn't having issues with control, then he's having issues responding to a direct order," Sam said.

"Actually, I believe I've addressed this. I've requested his reassignment," Chang said from behind us. "I would think that you just hadn't bothered checking your mail. The messages were sent down the line yesterday. Doyle is now officially under my command."

"Ease up, Chang," Damon said easily. "I'm sure Sam is still just a little tired. She has to pull extra duty when I'm not here and all. Maybe it's too much for her. Is that it? You tired, Sam?"

"I'm not—"

Damon arched a brow. "You're not tired, huh?" He shrugged. "Okay. I was trying to throw you a rope, but you don't want it."

He nudged my foot aside and I drew it away, shifted on the couch so I could study the rest of them. And although they were being pretty subtle about it, they were studying me, too.

I felt like I'd been dipped in neon paint or something—or rather, my neck. Two of them noticed almost right away.

I knew them. One was Thomas Buxton. The other was Kingston Reardon. Together with Chang, they made up Damon's advisory committee. I knew them more than anybody else, except for the guys that made up his bodyguard detail when he bothered to *let* them.

Reardon and Buxton were typically polite to me, but they reminded me of the wolves. They'd treat you with courtesy as they relieved you of the burden of your head.

I was a little freaked out when their gazes immediately dropped like they'd development an obsessive interest in the toes of their shoes or the pattern of the rug.

It was plush and thick and nicely padded, but it had no pattern, so that didn't make sense.

I brushed my hand across my neck. Were they going to try and relieve me of the burden of my head now? Nah. That didn't make sense. One, my hand didn't itch—if I was in danger, my hand would be itching, the magic that connected me to my weapons firing up. Two, I wasn't going to be in danger *here*...even if Damon wasn't sitting a few feet away, I was in his rooms. Still, they were acting *weird*.

"Sir, I'm not sure what you mean by the woman being part of the Clan." That came from the diminutive thing standing on the far side of the room. She was the direct opposite of Sam. Where Sam was all lush elegance and power, this woman was sleek and lean. She made me think of a bobcat.

I glanced over at Sam and studied the pacing energy around her. I hadn't taken notice of it earlier, but now that I was looking, I could see it. Panther. Black death in the night. She'd crouch in the trees and drop down on her prey.

Reardon touched the smaller woman's shoulder. The look he gave her was telling. She glanced at me and her eyes were puzzled. Blood rushed to my face as her gaze locked on my neck.

"Oh." Her eyes rounded. "Sir, I—"

She said nothing else, just looked away.

One by one, each of them noticed.

Except Sam.

She was oblivious as she took a step toward Damon, head cocked. "Sir, you've been away or busy for quite a while. I realize your *friend* would like some of your time, but the

Clan needs you and this is Clan business. If I may just show her to the guest chambers, then we could—"

"Sam."

Buxton stepped forward, an apologetic look on his face as he glanced my way.

Hell, what did they think *I* was going to do?

She shot the guy an irritated look and he gave her a squinty-eyed one.

My phone rang. I recognized the ring from clear across the room. The Imperial March...not a good sign. I only programmed that ring for certain people and while it was *possible* Linc from the local human police department was calling me, I wasn't going to bet on it.

It rang again before abruptly cutting off as we all continued to sit there.

As Sam took another step away from Buxton, and another step *toward* Damon, I decided I'd had enough. I looked over at him. He flicked a glance at me and shrugged.

I took that to mean...*I don't care.*

Good. I didn't have time for this. My discovery from earlier was weighing on me like a stone and I had to get to work, I had to call Justin, because I *knew* who'd called me, and I couldn't do *any* of that while we were having a pissing contest.

Since I *didn't* have time, I went for the direct approach— I decided to piss her off.

"Damn, Damon. Either she's deliberately obtuse or she just wants in your pants so bad, she can't see what's right in front of her face."

Damon looked over at me and there was a look on his face, brows arched, eyes opened just a little too wide. He almost looked a little surprised there. *Oh, come on now.* I stared at him for a second. *You had to know.*

Then I looked back at Sam and met her furious gaze.

A growl trickled out of her throat, but she continued to stand there, hands flexing and curling at her sides like she was imagining my throat in her grasp. Not good enough.

I slid Damon another look. "Think she's nearsighted?"

Another growl escaped Sam, a little louder this time. I shifted on the seat, readied my body, measuring the distance between us. Yes, it was enough. Not by much, but it was enough. Heat gathered in my palm, but I didn't focus on the song of the sword just then. That wasn't what I needed. I needed something else...tribal beats. Deep, rhythmic, pulsing in beat with my heart.

"What did you just say, bitch?"

"Sam, be *quiet*." That came from the only other woman in there—the little bobcat. If she'd been in cat form, all her fur would standing on end.

"Ella, shut up," Sam snarled, still not taking her eyes off me.

I smiled at her and blew her a kiss.

That did it.

She lunged for me.

It was the smart-ass things that had done Damon in, too. Muscles pulled and screamed at me as I moved, springing into a crouch onto the couch and then jumping backward right before she would have grabbed me.

Somebody shouted at her but Damon snarled.

Everybody but Sam and I froze.

I figured he wasn't directing it at me. He knew I didn't respond to the growling—he'd have to physically stop me to keep me from a stupid course of action and since he hadn't—

She paused and something that might have been surprise flickered in her gaze for just a moment as I landed on the balls of my feet right behind the couch. Then her eyes started to glow.

I knew what that meant.

I gave into the tribal beat of drums right as Sam's bones started to shift. Damn. She must be young if she was letting herself do that now. In the middle of a fight, it was a waste of energy. Either do it *before* or wait until you had no choice.

My bow was in my hand before she finished her shift and I sighted, released.

Her pained scream ripped through the room and her shift froze. I had the disconcerting pleasure to watch as she went from nearly a full shift back into human, bit by excruciating bit.

I'd used silver.

And I'd shot her right through the throat.

Again, everybody but Damon was glaring at me.

Even Chang looked surprised as I passed by him to stand near the couch, a foot away from Damon. I met Chang's gaze and shrugged. "I didn't shoot her heart. She'll heal once the arrow is out," I said, still holding onto my bow.

Buxton was holding her upright, careful not to dislodge the arrow.

The woman—Ella? Yeah, it was Ella—looked at me like she'd like to just run away and hide.

"Ella, get the arrow out," Damon said, his voice still level.

As he came off the couch, I ran a hand down the carved surface of my bow. Her drums beat in the back of my mind and the sound of them soothed me. Listening to that beat as he shot me a look, I held still and met his gaze.

All he did was smile.

I absolutely would not admit that the sight of his smile made me feel a little more at ease.

I stayed where I was, busied myself with examining my bow, checking the string, even though she was perfect. If anything was wrong with her, she'd let me know—

Sam screamed. A woman's scream mingled with a cat's; the sound of it made my skin crawl.

Looking away from the bow, I watched as Ella finished pulling the arrow from Sam's neck. "Be still, Sentry," she snapped and that nervous hesitation I'd seen earlier was gone. "If you move, you'll make this worse."

Ella was good. There wasn't any mishap, any careless moves and she didn't hesitate, either. The arrow was out in an instant and hot, black blood flowed for just a moment before it gushed red. Ella clapped her hand over the wound and somebody shoved a white cloth into her free one. As she covered Sam's neck, she looked over at me. "Either you're a very good shot, or a lucky one."

"I've never had a lucky shot in my life," I said softly.

She nodded and then looked back at Sam, who was arching off the ground and whimpering.

I looked away. It hurt. I had no doubt of that. Sam was a were and I'd shot her in the throat, deliberately nicking one of her major vessels with something that was poisonous to her kind.

She could handle the loss of blood. It was the poison that was making her whine and cry like a baby.

Absently I wondered what my grandmother would think. *Useless waste—*

In the back of my mind, I heard the crack of a whip. *Does it hurt? Tell me it hurts...*

Fanis's voice was an evil whisper in the back of my brain. I pushed it out even as I allowed myself to acknowledge a simple fact. If it had been one of my cousins lying there on the floor, writhing, whining, whimpering, she might have kicked them in the ribs and told them to shut up. Petty cruelty, yes. But if it had been me? Another whipping.

One of the reasons I didn't like to let myself scream. That conditioning was hard to break.

I moved back over to the couch, leaning against the arm by where Damon stood and resting my hip against it. The expression I pasted on my face was bored, but inside I was crawling with nerves, anxiety and impatience. There was no *time* for this, damn it. No time at all. I had to get out of here and—

Damon rested a hand on my back.

I shot him a look.

He wasn't looking at me; his gaze was locked on Sam.

And his thumb was rubbing the base of my spine.

Perfect. Now he was picking up on my anxiety and thinking it has something, *anything* to do with this female cat I could kill blindfolded.

149

No. She didn't worry me. There were much, much more important things worrying me…like the cat sitting down next to me. Rubbing his thumb along my back and trying to soothe me.

"Sam, are you going to quit crying like a baby and get up or not?" Damon said after another thirty seconds passed.

Mid-whimper, she stopped and rolled to her feet. Her movements were stiff and awkward; I could tell she was burning and hurting. Enough of the silver's effects had hit her blood stream now that it would take her a few hours to burn it all off. Shifters reacted to silver like an allergic reaction. Shove enough of it in them, and it could kill them. She hadn't taken enough to kill, but it would sure as hell hurt.

A human doctor had once explained that it wasn't too different than a bad, but abbreviated case of the flu. There was the expected pain at the point of entry, but it was worse than that. Aching joints, stiff muscles. The works.

As she shot me a hate-filled look, I smiled. "Ready to go again?"

"I'm going to kill you," she said, her voice ugly and raw. "Fucking him doesn't give you the right to attack."

"Enough," Damon said. He rose off the couch and moved to my side. "Sam…you're either too fucking stupid to serve as second in charge, or there's something else eating at your ass. I don't know which, but I'll damn well figure it out and address the problem because I won't have an idiot helping to train my fighters."

The hot wash of blood stained her face red as she dragged her gaze from me to him. "Sir?"

Buxton leaned in, muttered, "Look at her fucking neck, Sam."

Her gaze landed on my neck and once the shock faded, her gaze went cold and black.

Somehow, I didn't think the two of us were going to be friends.

CHAPTER ELEVEN

"He bit you again." Colleen laid her fingers over the bite at my neck and before I could say anything, I felt the warm pulse of her healing magic run over me, through me. Moments later, her hand fell away and she sighed. "I'd like, more than anything, to take that mark completely away. But you'd be pissed."

I didn't respond. I wasn't about to tell her that I hadn't exactly *planned* on this happening. I wasn't really upset over it, but she'd see it as splitting hairs. Damon and I already had this discussion. Nothing for me had changed. If this mark made things easier for him, for us both? Fine. I might punch him when this was done, but for now, if he'd cope better this way, so be it.

When I didn't answer, she turned away and started gathering up her supplies while I finished getting dressed. There was a lingering ache in my side. I was still tired. But I could move, a lot better than I had.

"Drink."

I wrinkled my nose at the cup she pushed in front of me and then sighed, reaching for it. There was no use avoiding it. I needed it. I knew it. I bolted it back as fast as I could and then concentrated for the next two minutes on the very pretty, pale green of her walls.

Pale. Green. Soothing. Nice.

Almost like the color of the vile brew she'd made me drink. The brew that I was certain I'd hurl—

No. No hurling. Okay. So no thoughts about anything green. Think about—

The soft pad of footsteps caught my ears and I looked up as she came to a stop a few feet away.

"You need to eat."

I ignored the wrapped sandwich Colleen tried to shove in my hands. The healing tonic, the vile, green brew continued to gurgle in my belly. Try to eat? Oh hell. No.

That stuff needed to stay down. I had to be moving faster than this and the tonic would help. Puking wouldn't. So as much as I needed food, the sandwich would have to wait. I couldn't do what I needed to do if I was moving at this speed.

"Damn it, Kit."

I glared at her as I pulled my vest on. "I had a banana and a protein bar on the way over. I'll grab a meal later."

"You need more than that." Her eyes all but snapped with fury as she stormed over to glower at me. I had to tip my head back to meet her gaze. "You look like death and *he* moves faster than you do right now."

"Oh, you know how fast death is? Really?"

"Ha, ha." She smacked me against the chest with the sandwich. "It's just ham and egg. But you need the fuel and don't tell me you don't."

Sighing, I scooped my hair back from my face with one hand and accepted the sandwich with the other. I *did* need the fuel. "Yeah. I know, but if I eat it now, I'm going to puke. Look, I'll eat it at the office. My gut will settle by then...fair?"

"Promise?"

"Yes."

"Okay. Fair enough." She eyed me narrowly and then nodded. "What's this case, Kit? I can't..."

Then she shook her head. "You've been working with Banner. I know the feel of their blocks."

I said nothing.

"Kit, what's going on? Something's got you worried. I can feel it."

"I can't talk about it," I said, shaking my head. Even though I really, really wanted to.

"You mean that literally." She pressed her fingertips to my temple and sighed. "Those blocks—why did they do this, Kit? I could get around them, but..."

"No."

If she messed with Justin's spells, he'd know. Colleen wasn't skilled enough to hide her magic from him. I have no idea what kind of repercussions that would have.

She studied me for a moment and then nodded. "Okay. Look, if you're having problems, you know you can come to us. That's why we're here."

"I can get around it, but..." then she shrugged. "You've got to work. Go work."

"I know." I made myself smile before I headed for the door. "Thanks. For the sandwich and...well, everything."

"Kit, are you okay?"

I wasn't sure how to answer that.

As I closed my hand over the doorknob, I sighed. "It's a lousy job, Leenie. I hate it. I have to do it, but I hate it. I'm tired and I'm stressed...but I have to work this miserable-ass job."

I felt the probe of her magic against and pain shrieked through my head. Okay...the spell Justin had laid didn't like that. Not at all.

"I gotta go."

As I stepped outside, I caught sight of Chang, waiting by his car.

Starting down the walkway, I hoped Colleen would be quiet. Chang wouldn't have heard anything she'd said *inside* her house—she safeguarded against that—but if she said a damn thing now, he'd hear.

And it would get back to Damon.

The ham and egg sandwich was a nasty lump in my stomach and there was a headache at the base of my scalp as I sat down at the computer. All in all, I felt better. My body no longer ached.

Justin was meeting me in twenty minutes.

I was to *'keep my ass in the office, wards up or else'*. A mean, contrary streak a mile wide had me tempted to pitch a tent in my parking lot, but that would contradict what I'd promised Damon when he'd sent me off—with Chang as my guard. He was to watch my cute ass, Damon's words, not mine, until I was safe behind my wards. Chang had been agreeable about waiting outside Colleen's house, but only *after* he'd checked in with Damon.

Damon had told me: *Stay safe.*

So that was what I'd do.

It had nothing to do with Justin or anything else.

The computer came to life with a quiet a little hum and I went online via a stealth site that Colleen had showed me. It was a cyber-witch's creation. They couldn't *cast* spells online, but the cyber-witches were hackers of the highest caliber. If you needed to do an untraceable search, this was the way to do it.

I tapped in the first of the two names.

Cedric Marlowe.

The information that came up on him was some of what I'd expected, and a lot of shit that made my stomach turn. Yes, he'd been one of the ones who'd opposed the whole 'coming-out' plan. Since then, he'd apparently been practicing mind-wipes. Quietly. Very quietly.

Even worse, *successfully.*

Bile churned a nasty mess in my gut and the more I read, the worse it got.

Okay, if this guy wasn't on Damon's list for a legit reason, then he needed to be on Banner's. If *they* didn't take an interest in him, I was going to. He'd be a hard mark, but hard marks made life interesting and I hadn't ever taken out anybody quite like him. All it would take was the right weapon—which I had—and the right distance, so he didn't pick up on my presence.

Mind wipes. Scum-sucking dick.

I saved the info to an encrypted file and went to the next name, almost scared at what I'd uncover.

But a heartbeat later, I wish I'd spent longer looking at Marlowe's info.

Because I knew this face.

Delores Richards.

Delores.

That was her given name.

But the rest of the world...including me, knew her as *Es*.

"Oh, no, Damon."

Screw the fucking wards. Screw the wolves that *might* try to come after me.

I wasn't waiting for this.

* * * * *

"Where in the *hell* are you?" Justin demanded.

I checked the mile marker and told him.

"*What?*"

"I have to go see a witch."

"I'm a fucking witch. If you need help? Talk to me or Colleen."

"A specific witch."

"Get your ass back here, Kit," he said, voice vibrating with intensity. "There's no time for this. And did you forget? You might have a pack of drug-dealing wolves on your ass?"

"First...if somebody was tailing me, I'd know. Second, I know how to do my job, Justin. Sometimes I think people forget that." I hung up on him and checked my mirror, focused and let myself just...*feel*. Nope. None of the drug-dealing wolves on my ass. I'd been paying attention.

I'd been paying attention the entire time I'd sped down the highway. At the speed I was going, I'd be at the house where Es lived in a matter of minutes. Too late to hold me back now.

Es.

Please be safe…

* * * * *

She was waiting on the porch.

Her hair, white as the driven snow and straight, hung down her back.

She sat with her legs drawn up to her chest and a fat mug cradled in her hands. As I climbed out of the car, she took a sip of the steaming brew and then sighed. "I had a feeling there were problems when I woke this morning."

My gut dropped to my knees and automatically, I popped my wrist.

If he was coming, I'd just have to plant my ass here—

"Oh, Kit, you worry too much," she murmured. She stretched out her legs and crossed them at the ankle. After her next sip, she lowered her mug to her lap and stared into it like it held every answer the world had ever asked. A moment passed and then she added, "I do understand your fear. You wish to protect him. You wish to protect me. Even though your mind is already moving on a logical process that he has reasons, you don't see one for me."

The logical process she'd mentioned wasn't functioning well right now. I shook my head and barely resisted the urge to drive the flat of my hand against my temple. The headache was already raging close to out of control and I hadn't even said anything. "You…you know what's going on."

"Oh, yes," she said, nodding. "I've known for a while."

She glanced at me and smiled. "I was the first he spoke with. Didn't you know that?"

"No," I snapped. "I didn't know that. Now tell me, what in the hell is going on?"

She took another sip from her mug. "He asked that I not speak of our discussion with anybody in the Assembly, you know. He told me that he didn't see me as a threat. I'd already seen what he was planning and Damon is a smart man...he knew what I'd sensed. Then he told me that unless I was a threat, he wouldn't treat me as one, so I was safe."

"Tell me."

She rose with another one of those tired sighs. "I guess it's a good thing you're not working this for the Assembly, hmmm?"

* * * * *

She didn't take me to her workroom.

I found myself inside the medical ward and she gave me a deprecating smile. "If I want the assurance this conversation will stay private, then we go to the most private room I have...which is here." She brushed a hand down one of the walls. "This is one of my finest accomplishments, you know. I sank ten years worth of magic into these walls. Unwanted souls cannot come through. Even a witch stronger than I can't break these magics without doing herself harm...fatal harm."

She settled on one of the beds and smiled at me. "We can talk in peace here. Undisturbed. And undiscovered."

The kindness in her eyes was almost my undoing. The understanding. And *damn* it, I could feel the words I wanted to say boiling up in my throat, but even that was enough to ratchet up the pain. As it tore at me, I forced the words out. "I can't *tell* you anything—"

Her hand touched mine and her eyes, near colorless pools of gray, started to glow. "You needn't say a word, Kit...oh. That's displeasing," she murmured, her voice echoing around me. Through me. "Who would lay an oath on you—Greaves. Why am I not surprised?"

I flinched as I felt something shift inside me. Magic working, shifting—

"I can break it, but it makes little sense," she said. "You never planned to discuss this with anybody and if I break it, Greaves will know and he'll feel bound to let his superiors know. It will compromise things."

I opened mouth to answer, but she was already moving on to something else. "Yes, yes...I knew these people and Damon was right to suspect them...Marlowe is the last one, Kit. After him, it's done."

Then she let go of my hand and instead of moving away, she placed it on my side. I tried to recoil, but she was already acting, shoving her magic inside me, like she had a right to and I was caught, trapped in it and swearing at the heat of a healer's magic went to work on the lingering damage inside me. Colleen was good. She was damned good, but she couldn't undo what had been done to me with a few tonics.

Es, on the other hand...

As the supernova force of her magic hit me, it felt like I was dying inside. It burned through me and when it was done, I sagged to the floor and she went with me, never once breaking contact. Distantly, I heard her talking to me, but I couldn't make out the words.

And then, for a few minutes, I was too weak to do any damn thing. Swearing, I slumped to my side and eventually rolled onto my back, staring up at the ceiling. "Damn it, Es, you aren't supposed to pull that shit without my okay," I grumbled

But as the rush of her magic faded away, I felt better. Stronger, clearer.

Not only physically, though. It was deeper.

"I made a few...adjustments," Es said quietly. "He shouldn't have placed the grip so tightly. Your thoughts should be your own."

Bonds I hadn't even been aware of loosened. Swiping the back of my hand over the back of my mouth, I finally found the strength to sit up and glare at her. "Damn it, Es, what the hell?"

"What? Would you *prefer* to have to censor your own thoughts?" she said.

"Not what I'm talking about," I snapped. And immediately, I wanted to kick myself. "Ah..."

She arched a brow. "Go ahead. Try...think anything that would have caused you pain this morning."

I pictured myself standing in front of Damon and telling him *everything*.

And there was...nothing.

"Oh..." I covered my face with my hands as relief slammed into me.

"This isn't a complete fix, my dear." She curled an arm over my shoulders. "You need to understand that."

Not a complete fix. Got it. But still, for the first time, though, ever since this had started, I could actually *think*. I could think it all through.

And that meant...

Relief made my legs boneless. I sank back to the floor and drew my knees to my chest. Sitting there, I pressed to my face to my knees as all the implications sank in. I could think clearly, which meant I could plan. But I could think clearly...which meant I could easily picture myself *failing*.

* * * * *

It felt like hours passed. It was really only minutes. Not long enough, but yet each second was a precious waste. Finally, I shoved myself upright and faced her. She'd settled back on the bed, allowing me a modicum of privacy while I had my miniature collapse.

"Can you help me?" I asked softly, flexing my hand. The one thing that mattered *here* was taken care. Damon wasn't coming after Es, so she was safe. Now I had to focus on making *him* safe.

"I can give you the answer." A serene smile curved her lips. "It lies in the charter. Article 7A. Acting in defense of—"

"Family, spouse, clan, dependent, yadda yadda yadda," I said, shaking my head. I knew the fucking charter, but that wasn't giving me an answer, because I still didn't know the damned question. "Why in the hell would a couple of witches

159

and a vampire be a threat to his Clan? They are the largest faction of NHs in all of the eastern US."

"His *Clan* isn't at risk." Her pale, nearly colorless eyes held me all but spellbound as she watched.

My heart slammed against my ribs and part of me wanted to leave. It was time. Time to run, I knew that now. My instincts had always whispered when it was time to move on and although I'd been in this area for a long, long time, that didn't mean I had to stay.

I didn't even know *how* I knew; I just knew it was time to get away.

I could get away before I made things worse—

Es leaned forward and caught my hand. "For Damon, this is more important than the Clan. It's your safety he's protecting, Kit. It's you...it's been you all along."

"What?" Her answer bounced inside my head, not connecting. "That doesn't make sense. I'd only briefly met a couple of them and it wasn't like I was going after *them*." Not that I knew of anyway.

"No, you weren't. And none of them were that interested in you. But..." she rose from the bed and paced over to the window, staring outside. "I, like them, knew Fanis."

The sound of her name on the lips of another struck me in the heart. The weight of my sword hit my hand and I looked down, a little dazed. I didn't even remember calling her—

Go back, I whispered to her. *Go back—*

I didn't need the blade just because somebody had said her name...

Fanis—

Useless waste. I'll make a warrior out of you yet—

"You have to stop letting her inside your head," Es said and her voice, for once, wasn't serene, quiet or gentle.

It sounded through the room like the peal of thunder and struck me right in the heart, slashing the threads that were trying to jerk me back into the past.

Gasping for breath, I shoved the heels of my hands against my eye sockets, hoping it would block out the memory of her face. So similar to my own. Lovely. More elegant, though. Very refined. So very evil.

"What does she have to do with anything?" I demanded.

"It seems she's only now realized that you're still alive," Es said softly. "And she's been making...inquiries."

"Inquiries." I shook my head and lowered my hands, staring at Es. "Damon wouldn't kill over *inquiries*."

"A few people have made mention that she's approached the World Council." Es stared at me. "She claims you stole a blade and you're to be returned for discipline."

Stole it? And now, I didn't even bother resisting her when she came back to me. She came to my hand, a brilliant gleam of enchanted silver, as much a part of me as the color of my hair, the color of my eyes. As much a part of me as *me*.

"The sword *came* to me."

"Oh, I know this." She smiled a little as her gaze dropped to the blade. "It's a blood bond in that blade and I've already written the World Council my thoughts on the matter. I did that at the very first whisper of her name, Kit. The blade was your mother's, was it not? Bonds like that come *down* the line. They never go back. Nobody who understood that sort of magic would refute this. But she won't let it go so easily if she's determined. And it would seem she is. I heard that she's made...overtures to some. Then she made one to me. Offered to send one of her healers to teach us some of the older ways if I would return the favor and offer anything that might be of help when it came time to handle her wayward granddaughter."

My lungs burned. It hadn't dawned on me that I needed to be breathing, not until that moment. Sucking in a desperate breath, I popped my wrist and stared at Es. The blade's song was a gentle murmur in my mind, but not a scream. More of a reassuring stroke. I tightened my hand on her grip and then I slid her into the sheath I'd donned earlier. Right then, I felt better just having her with me. I had some serious issues.

"You talked to my grandmother." I was able to force the words out without breaking down into hysterical screams. A good sign, right?

"Well, I wouldn't call it a pleasant conversation, but yes. We had words. I told her she could get fucked," Es said, smiling. "Then I reminded her that you were well over the age of being 'handled' and nobody in the Assembly would see it otherwise. She laughed and said, *'we will see'*. I informed her I spoke for the House of Witches and I'd make damn sure that line wasn't crossed." Es shrugged. "Our conversation didn't end happily."

Turning away, I stumbled over to a bed.

She knows...she knows where I am—

"She thinks she knows."

I jerked my head and stared at Es as she sat beside me. "She doesn't often come into this...bit of reality," Es said.

This bit of reality—

I stared. "You know..."

"Yes." She shrugged and said, "If she were to try and successfully locate you, she'd have a hard time of it. She knows *vaguely* where you are, but finding you easily...wouldn't happen." She caught my eyes and held them. "You consider it a weakness and I know it sometimes hampers you, but that human blood that you hate so much made it easier for you to adjust to...living here."

"I don't hate having human blood," I whispered. "I just hate..."

"Hate being weak." She sat on the bed across from me. "There are different kinds of strength. Different kinds of weakness. If you were truly weak, you would have broken under her *care*. Don't forget that. And *don't* forget—you have allies here now. You are not the broken, solitary child who fled from her. You made yourself stronger. You made yourself more. And you're not alone."

I gave a tight nod, even though it felt like I'd break if I moved.

The words might be a comfort later on. Right now, it

was all I could do to keep myself together.

"The real danger to you came from the few who didn't realize just *what* you were," Es murmured. "Maxine, Silas and Cedric? They wanted you simply because they believe you can show them Aneris Hall."

I closed my eyes. "None but our blood can find it. It's like the fabled Fountain of Youth or Pandora's Box."

"Well, those aren't quite so fabled," she said, shrugging lazily. "But their powers are...well, we'll say they've not been fairly labeled. And this is all irrelevant. They *think* you can show them a hall of warriors who might be able to overtake any enemy. Plenty have searched for warriors like the *aneira*. You'd think they would have learned after..."

She grimaced and rose. "Never mind. But they won't listen when you tell them otherwise. So they gave lip-service to her while they gathered information. She knew it and she laughed."

"Sounds like her," I muttered. "If I'm dead, I'm not her problem."

"Why aren't you surprised?"

I blinked my burning eyes and stared at the floor. "Because part of me always feared she'd come for me."

"I don't understand why she would. Unless it's sheer cruelty that drives her."

"Well, sheer cruelty is reason enough, for her."

"For some reason, that doesn't shock me." She pushed my hair back from my face. "In the end, it doesn't matter. What matters is this...Damon heard. I don't know how. He has ears in the Assembly and I think that sleek piece of work that he calls his *Adviser* is behind much of the information he ferrets out. But he has ears. And he heard. It was the single biggest mishap any of them could make. He's down to one final name now."

"Your name was on his list."

She blinked. "He made a list?"

I swallowed and jerked my gaze away. "In his private chambers. Nobody but me is likely to ever see it, but..."

"And he isn't likely to realize the impact of you seeing it," she finished.

The stone in my chest weighed so much heavier. I think it used to be my heart but now… "This is all my fault."

"No. He is doing the same thing you are, Kit. Protecting what is his. Just as you're protecting what is yours. It's a dangerous game on all sides."

Coming off the bed, I started to pace. "The Banner squad has him down for execution if I don't find justifiable cause for what he's done."

"And I've given you one."

I snarled, stopping in my tracks as I turned to glare at her.

She was holding a letter.

I blinked as I stared at it. "What…what's that?"

"Something I wrote the day after he left. There's a notarized copy in my files at the Assembly House. This is your copy and I have another for my files here." She inclined her head. "Once upon a time, I briefly worked with Banner. I was one of the witches they'd called to read a mark. They will not refute what I've given you."

The knot in my chest tightened.

"He's still going after one of the Assembly members."

"Yes. Cedric." She shook her head. "You won't be able to stop him, Kit. Maybe you shouldn't try."

"I have to see this through," I said quietly. "If he kills another one, they'll move up the damned timetable. I'll call Justin, let him know I have this…" I looked at the letter I held. "But I can't just ignore it when I know he's going after somebody else."

Her eyes were terribly sad as I walked away.

But I couldn't let it stop me.

Damon was risking his life to help me.

I was going to give everything I had to help him.

* * * * *

164

The *aneira* are the world's greatest assassins for a reason. It's the same reason we are good thieves, good treasure hunters, all that jazz. Give us a target and we *find* it.

I hadn't lied when I said I'd never had a lucky shot in my life.

However, luck had guided me more than once in my life.

Maybe I was a watered-down offshoot and so far, I'd only done a handful of assassinations and I'd much *prefer* a different way of earning a living, but still...I am what I am. The descendent of Amazons, and something whispered to me, tugged at me.

Warned me.

Damon wasn't going to wait long. Was maybe even on the move—?

*Yes...yes...*it was an odd little tug inside me. Drawing at me. I'd felt it before. Pulling me in and drawing me toward my target. We were the world's greatest assassins because we *always* found our target and we *never* missed a mark.

This time, my target was my lover and my goal wasn't to kill him.

Just stop him.

Halfway between East Orlando and Es's, I had a call.

"I've got your proof," I snapped into the phone. "But I'm on a—"

"He's on the move," Justin bit off. "And I can't come to you. They've got me watching *him*."

The pit of my stomach dropped out.

"Kit...if he kills another..."

My belly went cold. "He's got a reason. It's justified by the charter and I can give you proof. I'll get it to you and if I *don't*, tell your superiors they can't do a damn thing without conferring with Delores Richards. She used to do work for Banner and they should listen to her."

"What's the reason, Kit? And I need *more* than a reason. I need proof of it."

I stared at my reflection in the mirror. "I'm the fucking proof...he's doing it for me."

"You?"

"Yeah. You can thank my dearest grandmother for this mess. There's no time to explain this right now, though. Where the hell is he?"

"Your *grandmother*?"

At any other time, I might have appreciated the pure, undiluted hatred in his voice. "Justin, tell me where he is, or I'll kill not only your bike, I'll break into your house and destroy every single thing in there. And you know I'll do it. You know I *can*."

"Kit, what the *fuck* is going on?"

"Tell me what I need to know," I shouted.

"He's heading south, that's all I know. Now tell me about that evil bit—"

I hung up the phone. South. That told me everything I needed to know.

Justin couldn't help me. I was hoping like hell somebody else could. As I dialed another number, I prayed.

Colleen came on the phone.

"I need a cloaker and I need it so bad, I'll give you a kidney if you can make it happen."

"Ah...that's a bit extreme," she said. "And gross."

NIGHT BLADE

CHAPTER TWELVE

My plan was simple.

I had to get to the Assemblyman's house before Damon and head him off.

I had to do it without being seen or sensed or detected.

That required something *my* handy little knack wouldn't cover. I could go invisible for short periods of time, but I could still be heard. I was quiet, but I couldn't stop the beat of my heart or hold my breath. Nor could I eradicate my scent trail.

A cloaker could hide all of those things.

The ability wasn't common among witches. Those born with it tended to be their warriors or have a lot of pent up aggression. I think that's why they didn't see the cloaking skill very often.

The man coming toward me had a swaggering gait, buzzed blond hair and an *aawww-shucks* smile. He also had power coming out of his finger nails. I didn't like the look of him or the feel of him, but I didn't have to. All I had to do was tolerate him so he could help me get to Marlowe's, a sprawling piece of real estate forty-five miles west of here.

"You need to hide?" he said, smiling at me.

I stared at him, doubt shivering through me. Something about him felt off. If he came to me wanting me to do a job,

I'd turn him away. His type tended to do things outside the law, and they tended to go…well, wrong. *Very* wrong. "You're with Green Road?"

"I freelance." He shrugged. "Colleen knows me and knew you needed a hand so I volunteered…although you are paying me."

"Yes. I'll pay." I wasn't doing a favor for him later on the down the road. That was how witches worked. "What's your name?"

"Xavier." He exposed his wrist and showed me a wrapped twig. I had to smile a little. Colleen had bound him. "She's not taking it off until you call her, so I'd appreciate you doing it as soon as we're done. It's going to apply more and more pressure and she's timed it to twelve hours."

It looked like a twig, all right. But it was a Green Road charm. A ticking time bomb. Colleen really loves me. And she must not trust this guy at all. "Wow. You must not be on her good side."

He smiled. "Nah. She's just the cautious type."

That wasn't it. Not by a long shot.

Colleen was pretty good at judging people and she wouldn't put one of those on anybody, outside of an emergency. So it meant one thing—she knew I'd had an emergency and she was giving me the backup I needed, even though she didn't like it.

"Well, then." I smiled at him thinly. "Let's go."

I started toward my car but he caught my wrist. "Sorry, sugar. We need to be in close physical contact and I can only cover small area of space if we're looking at an extended amount of time." He pointed to the bike he'd arrived on.

"No."

"Fine." He turned and started back to the bike. "Make sure you call and let her know you refused the service, sugar. I want the charm off if you aren't using my services."

Shit.

* * * * *

I kept feeling him pressing at me.

I was sensitive to magic and I knew what he was doing, and it pissed me off, although I didn't know *why* he was trying to get a feel for what sort of power I had.

It wasn't something anybody other than a witch...or somebody *like* a witch...would feel. Weres could feel active magic, but this wasn't active. Vampires were the same way. This was calm, passive...rather like he was breathing me in as we sped down the highway. Breathing me, taking my measure.

And I didn't like it.

He wouldn't pick up much. Colleen, even Es, had done similar things. I *felt* sort of magical, but I didn't feel like a witch. If I had any active protection spells on me, he might be able to break those with his poking and prodding, but I didn't carry active spells. I left those on my home and office and it would take more than a few pokes and prods to break them.

This guy was strong, but if he tried to break what half a dozen Green Road witches had crafted, he'd be in for one hell of a shock.

I doubted he was aware that I knew what he was doing. Colleen hadn't realized I could feel all her little pokes and prods until she'd *sensed* it with her empathy. This guy had about as much empathy as a piece of roadkill. I wasn't going to enlighten him, either.

One lesson I'd learned rather well under my grandmother's brutal hand...*Never show your weapons until you need them.*

While my ability to feel his magic wasn't really a weapon, *knowledge* always was.

I wouldn't show my hand until there was a need to.

But if he thought he could stick his magical fingers inside my head and not pay for it...

Something tugged me. *Hard.*

"Stop the bike."

"Thought we were in a hurry, sugar." He guided the bike over the side of the road and propped a foot on the ground while the engine rumbled beneath us.

"Nobody sees or hears us, right?"

That was the problem with a cloaking witch. One had to *trust* in them and I didn't trust this guy. Although I had felt it when the cloak settled over us earlier at the out-of-the-way diner where I'd left my car. It was like I'd had my head plugged with cotton—ears, nose, mouth, and my eyes were hazed by a greasy, white smear. All of that faded in the background as the cloaking settled in but it was still unpleasant.

"Yes, it's up. Why?" He scowled and tugged at the twig wrapped around his wrist. It didn't move. "I want this thing *off.*"

"Something…"

The word died in my throat.

There was a singular sensation that nobody else could cause.

His energy—*Damon's* energy—that warm, rolling cloak that spread around me like a mantle. But it wasn't comforting now. Nor was it warm. Icy. Focused. And bearing down fast.

I gulped and turned my head, staring down the road.

It wasn't even sixty seconds before I saw Damon's car, that long, sexy black car come hurtling down the road. A Dodge Challenger, made in a century past, when non-humans still hid in our closets and man still thought he was at the top of the food chain. Back then, mankind had put out some seriously kickass pieces of automotive equipment and this one of the finest, a classic piece of work from the 1970s, the engine modified to run on cleaner fuels and eat up the miles like it was starving.

"Sugar, he can't see us," Xavier said, his voice grouchy. "Trust me. The last thing I want is for that fucker to rip my face off because he saw me with you. I'm not going to fight that bastard, so I'm keeping this up good and tight, trust me."

He knew of Damon. That didn't completely surprise me,

but I was a little caught off-guard that he knew about *us*.
Another reason not to trust him, not that I needed it.

Even after the car had shot past us, I was still breathing
shallowly, each breath coming in an odd, hitching little pant
that made it almost impossible to really get oxygen where it
needed to go.

"We going to move or just stand here so you can have a
panic attack?"

I gave Xavier a dark look.

If I had to hurt somebody in the next few hours, I'd
really like for it to be him.

* * * * *

Keeping the black car in my sight wasn't hard.

Listening to Xavier bitching was harder. "It would be
easier if you could just let me do a trace on him and we could
drop back. It's hard keeping a cloak up this long."

"No. You want me to pay you? I asked for somebody
who could cloak and that's what I need." It was only the
tenth time I'd explained it; hopefully it would be the last.

Damon had just exited the expressway.

"We're almost there. We need to get around him," I said.
I had an idea. It was insane but if I could just get there ahead
of him...

"Ain't happening."

"If you want me to pay you a red cent, you're going to
do what I need you to do."

"I *can't*," Xavier snapped. He pulled over and pointed off
into the distance. "That's Cedric Marlowe's turf. I even *try* to
cross his boundary line and he can fry my ass. High magic
can't cross it. Now *you'd* be okay. Your cat? I don't know. But
I *can't*. If I try to cross his wards, he'll feel it and he'll fry my
ass. He's old magic, sugar, and I'm *not*."

"Fine." Snarling, I shoved a hand through my hair, trying
to think. "Get me as close as you can."

Long seconds ticked by and then he shrugged.

"Whatever you say, sugar. It's your funeral."

We drove a few miles before we reached the turnoff. "It's coming up close. I can wait for you, but once you're two feet from me, I can't cloak."

"I know. I—"

The world exploded around us.

At least that's what it felt like.

Xavier must have had magics laid on his bike because with the brilliant blue explosion, the bike went into a skid. Only thing that saved us from crashing into that expanding wave of furious power was the fact that I could feel his magic grabbing us and jerking us back.

The bike was propelling us forward, his magic was jerking us back and the pavement was chewing a hole through my jeans, my skin and then I hit my head and for a few sweet, sweet moments…everything was blanketed in gray.

* * * * *

By the time those gray clouds cleared, it was like the whole world was burning. Even though everything looked *normal* to my eyes, it didn't *feel* that way. I could feel the heat slamming against my shields and I could feel the air as it was being squeezed out of my lungs and I was certain that if I didn't move, didn't get away, I was going to die.

Rolling onto my belly, determined to do just that—get away—I went to shove onto my hands and knees.

Somebody forced me back onto my face in the dirt.

"You move, you die."

The voice. I knew that voice. Didn't like the owner of it. Didn't know why, but after a few seconds…

Oh. Yeah. Sleazy son-of-a-bitch witch.

Evil witches were bad.

This guy had *wrong* written all over him. Bad news.

In my pain-driven state, I think maybe I saw a little more clearly than I had earlier and that spell Colleen had cast on him now made more sense. I flexed my hand, ready to call my sword but his voice stopped me.

"Marlowe and your cat are at each other's throats—son of a bitch is throwing magic out like he doesn't care who lives or dies and I'm not strong enough to do anything more than buckle down and wait it out." Xavier's voice was a disgusted mutter just a few inches away from my ear. "If you leave the circle I've got down, you aren't going to live and I am *not* responsible for your stupidity. You hear me?"

I tried to think past the roaring in my ears.

The air was thick with magic and it was the angry kind. Careless. Careless didn't fit the image I had of Marlowe, but if Marlowe thought he was about ready to go down in a blaze of glory? Behind my eyes, I thought I caught flickers of something virulent and red, ricocheting through the air.

All the oxygen seemed to disappear from the world and Xavier muttered, "Aw, *fuck*—"

I forced myself into a crouch. I could see past the circle Xavier had cast and just a few dozen yards away, there was a dead hawk lying there. "What happened to it?"

"Marlowe," he said thinly. "He's got an affinity for death magic. It's forbidden but he doesn't care."

Beneath us, the ground shuddered and then he looked at me. "Your cat isn't going to make it if this keeps up. I'm barely holding the shields and I'm not in the thick of it. If he—"

Despite the wild magic rippling all around us, a surreal quiet had fallen but the sound of a weapon firing through the night had suddenly shattered it. Yeah, no mistaking that sound.

Ammo.

My brain kicked into gear and I started processing. No. I didn't like modern weapons, although some of the weapons manufactured back in the 1800 and 1900s weren't bad. They usually needed work when I got a hold of them, like my Desert Eagle—they were in bad need of repair, some TLC and I usually had to have my ammo specially made.

Weapons, though, regardless of their craftsmanship, or lack of, were my stock and trade and I knew them.

The one being fired now wasn't new—the typical gun of today was quieter and operated with either a laser or an electric discharge. Most. Not all.

There were still plenty that fired ammo like the old school weapons, but my ears told me this was an older one. The kind that would cut through a tank. The kind soldiers had carried when they walked through deserts back in the wars fought in the earlier part of the century, right before our presence had been brought into the open.

They were rare these days, but I knew what it was: an old-school assault rifle with armor piercing capabilities. Loaded with the right kind of ammo—*magically charged* ammo, a weapon like that could take down just about anything...an elephant, a tank, a homicidal vampire. Or an enraged witch with a knack for death spells.

Magic ripped through the air—fuck. That was the right kind of ammo. I gasped as I felt it in it the pit of my gut. The screaming started almost instantly.

"Something charged in that weapon," Xavier whispered. "Where in the hell did he get that idea?"

I swallowed, staring at the ground. The weapon fired again and each time, the power built in the air. Higher and higher.

"He's going to bring down the fucking ward. Son of a bitch..." Xavier's voice was full of shock, amazement and a little bit of horror.

I clamped my hands over my ears, because I knew what was coming. I could hear something shrieking—the wards, maybe. I could hear somebody screaming off in the distance, even though I knew the firefight was easily a mile away.

The magic built and built, and built—

When it broke, it was like a tsunami and I swayed under it. Blood trickled from my nose and I huddled there, convinced that somehow, the dying magic would get in and grab me.

* * * * *

"It's over."

I watched as Xavier rolled to his feet and kicked at the circle.

The air smelled of death and scorched earth and over it, I could smell hot grass, ozone and the scent of a coming storm.

Had I been human, I never would have noticed the magical, deathly storm that had just passed. Not until it killed me, at least. Flat on my back, I held a cloth to my nose and waited for the bleeding to stop. "Did Marlowe kill any people?"

Xavier was mopping up the sweat from his brow and paused to look at me, an irritated look on his face. "How the fuck should I know?"

Colleen. This guy is an asshole. I want to play slice and dice.

Instead of doing that, I climbed to my feet and took a few seconds to check my nose. The bleeding had eased up, although I had that disgusting sticky feel inside from the clotting. Wonderful. Folding the cloth inside itself, I tucked it back into my pocket and stared at him. "You're a witch. You can sense death pretty damn easily, if you'll exert yourself for a minute." I waited a beat. "Exert yourself."

"I think I've exerted myself enough," he replied. "Fucking crazy bitch. Nobody said I was going to have to do any of this shit."

"This wasn't exactly what I was planning, I'll agree, but you said yourself. You freelance. That means you should be used to changing up your job on the fly and that's what you did." Taking a step toward him, keeping my gaze locked on his face, I tried again. "I want to know if anybody died."

"You owe me money," he warned, jerking at the twig that seemed to be embedding itself in his wrist.

"You'll get paid. But the question is how much? Do a good job and you'll get paid for it. Do a lousy job and I might just reimburse you for the gas and the damage done to your bike."

The look that crossed his face was ugly and it might have scared me, if he was anything more than a half-assed witch.

Not that being afraid would ever stop me.

"Do your damned job," I said quietly.

The look in his eyes was pure venom but he turned away, staring off toward the now-silent battle zone. Tension rippled through him, wrapped around him. I could sometimes feel the echoes of death, but I had to be a lot closer than this and that was one thing I couldn't do right now.

"A handful of his people are dead," Xavier said. "They've got his signature all over them and they stink with his power. He's dead, too. It's on his head because he should have taken better care of his people when he went into a fight with a high level NH. Charter covers that and money from his estate will have to be paid to their families." A sneer curled his lip. "Your cat ain't responsible for anybody's death. Well, except Marlowe's but the high-levels get into fights all the time."

The big problem here...he knew what Damon had done.

The bond on his wrist could cover that.

I'd meant to *stop* the fight, not give another witness.

I'd inadvertently done that, but I could possibly get Colleen to work this...yeah. I think I could.

She couldn't do it indefinitely, but I didn't need that.

I just needed time to get—

"He's coming." Xavier unceremoniously shoved me to the wreck of his bike a few feet away.

"You have to cover the entire area," I warned. "If he catches my scent, we're fucked."

Before he could argue with me, I added, "If he can smell *me*, he'll smell *you*. And he can hunt, can track...and he just killed a witch you were apparently terrified of. I'd suggest you cover *your* ass, if nothing else."

When the cloaking fell around this time, it was so all-encompassing, I felt like I'd been shoved into a vat of cotton. I was still struggling to think past it, see past it, feel, smell, when I heard the powerful engine of Damon's Challenger tearing up the road.

I don't even know if I *breathed* when the car slowly came to a stop.

Not by us. It was a few feet away, probably twenty and from here, I could see the path the bike had taken when it had wrecked.

"Not good," Xavier muttered and his head cut to me, his gaze raking over me. "You bled, sugar. I can't completely mask that smell."

All the oxygen dwindled out of my lungs as Damon climbed out of the car, his eyes narrowed, head tipped back.

I knew what he was doing. He'd caught a scent. *Mine…?*

"Can he smell it?"

Xavier's jaw clenched. "Not entirely. It's more like…something he forgot. Smell and memory are pretty tightly linked, but the cloaking is screwing with it so he's not sure—"

Both of us froze as Damon knelt in the dirt, studying the track the bike had taken. He followed the path with his eyes and although he couldn't *see* us, he was looking right at the bike, his gaze puzzled as he tried to think it through. He couldn't see the bike, but if he walked over there…

Oh, *shit—*

Xavier's breathing hitched. He lifted a hand and I did the same. Leveling my blade at him, I said quietly, "Do a damn thing to hurt him and I'll carve your dick off, you hear me?"

"Give me some credit." He flicked his wrist and Damon stilled, looking back toward the interstate.

I didn't hear anything, but Damon apparently did.

His phone rang in the next second. He answered it, straightening from his crouch, still staring at the earth.

Only thirty feet separated us.

My ears weren't as keen as his, but the cloaking spell didn't affect me and I could hear the phone call just fine.

It was Chang on the other end. "Is it done?"

"It's done. She's safe for now, but keep your ears open. And if you hear *anything* about where in the hell I can find that evil bitch…" Damon was staring off into the distance now, but the look on his face—it was enough to freeze the blood in my veins.

Looking at him, even knowing him, see the sly humor, the way he interacted, one would probably think his fury would be all fire and heat. But it wasn't. It was ice. Pure, glacial ice, like the icecaps that were receding more and more every year.

Right now, the storm clouds in his eyes were so cold, it was a wonder the very air hadn't frozen along with his rage.

"I'm still searching, Damon," Chang said and his voice was that low, almost soothing tone I'd grown more accustomed to. "But I don't think it's a place people like us, or even the humans can find. You may never find her unless Kit can find her way back, or unless her grandmother comes out looking for her."

"Kit won't go back," Damon said. He scraped the toe of his boot over something in the dirt. I was pretty sure it was some of my blood. I could still see the bemusement on his face, but it had faded away into the background under the fury. The one time in my life I could actually be grateful for my grandmother, I thought. "But that woman may come looking for her. Keep alert, Chang. I'm counting on you."

Closing my eyes, I gripped the hilt of my sword.

And the sick feeling in my heart spread.

For me.

All of this was for me.

I had to get back and talk to Justin.

CHAPTER THIRTEEN

"Call Colleen," Xavier said as I dismounted the busted-up mess of his bike. I think he'd whispered and spelled the wreck into getting us here.

I smiled at him. "I'll go by her house. Straight from here." I had to. I'd call Justin and ask him to meet me there, but I had to go there and get her to heal my leg, change into a spare set of clothes that she kept on hand...*and* tell her what I needed her to do about Xavier.

"Call her," he snapped, jerking fitfully at the brown thing on his wrist.

It had gotten darker, I realized and it no longer looked *exactly* like a twig. Blood oozed out from it but it never fell. I stared, mesmerized as one of the little stump-like protrusions snaked out as a bead of blood welled up. It started to roll down his wrist but the stump of the twig lapped at the blood like a tongue.

What in the hell kind of magic had Colleen used?

"I'm not calling her," I said quietly.

His arm shot out.

I pulled my blade, leveled her before his fingers even got close. I let her point kiss his flesh as I smiled at him. "You don't want to do that."

"Bitch, you cut me and I'll hurt you," he warned.

"Hurt doesn't faze me. I'll talk to Colleen. It's forty minutes away and that thing isn't going to kill you from here to there. You said you had until nightfall and it's not even close."

Something powerful and frightening danced in the back of his eyes.

"You're not going to freak me out or scare me into changing my mind and if you keep this up, I'll have a nice little chat, not just with Colleen but with every damned witch I can find," I warned him. "Don't expect to find a lot of work in the near future when I'm done."

Freelancers relied on references and word of mouth. A *bad* reference would hurt him. A lot.

"Yeah? Maybe I've already got worked lined up. Very profitable work. Maybe I don't *care* what sort of talks you have, bitch." Ugly hate roiled in his eyes.

Magic tightened in the air around me and I readied myself. "Try anything and I cut you open."

"I ought to just load that blade of yours up with so much magic, it fucks you up from here to Sunday." He sneered at me.

I nudged his throat with the tip, all too aware of the fact that we had people staring at us. Once Damon had sped on past us to East Orlando, Xavier had dropped the cloaking and now, we were across the street from the little diner where I'd left my car. We couldn't do this here. *I* knew that. Xavier didn't seem to get it.

This was human territory.

"You think you're the first idiot to think they can break me or my blade?" I asked him quietly.

"Sugar, I don't have to *break* it to seriously *fuck you up*." A smile, dark and evil, lit his face.

"And I don't need magic or even this blade to do the same to you."

He closed a hand around it and I felt the pulse of magic race through it. Banishing it, I spun around, checking myself at the very last second as I smashed my foot into his head.

The spinning heel sent him to the ground. Idiot witch. So many of them were so used to fighting with spells, they never bothered to brace against a physical attack. I could have broken his neck if I'd wanted to.

He was still lying there, probably wondering what had hit him as I walked off. Pulling my phone out, I made a call, talking loud enough so he'd hear. "Leenie?"

"Yes..." her voice was hesitant.

"That witch is an ass. Don't let that bind off of him until you see me, at your place, in the flesh."

I smiled as I heard him cursing behind me. Low and ugly.

That described him rather nicely. Low. And Ugly.

* * * * *

"Can you *ever* come here just to talk?" Colleen wielded a pair of tweezers over my thigh. Her hair was pulled back from her face and she was scowling. She'd been worried when she opened the door, but then she took a look at me and the worry went straight into frustration and aggravation. When Xavier had come peeling up, laying rubber on her driveway not long after I'd arrived, she bellowed at him so loudly, I was surprised the glass in the windows didn't break.

"I come over to visit," I said defensively. I'd been over several times. Usually when I was feeling freaked out by how things were going with Damon. By that point, I was in the need for a jumbo sized pitcher of margaritas—for me. Colleen made do with a beer or two. With a frown, I thought and calculated. "It's only been...ah—three weeks?"

"You used to come over two or three times a week." She looked up at me and smiled a little. "But that was...well. Before."

She pulled another piece of the interstate out of my thigh and I managed to keep from groaning by digging my hands into the arms of the chair. "If you tear my furniture, Kitasa, I'm going to heal this the hard way," she warned me.

181

Groaning, I clenched my teeth and uncurled my hands from the plushly padded fabric. "Just hurry it up," I said raggedly. Pain streaked through me and I slammed my other leg down on the floor. "Damn it, how can this hurt so bad? It wasn't hurting like this earlier!"

"You want it healed with no scars. I have to clean it. I have to do all of this fast. The longer we wait, the harder it is to heal—"

Xavier chose that moment to slam a hand against the door. "This is fucking painful, Antrim. Get this the *fuck* off of me," he snarled through the door.

"He has control issues," I said soberly.

"Xavier, if you want me to take that off before it amputates your hand, you might want to shut the hell up," Colleen said without raising her voice. She bent closer to my leg. "Kit, this will hurt. Hold still."

Her hand moved so fast, I barely saw it coming and then I bit my tongue bloody trying to keep quiet.

A few seconds later, it was done. She dropped the tweezers into a metal pan. "That does it. The last bit was some glass. Sorry."

Her hands covered my leg. "Last chance, Kit. This is going to be rough. You're pretty battered. Sure you don't want a full healing?"

"I can't." A full healing would drain me, leaving me out of the count for hours, maybe even a day or so, while my body recuperated. "But I can't scar. Surface healing and then...something?"

She blew out a rough breath. "I've got something that will do the trick. Surface healing to cover the scars and I'll slap a poultice on it while I deal with that dipshit out there."

I covered her hand. "I need five minutes first."

"Because of the dipshit?"

I nodded.

"That works. The longer the poultice stays on, the better." A tight-lipped smile spread over her face. "You're going to be sorry in a second, sweetie."

I already was.

Or so I thought.

She made me scream.

Very little managed to make me break that self-imposed limit. I rarely let myself make a sound when I was in pain. It was like I couldn't. It was conditioning of the very worst sort.

Scream for me, you useless waste...

But as Colleen healed the damage to my thigh, a scream ripped out of me and my grandmother's taunting voice rang through my head. *Scream...yes, little granddaughter, let me hear you scream...*

"It's okay, Kit...I'm done. Come on, now."

I don't know how long had passed before I actually heard her voice, but I knew she'd been talking to me for a while. Her hand was a soothing pressure on my brow and my hair was sticky with sweat, my heart thudding heavy and hard against my ribs.

"What..."

My tongue was glued against the roof of my mouth.

"Here," Colleen said. "Try this. It will help speed things along anyway."

I didn't even have the energy to fight her when she pushed the tea into my hands, and thankfully, it wasn't one of her more vile concoctions, either. It was astringent and strangely minty, but not overly repulsive. And once I'd gotten a couple of drinks down, I was able to squeeze out more than one word. "What in the hell was that?"

"Healing on several levels. I healed the surface tissues, so there was no scarring. There was damage almost to the bone, though so I had to heal the deeper tissues, as well, so I did that. The minor and superficial damage I left alone and it split my focus enough that I couldn't channel the pain *from* you...which is why you felt every blessed thing."

She touched my leg. The muscles bunched under her hand and I was relieved to realize there was very little actual pain. Lots of soreness, but the pain was mostly gone. "I'll get the poultice and you can get to work explaining…whatever."

I ran my tongue across my teeth. "I need privacy."

"Of course you do," she said, sighing.

* * * * *

"You get into so much trouble," she whispered, covering her face with her hands.

I hadn't been able to explain a damn thing. But Colleen, like Es, had picked up enough just through her empathy that I hadn't *had* to.

Once she'd laid a silence charm across the room, I'd felt safe letting her sink her slippery fingers inside my head and she was able to glean everything that had happened since Justin had made his appearance in my office.

"I didn't look for this," I said sourly. I rubbed my finger over the scar at my neck and stretched my leg out, staring at the pale surface of my skin. No marks. Thank God. "I didn't *ask* for this."

"You don't ask for *any* of the messes you end up. They just *find* you. Fuck it all, Kit. That cat isn't worth this," she said, shaking her head and surging upright.

I stared at her as she moved to the small metal stove she kept in her workroom and stirred something brewing there.

"He's worth it to me," I said quietly.

"Yeah, I picked up on that." She flicked a look my way, studied my neck. "Love the shiny new mark to bear…did he beat his chest after he put that on you?"

I sighed and looked away. "Coll, don't."

"He *marked* you, Kit. Wasn't one set of scars enough?"

"He's a shapeshifter," I pointed out. "They don't exactly operate on human levels."

"You're not a shapeshifter."

"But I'm not exactly human, either." Then I rubbed my thumb down my neck, brooding. No, I hadn't exactly planned on the second mark, but if I had issue with it, I could have come to Colleen while it was healing. She could have removed it. Damon would have gotten the point.

I looked back at her as she used a pair of tongs to lift a sopping cloth from a massive pot, waiting just a moment before taking the steaming mess in her hands. I winced instinctively, knowing it had to be hot. It wasn't hot enough to cause anything more than discomfort and the steam was crucial to the healing, but I still didn't want that thing on my leg.

I didn't have a choice.

As she spread it over my leg, I grimaced and swallowed back the dirty names that managed to burn a path up my throat.

"Kit," she said softly, smoothing the poultice down over my leg. "I know you're not human…or not entirely. I get what you are better than *they* do, I think. One thing I don't entirely understand is why you're *with* him."

"I…" I swallowed and looked away. "I'm with him because I want to be."

"Because he makes you feel safe or something? Because he wants you?"

I laughed. "Colleen, seriously…do I *look* like safety is my concern here?" Then I shrugged, something uncomfortable moving inside of me. I didn't let myself think about this too often, because it scared me. Being happy scared me, because I never trusted it to last. "I'm with him because I want to be. I'm happy with him. Yeah, having him want me is part of it, but *I* want it. That's enough for me."

She reached up and brushed my face. "It's more than that," she said, blowing out a breath. "I can feel it."

I glared at her.

She just shrugged. "Empath. What do you expect?"

She'd feel the things even I didn't entirely understand if I wasn't careful. "If you already *know*, then why are you asking?"

"Knowing isn't the same as understanding, Kit." She stood up and folded her arms over her chest, gazing toward the door. "What do you need from me about Xavier?"

"His silence."

She snorted. "I can't curse, Kitasa. Not even for my best friend."

"I'm not asking for a curse," I asked quietly. "But I do think you have a way of keeping him from talking about anything he saw or heard today. Justin placed a binding on me, without my consent and it's something I would have done willingly, you know it. Especially once I understood how important this is. You two fight the same kind of fight...even if you're different sorts of witches. If *he* can do it to me, bind me from talking, than can you...?"

"I can." She bit the answer off as if it hurt to say it. I caught her hand before she could move away.

"They'll kill him if I don't stop this, Colleen," I said quietly. "I have to get to Justin and that jackass doesn't *care*. If he talks to the wrong person? I can't risk it. I can't risk *him*. If you...if you know what he is to me, then you know how important than is. I wouldn't ask if it didn't matter."

Colleen stared at me, worrying something at her wrist. A charm, I realized. A twin to the one Xavier wore.

Hers wasn't biting into her wrist, but she didn't look happy about it. "I know, Kit," she said quietly.

She rubbed a thumb along the twig's surface and then looked to do the door. "I can bind him. Xavier's got a blood debt to me—one he's never going to get free of. But you need to understand...this is hard for me. I don't like using my magic this way."

"I'm sorry."

Her hand touched my cheek. "Don't be." A ragged breath escaped her. "I'd do the same damn thing."

* * * * *

I sped down the highway, with a few clear things in mind.

I needed to find Justin.

I needed to make sure I kept the hell away from

freelance witches in the future.

I owed Colleen, big-time.

And I needed, so desperately, to find Damon and just curl against him for the rest of my life.

The first thing, though, was to track down Justin. I'd been calling him, hoping he could meet me at Colleen's, but he hadn't yet answered.

I placed yet another call and checked my bag while the phone rang. I had to leave a message and I groaned, tossing the phone back down and consoling myself by touching the letter from Es. It buzzed under my hand and I wanted to just drop down, rest. It was over, right? Needed to be over.

Except I still hadn't gotten a hold of Justin and nothing was done until I talked to him.

I'd go to my office.

Justin would look for me there, I figured.

Lock myself up, keep calling him and maybe see if I couldn't find another damn contact at the Banner office.

Every mile that passed, I found myself checking my phone. Looking for a message from Justin, fighting the urge to call Damon. I never called him in the middle of the day unless there was a problem, so if I called now…

Well, there *was* a problem. I just didn't need to let him *know* there was one.

Which meant the very last thing I could do was call him.

Still, when my phone rang just outside my office and I saw Damon's name, my heart started to race, clenching in my chest until it hurt just to breathe. Turning off the car, I answered. It was a good thing he usually made me a little breathless because my voice was erratic as hell when I said, "Hey."

"Baby girl."

"What's up?"

An odd silence fell and I could count the measure of my heartbeats. *No fear…*Reaching up, I touched the mark on my neck, felt the ridged flesh where he'd sank his teeth into me. Marked me. "You calling to meet up for a quickie? Maybe you want to pee on my boots or something now?"

He laughed a little. "If I did that, you'd make me eat them. Besides…where would be the fun?"

"So biting me is fun," I muttered. Stroking my hand down the letter in my bag, I closed my eyes. *Justin. Where the hell are you?*

"Maybe it's a little more for me." He sighed.

In my mind, I could see him, rubbing his palm across his head, scraping it over his close-cropped hair the way he did.

"What are you up to do today?" he asked, his voice soft. "Gotten yourself into trouble or banged up much?"

Thinking back to the two or three pounds of flesh I'd left on the pavement, I made a face. "No more than normal."

"And this job you're working? How much longer until it's done?"

"Not soon enough." Even if Justin were to somehow magically appear in front of me—and I didn't think *that* was possible—this thing had still gone on too long. It needed to be done yesterday. It needed to never have *started*. I stroked the letter I held. Like it was a talisman. Justin. Had to get it to Justin. "It's wrapping up, but there's still a mess I have to deal with."

"And you're not in trouble."

I snarled and shoved off the car, turning around and driving my foot into the tire. "No, damn it. I *am* not in trouble." *You are. Because you're trying to fight my battles. And I…shit. I love you.*

The knot jumped into my throat and I had to squeeze the words out. "I don't think I've told you this, but I love you," I whispered. It came out ragged. Broken, almost.

Fear grabbed me and held me tight. I'd never let myself love anything, anybody before. Not really. What would happen now—*no. Don't think that way.*

"Kit—"

"Even when you are giving me grief over doing my job," I said, managing to make my voice sound a little more level. Almost the normal smart-ass me—maybe. "I gotta go. See you later, okay?"

"Kit!"

I hung up in the middle of his familiar snarl.

Swearing, I shoved the phone into my pocket and covered my face with my hands. It rang. And rang. And rang. I ignored it as I stormed into my office and set the wards. The past few days had strained my nerves to the breaking point and while I desperately *wanted* to talk to Damon, the things I *needed* to say? I couldn't tell him if my life depended on it.

My phone continued to ring in my pocket and I didn't trust myself to pull it out and not answer it so I grabbed the office phone and punched in another call. When Justin didn't answer that time, I was ready to scream.

* * * * *

Twenty-five minutes later, I tore out of my office like somebody had set it on fire.

When I hadn't answered my personal phone, Damon had taken to calling the office line and he alternated. Doing that *annoying* thing where he called just once. One single ring. My personal line. The office line. One ring. Every five minutes.

The good thing was that he was calling from his personal phone back at the lair. He wasn't coming after me…yet.

I could only thank God, because if he saw me anytime soon, he'd see what a mess I was. And damn it, I was a mess.

Such a mess that I didn't know where to go, what to do with myself.

My first stop was Banner HQ but if Justin was there, he didn't come out even after I stood at the desk swearing like a whore who'd just discovered she'd been short-changed.

Everybody there was giving me a very wary look and a wide berth and I left only because I knew I couldn't help Damon if I ended up arrested by Banner cops—might be hard to get the letter to Justin that way. It sat in the bag I carried, burning a hole in my hip and driving me insane.

There was one other stop I thought about making, one more question that needed to be answered. If I could figure out the right way to voice it. And maybe I could burn off some of the energy raging inside me while I waited for Justin. Justin, damn him.

Riding my ass about getting this job done and here I was, *done* and where the hell *was*—

A horn blared behind me and I looked up, realizing that I'd been stopped at a red light for I don't know how long.

Stopped, right in front of the rec club where I'd first met Chang months ago. As the driver behind me laid on their horn again, I darted into a parking space and parked haphazardly. The car shot past me and I climbed out, staring at the long, low building. It clung to the ground, squat and solid, and everything about it looked unfriendly. *Outsiders…stay away*, it practically screamed.

Four months ago, I'd been getting ready to go in there to question a bunch of punk kids about a missing teenager.

Damon had made me remove all of my weapons and then, because of my smart ass mouth, because he'd noticed I liked to tote around shiny objects and hide lots of weapons, he'd grabbed me, slammed me against the trunk of my car and threatened me…who says the path to true love is paved with roses? Then he warned me about what would happen if I caused him any more problems.

For days after, I'd been terrified of him. And yes, I'd still caused problems.

Now I was terrified *for* him and ready to cause so many problems, they might have to send a Banner unit out for me if things didn't settle down soon.

The phone in my pocket rang again and I tugged it out, checked—the single ring wasn't going to be Justin, but I had to make sure. Damon. My heart bumped against my ribs once, hard and fast and I curled my free hand into a fist as I waited for the ring to stop. After it did, I put in another call and this time, I also called Banner HQ and asked for Justin's immediate superior.

"Ms. Colbana, I'm afraid this is a bad—"

"I don't *care* if it's a bad time," I snapped. "I'm trying to work a job *you* hired me to do, a job I never wanted to work, that's almost impossible for me to do, and one that's gutting me *to* do—and I suspect that's why you assholes *chose* me. I need to talk to Justin, *now*. He wanted proof? I've got the fucking proof so why hasn't he come to get it? He'll know what I'm talking about. Get him the message. Now."

As I disconnected, I rubbed my thumb across the surface of my phone. One thing about the incessant calls. They were coming from the Lair. As long as he was tucked inside the Lair, I could trust that he was safe.

Banner would risk an inter-House disaster and it would be a disaster of epic proportions if they went after an Alpha on his home turf. They'd have to cut down too many of his people and they wouldn't do that.

They operated like a knife in the dark. They'd move when he was out of the Lair and not before.

A knot swelled in my throat and I rubbed the heel of my hand over my chest. My grandmother knew about me. I had to know how.

And Chang...somehow Chang and Damon knew.

Could I figure out a way to ask?

I didn't know. I just didn't.

One thing I had to do, though. I had to move. People were looking at me, including the men Chang had on the gate and they knew me. Which meant Chang knew I was out there.

* * * * *

"You look tired."

My visits here lately were a far cry from the first one. That time, *after* Damon had bruised the hell out of my windpipe, a sweet talker at the door had groped my tits. I'd busted his nose. Damon had then knocked him into the wall.

191

Apparently the groping hadn't been approved of.

Today, I was sprawled in a soft, plush chair that was big enough to sit five of me while Chang sat behind a carved oak desk that made mine look like even more of a disaster.

"I am tired," I said sourly.

"You should rest more." The phone rang, but he flicked a glance at it and ignored it. A curious little smile curved his lips as he added, "It's the key to a long life, you know. Eat right, a solid night's rest."

I curled my lip at him. "That applies to humans. I don't think the same goes for us." As his phone continued to ring, I glanced at it. "If I'm interrupting business, I can leave or wait outside," I said, absently rubbing a thumb down the scar on my wrist. I hadn't put the leather bracer on today. Didn't see the point, considering what my neck looked like.

"No. That's the beauty of being the boss." He grinned at me. "I can ignore them for a little while."

"As long as no investigators come and get groped?"

The smile faded from his face and for the first time, Chang looked...less than polite. He looked grim. "That will not happen again here, Kit."

Snorting, I shoved up and started to pace. "Oh, I'm not worried about it happening to *me*." I popped my wrist and realized I had the urge to rub my hands together—the heat was there, gathering and spreading. Even though I didn't feel threatened, I was...bothered. So very bothered. And the weapons always spoke to me when I was upset.

"I believe you misunderstand me," Chang said.

Turning, I glanced at him.

He'd come out from the behind the desk and I'd never even realized it. I hated that about him. All the other shifters I knew, I could read *something* about them, sense things because I could feel the energy of their beast and if they were angry, it was even better. I could even sometimes *see* the beast crouching above them in the air. It was a lovely, amazing thing...and one hell of a warning system, for me.

But Chang had none of it. I knew he was a cat. My gut

told me that and he moved too fast, with a grace that just wasn't human. But I could never *feel* anything off him and I never felt it when he was on the move.

Chang's eyes held mine steadily. "It will not happen within my establishment again. Ever. If it does, the man answers to me. I made this clear, and it doesn't matter who the person accosted is."

I studied him, wondered why he cared.

The question must have been written on my face because Chang said quietly. "You asked how I'd care if it was a wife, a sister, a mother." He flexed a hand and that façade cracked, for just a moment. "My mother died when both my sister and I were young. But my sister, well, perhaps life would have been kinder had she died with my mother. The men who hurt her didn't leave anything behind but a broken husk. She killed herself before I could rescue her. So I can tell you very much that it matters."

"I take it the bastard in question wasn't aware of this...issue," I said, looking away from him. Chang angry was disturbing enough. Chang *hurting* was just downright wrong. It was like seeing a statue weep.

"Irrelevant. He never made it out of my club alive." Chang shrugged and moved back behind the desk.

I blinked. Wiping a hand over the back of my mouth, I asked, "Damon?"

"No."

Okay, then.

"As much as it's always a pleasure to have you visit, Kit, is there a reason you're...hiding out?" he asked as I went back to pacing.

"I'm not hiding out," I muttered. The phone rang again and I cringed.

"That phone has rung like that exactly seven times. I'm something of an observer," he said.

"An observer." I smirked a little as I tugged the phone out, checked the display. Right on time. "Is that what they call nosy espionage types?"

193

"Spy is so much easier," Chang said, laughing. "But both work. I see things. I notice things. And I can't help my noticing you're acting the way you always do around Damon when you're nervous. Which makes me think he is the one calling you. And you're avoiding his calls. So that naturally leads to the conclusion...you're hiding out."

"Maybe I'm just hiding from wolves." I leaped on that with the desperation of the drowning and although I'd forgotten about them, it was a legit reason. One I could kick myself for not thinking up earlier.

Chang's lids flickered and I thought I could almost see that sharp mind of his whirling. "No," he said slowly. "That's not it. Because you wouldn't come to a club where the young are if you were really concerned you had a dangerous threat after you. That's not your way. You came here as a last ditch effort to get away from something that's bothering you. I assume you don't want Damon to know why you're upset. Try again."

"You know, Chang, I like you." I paused in front of the far wall and admired the katanas he had on display there. Some of them were *old*. I heard music from one of them and I wondered if he'd let me use him. I brushed my fingers down the hilt and smiled, closing my eyes at his music. Flutes...flutes and drums. Lovely. "I like you a lot and looking at the excellent taste you have in weapons only makes me respect you more."

Then I glanced over my shoulder at him and said softly, "But that doesn't mean I came here needing to confide in you."

"Then why *are* you here?"

"Because I'm trying to puzzle some things out. Wait something out so I can finish this job." I shrugged and went back to staring at the weapons. It wasn't a lie. I was still puzzling through a great mess of things, and I was still waiting on Justin.

I opened my mouth to ask about my grandmother. *How does she know about me? How do you know about her?* But the damn words were trapped in my throat.

Great.

Just great. It was too closely connected to the job and I couldn't utter those words without violating the binding laid on me. Swallowing, I shook my head. "But even if I *wanted* to explain what was bothering me? I can't. I've got an oath on me." Nerves tore their ugly hooks into me as I said it and I realized there was *another* reason I'd come. It was for a reason and not just because I wanted to pry information loose about my grandmother.

This was Damon's closest friend.

He trusted nobody the way he trusted Chang. Raking my nails down my forearm, I turned and stared at the man waiting patiently behind the table. "Have you ever had to do a job that you hated with every fiber of you being?"

He inclined his head. "At times. I usually try to find a way to avoid such jobs."

"Sometimes you can't. Because it's the only way to take care of things that matter most." I was able to force *those* words out, but just barely. The binding weighed in closer and closer, making it hard to breathe. "Sometimes, the only way to care for those things is to do something that leaves you feeling sick, twisted, broken inside."

"Whatever you're protecting, if it's worth that much...it will work out," Chang said gently.

I stared at him for a long, aching moment. "I hope so."

Then I headed for the door.

Before I could reach it, Chang said softly, "Kit...if I may? You've spent an extended amount of time in very close proximity to another male."

"I've been working with a witch," I said sourly. "One who doesn't know his personal space, but it was necessary."

Chang dipped his head. "I don't doubt that..." he said. Then he looked up at me. "If I had, we wouldn't have spent the past forty minutes chatting. You're everything to Damon. I owe him my loyalty. I won't see him betrayed."

"Somebody would have to have a blade in my gut and a

curse on me before they could even try to force me to betray him."

A faint smile tugged at Chang's lips. "I think you'd die first."

I will.

"However, be that as it may…you smell of another man. And he's had a trying day. He won't think clearly if he scents it. Perhaps you should shower before you leave." Then he flicked a look over me and added, "And burn the clothes."

I'd shower back at my damn office, thank you very much.

I still had calls to make.

Calls to avoid.

As I let myself out, I heard Chang sigh.

CHAPTER FOURTEEN

I should have taken Chang up on his offer.

My gut was a knot of nasty little tangles as I turned into my parking lot.

The light shone down on Damon's Charger and I looked down at my phone, tried to figure out just *why* his home number was still showing up—

He'd programmed it. Set a trap for me, like the cagey cat he was.

Fear knocked hard against my ribs as I glanced around. No sign of Banner. Would they make a move *here*? If they did, I could stop it. I had the letter from Es. But what was the deal with Justin? He *knew* how important this was, so why hadn't he called me back?

This was messed up. Had they discovered the death of Marlowe? Immediately, I wanted to kick myself. Of course they had. And that would explain why Justin hadn't returned my calls.

He was busy investigating my boyfriend—Banner was trying to find a way to slip a noose around Damon's neck and Justin was trying to work the case so that didn't happen.

Fuck this mess. Sideways and to hell and back.

Had somebody seen him out there? Well, other than corpses and Xavier. Marlowe and his men had seen him, but

197

they were dead. Somebody must have reported *something*.

Other than Xavier, I hadn't seen *anybody* and the witch wasn't going to be doing any talking.

Not until Colleen released him from that binding oath.

Fear danced a wild song in my head but I shoved it down. If I faced Damon like this, it was over. He'd know something was wrong and it would only be worse since I couldn't tell him.

Although this wasn't going to be good anyway since he'd smell Xavier on me.

Damn that son of a bitch.

Parking the car, I snagged the bag and caught my blade. Everything else, I left. Hooking the strap of my bag across my torso, I started across the pavement to Damon. I hadn't even taken two steps before he was there, closing the rest of the distance with eerie, feline speed that left my head spinning.

"Damon, I—"

His mouth crushed mine.

And for the second time that day, all the oxygen was sucked out of the world.

But this time, it wasn't a battle that caused it, unless you counted the way his tongue tangled with mine, the way his hands streaked across my back, jerking my shirt up and splaying across bare skin.

Thirty, wonderful seconds and then it ended as he jerked away and glared down at me. "What in the fuck, Kit? I smell—"

"My case," I said. I cut him off. If I said something before he asked, then maybe he wouldn't ask me questions I couldn't answer. "I got stuck with a witch who does cloaking and we had to do some messy work, but it only works if we were close."

"Close?" He pressed his hand to my collarbone, splaying it across my skin so that I felt the very heat of it rushing through me. "He had to fucking be *touching* you?"

"Close quarter detail sadly means just that—cloaking

doesn't work otherwise." I plucked at the hem of my shirt. I really should have had that shower—and burned the damn clothes. "Once the job was over, I kicked the asshole in the head. It wasn't enough."

Damon's eyes flashed. Light reflected back at me. *Cat's eyes—*

I held his gaze. "This wasn't a job I picked. I had to take it—lives are at stake—and once it's done, I'm going to bloody somebody over it. But for now, I have to finish it."

"And this?" he asked, fisting his hand in the front of my shirt, tugging me close. "Does this have to happen again? You stand there smelling of another man again? Kit...I—shit, Kit, this is gutting me."

I curled my hand around his wrist. "If I could tell you what it was doing to me, I would."

His eyes searched mine. "Why can't you?"

"If I tell anybody, Banner is going to know. And people die. I can't do that, Damon. I can't." *I can't let you die—*

He groaned and pressed his forehead to mine. "Inside now, baby girl. Inside, okay?"

His presence was a burning ache at my back and my breath came in hot, harsh little bursts as I made my way to the door. "Don't forget the wards," I whispered as I dealt with the locks.

He stood there waiting, his eyes on my bowed head as I went through the process of disarming the protections wrapped around my office. "Put them back up," he said as he shut the door behind him and locked it.

I put the bag on the desk, carefully touched my hand to it, too aware of the precious burden it carried.

I licked my lips and then went to the door. It was a simple design to arm the wards. My touch alone, on the locks in a certain way, did it. As I flipped the deadbolt, magic skittered around the room. One ward in place. Damon's fingers brushed across the back of my neck. I put the chain in place. Second ward. He laid his hands on my waist. I unlocked the lock he'd turned and then locked it back up and the wards burst into life with a whispering sigh.

Damon shredded my shirt.

Turning around, I reached for him and all those nasty, jagged places inside me faded away. This felt real to me. Felt whole. Felt right. And I was going to make sure I kept this.

"Baby girl," he muttered as his mouth pressed to the mark on my neck. It was sensitive, still sore, but that light caress felt so good.

He boosted me up and I groaned, wiggling against him and reaching for the waistband of the BDUs I wore. "Be still," he rasped against my mouth. He shifted and reached down. Seconds later, the sound of cloth ripping filled the air once more. "I don't want you ever wearing these clothes again."

The scraps of my pants still clung to my legs, but neither of us cared.

The rasp of his zipper was terribly loud and then he was there, pressed against me...*in* me, driving so deep and so hard.

"Tell me again," he muttered. "Tell me, damn it. Without hiding away this time."

"I love you."

"I love you, too. And stop *running* from me, Kit. Stop running...aw, hell..."

His breath hitched in his chest and I felt it against my own, felt the massive pressure of need swelling in us both. As it exploded and swelled and built again, I clung to him.

He was the only real and solid thing in my world.

I couldn't lose him.

* * * * *

It wasn't as easy to get out of a pair of torn BDUs as one might think. Especially since my belt had ended up in a tangled snarl around my waist. In the end, I just used a knife to cut the ruined pants off and dumped them in the trash. As I sat down to deal with my boots, I looked up and saw

Damon sprawled in the chair behind my desk.

The dark, brooding look in his eyes made my heart skip a beat. Even the sly smile curling his lips didn't help much.

"You know," he murmured, staring at me hard. "That right there is a picture. Maybe I should get one like that for my birthday."

"Pervert." I made a face at him and finished stripping away my boots, leaving them by the couch. I opened the small closet and grabbed the first thing that came to hand—a plain black T-shirt. Jerking it on over my head, I made a concerted effort to ignore the trembling of my hands. I'd just noticed the time. It was getting late. Sooner or later, Justin would have to call and my gut said it would be soon.

I had to talk to him—

"What were you out doing today, Kit?"

Closing my eyes, I scooped my hair out the neckline of the shirt and shut the door. "I already told you I was working a case." One that was breaking my heart. Breaking *me*—

No. I wasn't broken.

I was pissed, I was furious and I was *hurt*, probably going to be hurt more when this was done and I had to explain what was going on. But that didn't make me broken.

He loved me.

He'd understand that I was trying to protect him. He was doing the same for me.

He'd understand.

"I had to take care of something outside of the city," Damon said and his voice was a low, rumbling growl.

I heard that tone often enough. It was anger. Not that icy edge I'd seen earlier, but there were a lot of varieties of anger. And I'd faced this one of his before.

He'd figured it out—thought past the mask of Xavier's cloaking.

"Kit."

I turned around and I saw it in his eyes.

He knew.

As he came up off the chair, he shook his head. "I've

been trying to place it all fucking day and it wasn't until just now that it clicked. You said you had to work with somebody who...what, cloaked? What the fuck is that?"

"It's what it sounds like, Damon," I said levelly. The hell if I'd lied. Lies had never come easily to me anyway and if I even tried, he'd know. "I'm working a *job*. I'm doing the best I can and I can't *talk* about it. Let me work it, let me finish it and I'll explain."

The roar echoed around the room. Echoed...echoed...until I thought my ears would burst from it.

"Kit. Were you *following* me?" he demanded.

"I'm working a fucking job."

A muscle jumped in his jaw. "Is that the only thing you're going to say, damn it?"

"It's the only thing I *can* say." Tears were threatening to burn me now. *No crying, Kit...don't you do it.*

"I don't believe this." He spun away and braced his hands on my desk, the muscles in his back bunching and moving under his shirt. "Fuck—everything I've...shit. No."

The disjointed ramble of words bothered me as much as the pain I saw in his eyes as he turned back around to glare at me. "A job, right? Fine," he bit off, his voice a ragged, uneven snarl. "Day's done. Come home. With me now."

I opened my mouth to answer. *Yes. Please. Just yes...*

And my fucking phone rang.

Justin...I could hear the muffled ringtone of the Imperial March coming from the garbage can where I'd dumped the shreds of my pants. I wanted to scream. "I have to talk to him right now," I said, the words come in an awful, stilted mess. "I have the information I need to close this case and then I'm done. I just need—"

"I need *you*," he roared. "Now. Come with me now."

The phone rang again and anxiety rose to a wail in my mind as my office phone started to echo it as well. Calling both lines—not good.

And clear as crystal, I could see Damon speeding away

from Assemblyman Marlowe's house.

I opened my mouth… *I have to tell them you were doing it for me—*

That was all I had to say. That was *all*.

But the binding spell kept the words locked inside me and even when I tried to force the words out, it was like my throat was swelling shut on me while pain swelled like supernova behind my eyes, all but blinding me. *Justin, you son of a bitch…damn you.*

"Damon. It's two hours."

"No." He shook his head. "It's more than that. It's over, baby girl. Good-bye, Kit."

My heart cracked down the middle as I stared at him. I'd taking beatings that hadn't hurt like that. He…shit. He hadn't just said that, had he? *"What?"*

He backed away from me. "You don't trust me. Right now, you're half sick with fear and I can't get you to come with me when I need you like I need air. If we…if this is how it's going to be between us, then maybe it's better off if there *isn't* an us. It's done."

Tears blinded me as he turned his back on me.

It was probably for the best.

I didn't see him leaving me.

Something snapped, hissed. I flinched as I realized what it was—the wards. "Damon—" I swiped the tears away, made myself look at him.

He powered through it without sparing me a glance. They weren't designed to holding something *in*. They must have hurt like hell when he broke them. But as he stumbled down the sidewalk, he didn't much look like he cared.

He just wanted to be away from me.

And still, the damn phones wouldn't shut the hell up.

* * * * *

"Timetable has been moved *up*," Justin barked once I was finally able to answer. "He's slated for execution once the warrant is signed at the meet tomorrow and if they can get enough people together tonight, they may even try to get it going before then. Damn it, Kit—"

"I have the proof you need to stop it." I stood at the window, staring at the spot where his Challenger had been. He'd walked away. Just like that. "It was all about me. Charter decrees a were can't be executed for acting in defense of a mate, loved one or clan if he feels a threat is imminent. Alpha Damon Lee heard rumors that my grandmother was looking for me and those he killed were the ones who had shown interest in exchanging information about me for future favors from her."

There was silence.

"Your fucking bitch of a grandmother," Justin muttered. Then, his voice fell back into formal tones. "You said you had proof of this."

"He spoke with an Assembly speaker. Delores Richards. Es. You know her. She knows all of it and more; she read him when he confronted her."

"Why did he confront her?"

"Because my grandmother reached out to her and he was approaching anybody he thought might be a threat. He decided Es wasn't. She read him and she's willing to swear before the Assembly and a Banner court that he was acting in defense of me. He cannot lawfully be put down. Es has also made it clear that if Banner takes him out, she'll seek legal action. He's done nothing wrong."

"What's the proof?"

"Signed and sworn writ from Es herself. She has a copy and there's one at the Assembly as well, in the hands of somebody she trusts. If he goes down, people are going to burn over it, Justin. He was set up for the whole damn thing and Banner was manipulated. I haven't figured out *that* end of it, but this all …fuck it. I'll get there. But for now…how in the hell can I get you this letter?"

"I'm at HQ. Bring it. Immediately." His voice was edgy, tight. I knew him well enough to know it was kind of battle high he got when something big was going down. At least it wouldn't be my….Damon. He wasn't *my* anything anymore, I thought. Hours ago, he'd been my everything.

I'd been everything to him. And now I was nothing.

My heart simply shattered.

"Kit, you have to stay out of sight for a few days, okay? If this shit about your grandmother is legit, I need to check a few things, and TJ got in touch—she still hasn't dealt with all of the wolves. You got a place to go underground? Stay with your cat or something?"

"He's not mine anymore." I turned away from the window, unable to look out there anymore. But a fading spark caught my eye. I looked over at the doorway, saw the dying ripple of the magics from where he'd busted the wards.

I'd have to get them repaired. I'd have to…what?

What did I have to do?

"Kit!"

I blinked and glanced at the phone. Justin. Yeah. Had to focus and finish this up. "What?"

"What are you talking about, Kit?"

"Nothing," I said, swallowing the knot in my throat. I'd fall apart later. If I broke now, I'd never even make it out the door and Damon still wasn't safe. "Let's get this done and then I'll get out of sight. I'm good at hiding, remember?"

* * * * *

I made the drive in a numbed haze. Halfway there, something hit me and I put in a call to Chang. His voice was cool when he answered, but I didn't let it stop me.

"Do you remember what I asked you about working a job you hated? Then you said it has a way of working out?"

"I'm terribly busy, Kit."

Ouch. It was a distant thought, more of an afterthought than anything else. I didn't need to ask what his problem was. I already knew. He and Damon had talked.

I was now *persona non-grata.*

"Yank the stick out of your ass, Chang, and shut the *fuck* up," I warned him. I was mad enough to think about going back to the office and grabbing something with enough firepower behind it to make him do just that. But there was no time.

"Ms. Colbana, I'm afraid I don't have time for this right now. If you'd like to schedule an appointment—"

"Shove the appointment up your ass," I snarled. "I asked you a damned question—hey, you owe me a favor. Four months ago. One of your bastards trespassed on me and you owe me. Remember? I'm calling that favor in."

Silence, ugly and raw, fell.

His voice, when it came, was cold. "Make it fast."

"*You* said the things that matter that much usually had a way of working out. It didn't. The job's wrapping up, but I need you to make sure somebody stays at the Lair until after tomorrow. *Please.*" Razors blades gripped my throat and in desperation, I grabbed a knife from inside my vest. Adrenaline loosened many bonds. I plunged the blade deep into my thigh and twisted. Pain flared hot, while blood flowed like a river.

And deep inside me, something wavered—weakened.

"A life is at stake," I said, forcing the words out. "The Lair is safe from certain…entities. These entities, they can't *go* there." Those razor blades wrapped tight around my throat, but I gave the blade in my thigh another twist and managed to continue. "He's *safe* there, Chang. *They* can't go there."

Through the roaring in my ears, I heard him hiss. "Banner…" The word stretched out of him and through the roar of pain and nausea in my head, I heard his shock. "Is this about Damon and Banner?"

"They can't *go* there, right?" I demanded. He knew the ins and outs of clan law better than I did. He'd know.

"Kit, what is going on?"

"Just keep him there. Keep him safe. Give me time to finish this," I said, gritting the words out. It was enough. He'd get the point. Chang wouldn't take chances with

Damon.

I yanked the blade from my thigh and threw it down, blade still bloody.

He went to say something else, but I disconnected and hurled the phone down. Nothing else mattered now. Damon would be safe. Chang would see to it. That one thing was all that mattered. Fishing a couple of loose cloths from the bag I kept in the back, I slapped them against my leg. Hot blood gushed out, but I didn't care. It would slow in a minute and up ahead, I saw the bright, silver lights…Banner HQ.

And Justin was right out in front, pacing in front of his bike, a dark look on his face.

I wasn't even out of the car before he had his hand out.

I slapped the envelope into his hand and scowled as I saw the blood on it. My blood. Justin paused, staring at the blood and then my hand. His eyes dropped to the dark stain spreading down my leg. "Kit, your leg."

"Fuck the leg. The letter, damn it."

He sighed and broke the seal Es had placed on it. Both of us felt the whisper of her magic, but I suspected he felt it even more. As he unfolded the letter, her power started to scream.

"Yeah. This will do it." He looked back at me. "Now what's wrong? Damn it, you look like you've been beaten, Kit. What's wrong? You win."

"He knows," I said flatly. "Not why, but he knows I was following him and investigating. He…" I shoved harder against the wound in my thigh as I leaned back against my car. Pain screamed at me and I welcomed it. Anything to keep my mind from dwelling on the pain inside me. "It's over, Justin. He needed something I couldn't give at the time and I needed to make sure he was safe. The needs didn't meet and it's over."

Justin opened his mouth to say something but I didn't want to hear it. What did it matter anyway?

"I'll get lost for a while," I said, using the cloth to form a makeshift bandage. "I need to go pack up, but then I'm gone." I headed toward the car door, but stopped and looked back. "You…you'll call me when this is officially put to bed, right? I need to know. For me. I need to know he's safe."

His vivid green eyes rested on my face and he sighed. "You know I will. It shouldn't be a day. Look, Kit you can't just let it go so—"

I climbed back into my car and drove off. Whatever he was saying, it didn't matter.

* * * * *

I dumped the bag into my trunk and slammed it shut.

My house was locked up tight, light down and wards up. Although I couldn't do anything about the wards at my office, I went by there last, studiously trying *not* to think as I locked the doors and secured the valuable stuff. As much as it had hurt to go back, the majority of my weapons were stored there and I needed some of them.

The wards at home would hold for a few weeks without me being there to charge them. My office? Hell. Who knew. That magic—it was dead now.

It was time to get the hell out of East Orlando for a while.

It was a good thing I'd just wrapped up those courier jobs. At least I had money. Money…and no place to go.

I wanted to go to Damon—

Fuck this. I'd call. I could call, right?

I jerked my phone out.

It was a punch when the call was passed to Sam. "No calls from Kit, he said. Sorry, honey. He doesn't want you anymore."

It was a punch…right to the heart. I staggered, and fell back against my car, staring vacantly at my office as those words spun around in my head. My heart ached. My head…it was like the words bounced around inside it but they didn't connect. Everything inside me was free-spinning, free-falling.

And then *I* was falling and everything inside me burned.

The phone fell from my numb hand and I looked down, saw the dart protruding from my chest.

My ears popped and terror, adrenaline, nerves, all of it exploded inside me as I felt that familiar swaddling sensation settle over me. Cloaked. I was cloaked. Not by my own invisibility, but by a cloaker, one who could keep me from being scented, sensed, heard...all of it.

Clumsily, I reached up and tried to grab at the dart, but I couldn't make my hand rise above my waist.

This was bad—

"Hi, Kit."

My hand burned and I called my sword, but it was so heavy. So fucking heavy...

As Xavier stepped into view, I tried to lift the blade. Tried. Failed.

He laughed. "You won't be able to use that. I was warned, you know. Jude told me you'd be a fighter. So I figured I'd just suck the fight right out of you so I didn't have to deal with it."

Darkness danced around me. So close. So close—

But I couldn't go under.

Jude.

No...

Not...

CHAPTER FIFTEEN

Hello, darling Kit...

The voice in my head was one that made me shudder with fear. Even though I dreamed, I knew there was reason to fear that voice. He'd almost succeeded in killing me in a dream once. Or at least, he'd done a close enough job to make it look like somebody had *tried.*

Jude was deadly. In dreams. Awake.

I forced myself to lie there, waiting for him to make himself known.

But all I heard was his voice.

And a teasing sort of laugh.

I've been counting the days, you know, he murmured in the back of my mind. *I never expected it would be this easy. It was amusing, you know...sending the Assembly, chasing around in circles, watching as they stared at him, wondering. Waiting. All it took was a few whispers in the right places, at the right time. I wanted to see him burn. I never thought he'd help me like this.*

I tried to summon up the strength to push him out. I could do it. I'd done it before. But the cloying feel of magic clung to me, and I was so damn weak. And Jude was well and firmly trapped inside my mind.

A hand touched my brow. Even in my dreams, I felt it. Heard him laugh again. You made him so angry. And he

210

just...walked away. I was trying to get him out of the way, but he just walked and left you.

Denial raged inside of me.

Denial and grief...because Damon *had* just walked away.

Fear. Because only an idiot wouldn't be afraid of Jude.

Anger.

But anger was the best thing.

It gave me the strength I needed to fight my way past the spell. I fed that tiny kernel of rage until it grew and grew, spreading through me. Jude's voice continued to whisper in the back of my head, but I focused on the warmth of my rage, not the ice of his presence.

Finally, I had enough heat to struggle past the spell. It shriveled and faded and once I knew it was gone, I found the strength to shove him out of my head. As silence settled within me, I wrapped it around myself.

Damon... An ache spread through me.

I heard the echo of a promise he'd made me.

Nobody hurts you, Kit...

* * * * *

Kit...wake up. You need to wake—

I came awake to icy cold.

Water drenching me.

I rolled away from it and bounced to my feet. My body hurt, but that was nothing new. I knew how to fight when I was in pain and I could do it just fine. My hand heated— itched.

The water spray came at me again and I stumbled away. Hose. They had a water hose.

It took a few seconds to focus and fade away—the one true magic I possessed, that ability to go invisible. But finally I was able to calm my frazzled nerves and do it, blinking the water out of my eyes and smiling in satisfaction as one of them grunted and swore. "Fuck, where'd she—"

It was the last thing he said.

Idiots.

I lowered the bow I'd summoned to my hand and watched as a small bit of blood appeared under the arrow. Better to go with the bow. A friend of mine had once warned me. *Know your weapons—*

"Damn, sugar. You made it too easy…"

I felt something in my mind—a ripping, tearing sensation and I swayed, stumbling back as a pain like nothing I'd ever felt tore through me. It was like somebody had found some deep connection to my soul and just ripped it right out.

Gasping for breath, I hit the floor and felt stone tear into my knees. The pain grounded me and I slammed a hand against the ground for one precious moment, steadying myself.

That voice. I knew that voice.

Xavier—

Yes. I knew this. Memory came flooding back.

He was staring at me. Smiling.

Could see me.

I'd let the invisibility drop…? How had I done that…?

I bumped the heel of my hand against my head and wondered. It didn't matter though. I was going to kill that grinning bastard across from me. From the corner of my eye, I saw somebody lifting the hose and he glanced over. "Don't bother. We wanted her awake before he got down here. She's awake. I need to make sure it worked."

"Wha…" My mouth didn't want to work. Clearing my throat, I focused on his hated face. "Make sure what worked, you scum-sucking dickhead?"

He winked at me. "Don't you remember what I said? I don't have to *break* you to fuck you up."

Summoning the strength I needed to get to my feet was harder than I expected. Staying upright was even harder, but I managed. I braced one end of my bow on the ground, keeping it casual, like it was a walking stick…*not* like I needed to stay on my feet.

As I moved forward, I smiled at him. "You realize I'm

going to kill you, right?"

"Sugar, you don't stand a chance." He shrugged and glanced around, studying the bars. "You're trapped here." Then he looked back at me and the grim look on his face hit hard. "Just like me. But the good news, for me anyway? He doesn't want me the way he wants you. And I did a good job. That means I get a bonus. I get a few more days free, I get to go find a woman and—"

I smiled a little as I moved closer, toying with my belt.

Idiot. He'd stayed too close to the bars. "You've had your last woman."

None of them saw me grab him.

Now Xavier was flailing against the solid metal bars as I held him close.

As the others struggled to jerk him away, I wrapped my garrote around his neck. I jerked hard, felt his head smack against the bars as the wire dug deep. It was cutting in, deep. Something was missing—

I knew this, but it didn't matter. I could feel the wire digging in, biting, cutting.

"You won't ever get to spend that money," I whispered.

The guards bellowed, jerking on his legs.

Xavier kicked, fought.

And I used the strength so many didn't realize I had.

I severed his carotid and watched as it sprayed the men in front of us.

More came rushing in.

Utterly silent. *What's missing—?*

Xavier went to the ground, his head hanging off at an awkward angle. Witches are made of solid stock, but blood loss will do just about any mortal creature in.

If I could have gotten a little closer, I would have decapitated him. I wish I could have done so—I wanted to make his head into my personal punching bag. Jerking the garrote free, I backed away from the bars and stared at the men.

None of them spoke.

Not a single word.

That should have bothered me. Everything was terribly silent.

Why was it so quiet—but the puzzle had to fade to the background because the door opened. Two people entered. Two people I knew. Two people I hated. Evangeline was first, dressed in an immaculate suit the color of a ripe pumpkin. It clung to her curves like a lover and made her skin look a disturbing shade of yellow.

The man at her back wore black. Head to toe, like the proverbial vampire and he wore it well. He didn't cause any reaction in me except revulsion, though. And fear. I'd be a fool not to be afraid, but I could control that. The disgust was harder. I managed.

I hated Jude Whittier too much to ever let my fear show. But I wouldn't mind if he knew I despised him.

As he stood there, taking in the lifeless body at my feet, the blood spilling across the ground, I glared at him. "One of these days, you fucking leech, I'm going to rip out your heart and burn it to ashes."

Jude, the son of a bitch, actually had the gall to laugh.

"One of these days, Kit?" He smiled and nudged the body with his toe. "I don't think so. Xavier was right about one thing. You are, well and truly, trapped."

I flexed my hand. All I needed was a couple of arrows— But…they didn't come.

And the music at the back of my mind had gone silent.

Jude was staring at my hand. And he was smiling.

"Is something missing, Kit?" He reached for something behind a column and swung it up for me to see.

As the light danced off my blade, my mind screamed out in denial. *Mine—she's mine!* I waited for the magic to heat my hand. The connection.

But I was cold.

And her music was gone. The very soul of me felt empty. Jude smiled at me. "Yes…yes, I think it is."

He tossed the sword to Evangeline. "Lock it in my

chambers." Then he glanced around the cell. "Everybody...out."

* * * * *

I huddled in the corner as Jude rose. He stroked a hand down my hair.

I would have hit him again, except he'd already broken my right arm and my left shoulder was dislocated.

Everything in me hurt.

Blood ran in hot paths down my neck, down my thighs. If I had any tears, I might have wept, but I didn't want to cry because of what he'd done. I could live with being raped. I could live with being beaten. With having my bones broken, my body battered. After all, I'd lived through all of that before.

I couldn't live with showing him the fear he wanted.

"It doesn't have to be this way," Jude said, still stroking my hair. "All you had to do was come as I'd asked and you could have been a companion. Now...well, it's this way until you decide otherwise."

"Not..." I had to swallow to force the words out throw my battered throat. "Not happening, leech."

"It will, Kit." He kissed my temple. "Sooner or later, you'll realize that you have no place else. I'll be the one waiting when you see there's nothing else left for you."

Turning my head, I stared into that beautiful, demonic face. If I didn't understand how a vampire's soul eventually died, I might have wondered how anybody could be so completely soulless. But it was simple, when one didn't have a soul. As he went to touch me again, I spat at him.

Rage rippled over his face as he rose. "I think you want to drive me to kill you."

Figured it out, did you?

"It won't work." He left me in the cell and as he locked it behind him, he called out, "Yasmine."

A slim, pale woman with ash-brown hair came into the

room as he continued to watch me. "My healer is going to deal with you. When I come tomorrow, I hope you'll see the light. It won't take too long, I suspect, but we can go several rounds of this."

I just stared at him.

If he thought he could break me in a couple of days, he was sadly, bitterly mistaken.

A few days, really, was all I had to wait. Somebody would come for me.

I knew it.

He opened the door for the healer, eying me critically. "She's a pacifist. While I realize you're furious, I wonder if you're willing to harm a woman who would die before she'd lift a hand to protect herself."

I just stared at him. He already knew the answer to that. I'd let her heal me. It was better to be strong when the time came to fight my way out, anyway.

My hand, though, it felt terribly empty.

Terribly broken and wrong…and there was no music in my head. The sounds of my weapons were gone.

As the healer came forward, I sat there. Her hands touched my arm and her voice was gentle as she said, "I'll try not to add to the pain. I cannot offer any tonics, I'm afraid. I don't have the herbs I need to craft them."

Closing my eyes, I turned my head away.

Did she really think anything she did was going to be worse than what he'd already done?

Her hand touched my brow as she assessed the damage and then I had to stifle a gasp as she spoke clearly into my mind. *"I'm going to put you under after I do the full healing. You need a few days rest and I will tell the master so. Take the time to accept what has happened. It will go easier on you,"* she said. Her eyes, a crystalline blue, held mine.

If my mouth hadn't been starting to swell, I might have sneered.

Accept…no.

"I don't need—"

But before I could make the argument, she caught my arm in strong, unyielding hands and pulled. As bones realigned, anything I might have said was trapped inside as I struggled not to scream.

She was quick and efficient. If I hadn't been fighting the pull of the deep healing, I might have admired it.

But as she held my hand in hers, I battled against the waves of healing magic she pushed inside me, fought it the way I'd fought Jude's invasion of my body. I couldn't go under. Somebody would come for me—

"She needs a full healing, Master," I heard her saying over my head.

"She'll need rest after that," Jude bit off, his voice displeased.

"I realize you want to spend time acclimating her, but she's taken a number of injuries lately. I feel them on her body and her human blood makes her weak. If the full healing isn't done, and soon, the human blood will continue to weaken her—"

Weak, my ass...

I continued to struggle, but it was useless. Attempts to lift my newly healed arm were about as successful as trying to move a mountain. After another few moments, I was gone. Lost in a wave of unending blackness. Where I was certain nightmares awaited.

The last thought I heard was...*Sleep. Accept. There will be no nightmares here...*

* * * * *

I dreamed. The dreams that chased me couldn't be called nightmares, but they were far from pleasant. Nighttime forests, trees that rose around in a tangled spiral and off in the distance, I heard a familiar, slithering noise that should have sent trembles of terror dancing down by spine.

But the snakes weren't the thing that bothered me right

now.

Kit. Kit…where are you?

That voice. I heard it calling for me, but I didn't know who it was. Where it came from. And nothing mattered.

I could hear a giant cat out in the distance. Roaring. But the sound of his call wasn't one that made me think he was happy.

It's done…

His voice haunted me even as I moved through the night and tried to find some way to escape it. I had to get away. Had to find some peace.

I knew the nightmare that awaited me when I woke and I had to find a way to get out.

Maybe he was done, but somebody would come.

Kit…damn it. Voices raged in my head. Raged and crashed and made no sense. All my life, I'd suffered from surreal, *unreal* dreams, but this was even worse.

Kit—wake up! The very trees seemed to shout it. No. I didn't want to wake up. I was so fucking alone, but part of me still wanted to believe that somebody would come. Somebody would come for me.

But who?

I heard the roar of a cat—it wasn't Damon's beast. A different sort of cry, followed by a whisper, *Wake up. You need to wake up—*

No. I wasn't ready to wake up. I just wanted to get away from the voices that haunted me…

*Nothing hurts you, Kit…*now the memories were a bruise on my heart. He'd made that promise to me. It wasn't fair, exactly. Damon hadn't *been* there when Xavier grabbed me and it had been my own carelessness that led to this, but still.

I can't get you to come with me when I need you like I need air.

Trapped in a dream and surrounded by memories, I started to run. The growl of a giant cat's scream chased after me. And it lasted forever.

"Somebody will come," I told myself.

Somebody.

Kit.

Justin, maybe. He'd think to look for me when he couldn't reach me. I hoped.

Wake up, I can't find you like this—

Colleen…would she come?

No. She was a pacifist and even if she tried to search for me, she was bound from causing physical harm and that was the only thing that could get me out of here.

I had to face reality, even in the depth of a dream that broke my heart.

In the end, it all came down to me. If I was going to get out, I would have to rely on just myself. I could handle that. Jude's home was just outside of East Orlando. I could get out of here and get to one of the witch houses. They might be pacifists, but they knew how to guard themselves and I was an ally. I'd find safety there while I contacted the Assembly. Something…

I just had to get away long enough to do it.

I can't get you to come with me when I need you like I need air…

The memory of his words haunted me. Through the long, endless dreams.

As my body healed, my heart fractured even more.

Nobody hurts you, Kit…

* * * * *

Wake up, Kit. Come on, we can't find you if you sleep—

Once more, icy water was my wake-up call. Choking on it, I sputtered into wakefulness and tried to roll away. They'd learned fast though and I couldn't get away from it long enough to fade. The force of the water was brutal and I was gasping, choking when it finally ended.

A towel was thrown in at me and I stayed where I was, letting it fall to the floor in front of me.

"So you'd rather stay naked in front of the guards?"

Through the sopping wet hanks of my hair, I shifted my eyes up. I knew that voice. Knew it well—Evangeline.

Absently, I flexed my wrist but memory came rushing at me. The song of my blade was silenced. I couldn't call her.

She laughed, the sound of it so sweet and innocent, one might have thought she was a child at play.

I wanted to gut her. Wanted it so bad I hurt with it.

"You can't call that pretty sword now, can you?" she whispered. She paced forward to the bars and wrapped her hands around them, pressing her face against them, smiling at me. "How brave are you now, Kit?"

I shoved the hair out of my face as I took a mental inventory. I could move everything. Rising, I stared at her. I could stand.

That was good.

And there were still abilities they couldn't strip from me...the ability to go unseen, the ability to fight. As weak as I was, as tired as I was, I doubted I could maintain the invisibility for too long, but I only needed a few minutes. And I'd have to be dead not to fight.

Holding her gaze, I smiled and faded out of sight.

She sighed and shook her head. "That's not going to help you much. Jude can track the sound of your heart. If I try, I can..." She closed her eyes and judging by the look on her face she was doing just that.

Too bad she wasn't fast enough.

I shoved my hands through the bars. She was out of practice. She hadn't caught my location until it was too late. With every ounce of strength I had, I slammed her head against the bars and listened to the beautiful sound of bone crunching. I did it again, and again as her screams went from vicious to broken. She fought and she was strong, but Evangeline had come to Jude to be his little whore. She hadn't ever learned how to fight.

It took four of the guards to pry her loose and none of them wanted to come into the cell with me.

As they dragged her away, I moved over to the towel and lifted it up, used it to wipe the gore from my face. I was filthy again and I had to fight the urge to scratch at my skin.

Instead, I wiped away the blood, the brain matter and bone. Turning around, I listened to her moans. If she'd been purely human, she'd be dead, but a vampire's companion had a little more strength.

Crossing the cell, I smiled at her battered face. Nobody who knew her would even recognize her. "I don't know, Angie," I said, wondering if she'd heard me. "Just how brave *am* I now?"

One of the guards gave me a disbelieving stare. I threw the towel at him and moved back to the corner.

How much time had passed, I wondered. How much time had I been here?

It couldn't have been too long. I hadn't eaten a blessed thing, hadn't had anything to drink. Even after the healing, I could only manage a few days before I'd start to suffer the effects of that.

"He's going to hurt you over that," one of them said.

I looked up and met his eyes and just stared.

Hurt me? Jude had kidnapped me. Raped me. I was being held prisoner. And he thought I was worried that Jude would hurt me because I'd damaged his precious little Evangeline?

I curled my lip as I turned my back on them.

I'd settled in the corner where I could catch a glimmer of sunlight. There wasn't a window in here, but there must be out in the corridor because I saw a faint beam of light falling on the floor. If I kept my eyes on it, I could maybe keep track of the days. Maybe. There had been one day before Jude—

My mind spun away from that night, cringing in terror. The healer had said she'd put me under for a few days to heal so maybe three had passed? Today could be the fourth or fifth—

I gulped as it hit me.

Focusing on the face of the man waiting in front of my cell, I said again, "He's already hurt me. And he'll do it again. I might as well enjoy myself where I can."

Again, there was a flicker of disbelief in his eyes and he shook his head. "You're too fucking stupid to be alive."

It wasn't the first time I'd heard that. And for some reason, it made the ache in my heart spread. "How long have I been here?"

His mouth twisted. "Six days. Tonight will make the seventh."

Seven days—

My hands were trembling and I curled them into fists. But not fast enough. He saw that telltale tremor and something that *might* have been pity flickered in his eyes. "You don't have anybody coming for you," he said. "Jude's marked you as his own little bloodwhore and nobody around here fucks with him."

The title hit me like a fist. It was an archaic one that had been abolished with the writing of the charter. Some of the older vampires still clung to it. Bloodwhore. Just what it sounded like.

"There are plenty of people here who will fuck with Jude," I said, forcing the words out.

"Not here." He stood up and glanced down the corridor. I had the feeling he was eying the window I couldn't see. "You're not in your territory. You're just meat here. His meat. His property. Nobody will help you. Your only chance to escape is by dying. And he won't let that happen."

My nails dug into my palms as the full weight of what he was saying hit me.

Not in my territory...

Oh, shit. Shit. Terror gripped me, so hard, so fast. It wasn't just *what* Jude had done. Kidnapping me—that wasn't so much of a shock. The physical pain, the attacks, that wasn't even it.

But I was away from the few people I could trust. The very few, I realized.

Good-bye, Kit—

Suddenly, the weight of those words crashed into me even harder and I wanted to sob.

I'd just been trying to help him.

"Don't," I whispered to myself. It wouldn't help. Any

self-pity would have to wait, because it would *not* help.

I'd been trying to help him and he'd walked away from me. The one person who could have moved heaven and earth to find me no longer wanted me.

Now I had to acknowledge that fact, accept it so I didn't pin any misspent hope on it.

It was possible that Colleen could rally support for me among the witches, but there wasn't a strong bond there. They'd offered me kinship, but that only meant they'd give me aid when I called.

And how could I reach out to them now?

While I had friends in Wolf Haven who likely would care, none of them would travel that far from their particular safety nets—TJ would never leave the bar, and Goliath wouldn't leave her.

Which, in the end, left only one person.

Justin.

And one Banner cop, amazing as he was, wasn't going to be able to storm Jude's castle.

I'm fucked, I realized.

If I couldn't get out of there, I was fucked.

* * * * *

Bent over, I half-gagged, half vomited out a bellyful of blood.

Jude was on the far side of the cell.

I was acutely aware of his presence.

Part of me wanted to push him just a little more, because I thought if I *did*, he'd kill me.

Your only chance to escape is by dying. Something I was considering more and more.

"Call Yasmine," I heard him say, and his voice was a cold blade.

"Oh...come...on," I panted. "You're done, al...already?"

He closed the distance between us and fisted a hand in

my hair, jerking me up. "You won't get out of this so easily, Kit," he breathed into my face. "You've internal bleeding. I smell it. If you think I'll kill you and let you escape me like that, you're sorely mistaken."

His hand cupped my face and squeezed. Hard. The bones of my jaw shattered and despite my determination to never give into the need to scream, if I could have then, I would have.

"You'll stop this, Kit," he said, hurling me to the floor. He knelt by me and stroked a hand down my hair. "You cannot escape and you will not be *saved*. Surely you've figured that out by now. I've had more than a week. Even if your fucking cat could *find* you, he wouldn't want you after what I've done."

He raked his nails over my neck, over the raw, angry edges of the marks he'd left all over me.

I summoned up the energy to turn my head away.

The words were a knife in my heart.

He wouldn't want you—

And although he was still talking, it was no longer his voice I heard.

It was Sam's, when I'd called to talk to him.

Chang's, when I'd reached out to him.

His people, closing ranks to keep me from him. All because of a fight.

Jude was right…he wouldn't want me now.

It doesn't matter, I told myself and I tried to make myself believe it. I tried, so very hard. I had to believe in it, because I needed something to cling to. Something to focus on so I could get out of here.

The warmth of healing magic brushed against my skin and I knew Yasmine had entered the cell. More blood burned its way up my throat and I gagged on it, too weak, too hurt to move. Her hands rolled me onto my side and she stroked a hand down my back as the spasms gripped me.

"She's bleeding," Yasmine said quietly after it had passed. "Lungs, stomach, intestine. Her heart is bruised and numerous ribs are broken in addition to her arm. Again. She can't keep taking injuries like this without it doing harm, Master. Humans aren't made for it and she's half-human. I can only heal so much before there is permanent damage."

"She needs to learn her place," Jude said, and his tone was cold.

A gentle hand touched my brow and some of the pain faded away. I didn't welcome the kindness. I needed the pain.

As I turned my head to glare at her, Yasmine watched me with troubled eyes. Knowing eyes. "There was no lesson learned, I fear, Master," she said quietly.

More blood rushed up but before I could start to puke up the blood, her magic flooded me. Dimly, I heard her speaking. "She has a tolerance to pain that I haven't seen in anybody so young. There was a great deal of abuse in her life, Master. You will not break her or bring her to heel in such a method."

"Is that what you think?"

As Yasmine eased me into a prone position, her hands spanned my ribcage. "I pray you do not take this out on me, Master, for I can only tell you what I see when I look within her. But she will die before she breaks for you. And she'll do it happily."

As the magic chased through me, I closed my eyes.

Her voice drifted into my mind. *"I am not doing you a kindness, girl. He'll find another way. You should yield. If he thinks you've given in, then you have a better chance at healing, regaining your strength…then breaking free once you've lulled him into complacency."*

Even the thought was enough to make me feel sick again.

No.

Just…no.

CHAPTER SIXTEEN

Useless. Look at you...

I huddled in the corner and fought to see the slice of sunlight.

I wasn't quite awake, but I wasn't quite asleep.

Delirium plagued me and hunger gnawed at me, but I couldn't eat and I feared moving from my little spot in the corner. I hadn't moved since I had crawled away from Jude the past night. At this point, I was so weak, I barely had the energy *to* move.

He'd broken no bones, but it was becoming a struggle just to fight.

Every injury he'd left on me should heal within a day or so.

Except it wasn't. Blood still oozed from my cuts, the bruises were as vivid as they'd been when he had put them on me. I wasn't healing at all.

You're not eating. How can you hope to heal when you do not eat?

I rubbed my ear against my shoulder and tried to ignore that buzzing gnat of a voice. It almost sounded like Rana. One of my hated aunts.

Is this how you escape? Through starvation? A coward's way.

How can you be strong enough to flee from him if you do not eat? You have to eat, Kitasa—

226

I tried to get away from her voice, but no matter how hard I tried, the voice was still *there*.

The small panel of sunlight had traveled half way across the corridor. That meant it was noon. The day was half done. And that meant—

It means he is sleeping for a few more hours and you have those hours to eat, drink, and plan. Use them. Or are you the useless weak fool we always thought?

Useless…

I flexed my hand and thought longingly of my blade. I missed her music.

Dully, I turned my head and stared at the food sitting on a tray by the door. I couldn't eat.

Not yet.

But I was thirsty.

* * * * *

"You took some of it."

At the sound of Yasmine's voice, I looked up.

Drinking the water had been a mistake. It had brought a painful clarity to my mind, one I could do without. I didn't *want* clarity. I didn't want to think and I didn't want any more strength in my body, either. The weaker I was, the easier it was to drift away.

But I also knew that if I wanted to escape, I had to stop hiding. Had to do…something.

"Yes."

She nodded and studied the tray. "Can you eat?"

"No food."

"I'll send some broth down. They are preparing your lunch, but I can do that much." She turned and walked away.

I stared at her back. "Why?"

She paused. Without looking at me, she said sadly, "You are not the only prisoner here, Kit. I simply chose to make the best of my situation. I'm a healer. I heal the broken and the sick. I do what I must to survive. You'd be wise to do the same."

Disgust curled through me. "Survive...as his bloodwhore?"

"Would you rather die?" she asked.

Your only chance to escape is by dying.

"You already know the answer," I said. "Why bother to ask?"

If I had to choose between surviving *here* and dying, dying was the best option, no question. But if I could get away, that was my first choice. So I'd hang in there.

Reevaluate once I saw where I was. What was going on.

* * * * *

Broth and water for two meals made a disturbing difference.

I felt almost myself when Jude came in. Stronger. Clearer. And so terrified when he looked at me.

As the cell doors swung open, he came inside, that enigmatic smile on his face. "You look much better, darling Kit."

I stayed where I was. My hair was still damp from the daily dousing with the hose and I was cold; I'd been cold ever since they'd brought me here. I was almost used to it. Every instinct in me was screaming for me to run, or fight. Instead, I stayed where I was, staring at the wall.

"Aren't you going to say anything?" he asked.

I just stared at the wall. Gray stone.

Gray—my heart hitched in my chest, because that color reminded me—*No. Don't do this to yourself, Kit*—I bumped my head against the stone to knock the memory out. It didn't do much good, but Jude wasn't done tormenting me.

He came closer and stroked a hand down my hair.

"Aren't you going to fight?"

I didn't answer.

And to my dismay, to my humiliation, he started to laugh. "Oh, Kit...broken, already?" He patted my head, like I was a fucking dog. "You held on longer than I'd expected, but I was starting to think I'd have a real fight with you. You barely managed two weeks."

Two weeks.

Raped every day I wasn't unconscious.

Endless beatings.

Sure...you think I'm broken, you fucker. I kept my eyes closed, because if I looked at him, he'd see the rage in my eyes. See the hate.

"Come. Let's get you some place more comfortable to rest. I'll let you have a night to yourself. Tomorrow, you'll be bathed and fitted for some clothing," he murmured. And the bastard had the nerve to put his arm around as he dragged me upward. "Your new life begins tomorrow. It will be easier than the past few days."

* * * * *

There was no window.

I'd needed a window.

I missed the sunlight and I needed to get an idea where I was so I could start plotting my escape route. I'd hope I could even try tonight, even though instinct told me that wasn't wise.

Another meal was brought to me, but I ignored most of it. The rich pasta, the sweet desserts were more than I could possibly force into my long-deprived belly. I did drink the water. There was some fruit and I ate that.

I took a shirt and some trousers from the simple wardrobe. The servant who'd been sent to help me nervously said, "You won't stay here after tomorrow. The master didn't want you in your real quarters until you've been bathed properly."

I didn't care.

The door was locked once she left and I grabbed a blanket, searched the room.

Spying the closet, I went inside and shut myself inside.

Small, confining spaces might not seem ideal to some. Normally, *I* wouldn't like it, either. But after two weeks of sleeping behind bars, where anybody could see me, this sounded perfect. Locked behind a door, behind the illusion of safety…perfect.

Maybe I could sleep.

Kit…

I twitched at the whisper in the back of my mind. Most of the odd whispers had faded with the delirium. Now wasn't the time to let them come back. I had to get myself back on track. Focused.

Tomorrow I had what might possibly be the most hellish thing of my life before me.

I had to make Jude think he had me cowed while I began to plan my way out of here. I just had to get far enough away to find somebody who'd let me call the house of witches. Or Justin. One of them would surely help me.

That was all I needed. I had to keep up my strength long enough to do that.

Wake up!

It was a scream in my head. Louder than normal. I twisted away from it, huddling in on myself and moaning. The dreams…I'd actually almost had a pleasant dream.

Damon…

His hand touched my face and although he wasn't talking, I could see something in his eyes that looked like…love. He looked at me like he still cared and that meant I was dreaming of everything back before this nightmare had started.

Back before I'd tried to actually do something worthy of him.

I didn't want to leave this dream for the misery of my life. Instead, I rolled toward him and found a little bit of comfort in the warmth of his presence. It wasn't real comfort because this was just a dream. But if a dream was all I'd have, then I'd take it.

You need to wake up, the voice whispered in my head. Pleading and desperate. *It's too hard to track you like this.*

Grumbling, I shoved my face deeper against my dream Damon's chest. Nobody was trying to track me. Not after this much time.

So why did I have to—

Something smashed into the door and it shattered in front of my face.

Jolting upright, I rolled into a crouch, tensed and ready to fight. *No, I can't—*

The voice screeched at me from the very back of my mind. Had to play nice and calm and stupid and broken.

But it was so hard when I saw Evangeline standing there. Then she shot out a hand and fisted it in my hair, jerking me to my feet. "Hello, stupid little bitch."

I saw a hundred times I could have done something.

Kicked her feet out from under her. Snapped her wrist. As she dragged me down the steps, I could have shifted my weight and sent us both hurtling down them. It would have hurt us both, but I was fine with that outcome.

Instead, I just lay there, limp as a sack of grain, my scalp on fire from the grip she had.

Once we reached what looked like the great hall, she shoved me into the middle of the floor and stared at me, laughing. "Oh, this is just lovely, Kit," she said, clapping her hands. "He did break you. I knew he would."

With my face buried against the floor, I lay there. I hated. I planned.

All I had to do was get away. Evangeline wasn't one of the Assembly's dignitaries and she wouldn't be protected for her actions. Jude would burn for this—they wouldn't kill him, I didn't think, but there would be punishments. Evangeline, though. Her life was mine.

If I could just *get away.*

I heard her coming and instinct screamed. *Move, move, move—*

Instead, I kept still. Even when she drove the pointy toe of one small foot right into my gut. *Grab it, trap it, take her down*— my mind screamed.

I didn't.

I took it.

Whatever I had to do. Because I was going to get away from Jude. It was a burning, certain knowledge. I didn't know how. I didn't know when. But I'd get away from here.

Keeping my face blank, I stared up at Evangeline. The look on her face was one that might have been disgruntlement. "I can't say this is quite as much fun as I'd hoped," she muttered. "You won't even scream."

You don't have what it takes to make me scream, bitch.

She stared back at me, that haughty expression on her face. But after a moment, it flickered and then she curled her nose and waved a hand. "Come on, you lazy bastards. He wanted her bathed and it will take all afternoon as filthy as she is."

Moments later, I was being dragged toward the doors.

"You need to be bathed but you're too fucking filthy to grace the master's bathing chambers. We'll do what we can with you outside first."

The doors opened and the brutal punch of the frigid air knocked a gasp out of me. The shock of the cold bit into my skin and for a moment, I couldn't even breathe.

Snow swirled all around me, blinded me.

Evangeline looked back at me and smiled. "Have you ever been to the Canadian Rockies, Kit? Jude loves it here. It's so serene. So lovely and private...not a soul around for days." A disturbing smile curved her lips and she added, "You could run for hours and not see a single soul. There are no roads in or out. The fastest way in is by helicopter. The closest town is a human one and they don't welcome NHs of any kind. They shoot on sight."

Trapped—

As they dragged me through the fat, fluffy piles of snow, the hard, heavy reality of what she'd said hit me.

232

You could run for hours…

Even if I got away, how in the hell was I to reach anybody who'd give me aid?

The answer was simple.

I wouldn't.

I found myself recalling what the guard had said, just days ago. *Your only chance at escaping him is by dying. And he won't let that happen.*

* * * * *

Frigid water, dumped in a metal tub, was Evangeline's idea of *bathing properly.*

It was awful and painful, but I'd actually withstood that awful sort of torture before and it wasn't anything that would kill me. Wouldn't even harm me really. Stern stuff, us aneira warriors, even the half-breeds.

My hands were icy little sticks but I kept moving, kept moving everything. Eyes. Hands. Feet. Legs. And my mind…most importantly, my mind.

Canadian Rockies. He hadn't just dragged me out of the state, he'd dragged me out of the fucking country.

I caught a glimpse of the sprawling vista just beyond the courtyard. Rugged mountains. Very rugged. He'd built the damn house right on a mountain face. My heart stuttered.

Kit…get ready. It's almost time—

Almost time, I thought. It was odd. That weird delirium was returning, even though I wasn't suffering from lack of water or food. Maybe it was the cold. Or desperation.

Your only chance at escaping him is by dying…

From the corner of my eye, I studied the guard. Two weapons. Small handgun, discharged single shot ammo. And…I had to bite back a bitter smile. An assault rifle. A classic, too. An HK G36. It would take down just about anything that got in front of me…even Jude.

And this was where they'd messed up. Thinking I was so broken, they could put a weapon like that close to me and not expect me to use it.

Maybe I couldn't get out of here.

But if my only other chance was through a more permanent method?

If that was the choice, at least it was mine to make.

I climbed out of the bath and started toward the house.

Evangeline swore and shoved a towel at me. "Are you so stupid that you'd track water into the master's house?" she sniped.

I caught the towel, pretended to fumble, letting my teeth chatter.

"Madam," one of the guards said quietly. "She's half-frozen."

Evangeline sneered and gestured to me. "Then one of you help her. I'm not touching the little monster."

As the man came near me, part of me felt some guilt. He'd shown a bit of kindness there. But I had to get away.

And this was my only chance.

As he came near, I dropped the towel, and stammered out, "Suh-suh-sorry…" watching Evangeline from the corner of my eye. She was staring toward the house. The other guard was watching the perimeter. A grim look was on his face. He reached up to tap the earpiece he wore, turning his head away from me.

As my guard stooped to pick up my towel, I slammed my fist into the back of his head. He went sprawling and I swiped the first gun and leveled it on Evangeline. A quick death wasn't what she deserved, but I had no time now. None at all.

Her head exploded in a mist of red.

I shifted to the other guard and unloaded on him before he'd even saw that I'd moved.

Some humans are fast.

Humans bonded or enslaved to a vampire are faster. But I leave them in the dust, even if I'm starved and tired and wishing I'm dead. I caught his weapon and jerked it free as he started to topple to the ground and then I was running.

One person fired and I heard another screech. *"Don't fire! If you kill her, we're all dead!"*

Perfect.

It made it that much easier to get away.

The snow was a stinging blast against my skin as I hurtled across the courtyard and everything blurred by me. The brightness of it stung my sensitive eyes and it took a moment to even get my bearings, but I didn't have to search for what I needed. There was a yawning chasm less than a quarter mile ahead and from what I could see, the drop was steep enough that it would likely shatter even my sturdy physique.

I'm made from solid stock. But I'm not made like a vampire or a were. I'm not immortal.

And I wasn't planning on the fall to kill me.

There were guards chasing me now, but it didn't matter. I just had to get there—

Memories chased me as well.

TJ and Goliath, sitting at the bar as they showed me how to pull drinks. *You can hold a fucking blade but you can't pour a beer? That's shit, kid,* TJ had groused. And Goliath had laughed. *She don't want to, TJ. But she'll do.*

Then TJ's hand on my shoulder, years later. *It's time you try to do something else, Kitty. You ain't made for hiding in a bar.*

Justin, all fire and flash on the surface...and he'd made me realize I could come out of the shadows. *Come on, Kitty-kitty. If you find that runner before I do, I'll let you try to beat me up. You won't win, though...*I had. It was the night he kissed me the first time.

Colleen. Sitting at her daughter's bedside as Mandy had breathed her last. The girl hadn't died easily...but Colleen had looked at me with a thankful smile and held my hand, cried on my shoulder and whispered, *Thank you...*

There was even a flicker of a memory from Rana, one of my aunts. *We could make a warrior of you yet,* she'd remarked as she'd stared at the bow in my hands and shook her head with something like admiration in her eyes.

Memories, slamming into my mind...and then one nearly sent me to my knees.

Baby girl—

I stumbled to a halt as I reached the lip of the chasm. It was so far down, I couldn't see the bottom for the blowing snow.

The wind howled, raging and furious.

"Don't!"

I turned and looked at Jude's men, creeping closer.

I barely felt anything as I lifted the HK. Their blood painted the ground red and I went back to staring at the drop. Slinging the weapon's strap over my shoulder, I lifted the handgun and pressed it to my chin.

*Shhh, it's okay, baby girl. It's okay...*Damon. After the first time Jude had fucked me over. Damon had been there. Had saved me. Hot tears burned my face but I managed to smile a little as another memory flickered through my mind.

Reluctant humor in his eyes as he dragged me out of a drugstore after we'd narrowly avoided a run-in with those humans who'd helped hunt kids like Doyle. *Come on. I'd rather not continue to lurk in the feminine hygiene area.*

The look in his eyes the first time he'd marked me.

Good memories, I thought.

Not all of them were hurtful.

I needed to focus on those. They were more than I'd really ever expected when I'd broken free from my grandmother's iron grasp.

I squeezed the trigger, felt it giving way.

"No!"

Shock had me easing up. That voice...familiar.

A trick. I wheeled my head around, searching for Jude. The fucker was awake and screwing with my head—that son of a bitch loved to fuck with my head.

I saw his men creeping toward me, another wave of them and I lifted the HK, fired. Screams rose in the air and I realized I'd missed. *I don't miss—*

But the tears...I gasped out past the knot in my throat.

Hard to aim with them blinding me. I knuckled them away and fired again, taking down anybody still on their feet, then I lowered the HK and looked down at the handgun I carried in my left hand.

The way out. This was my way out.

I jammed the muzzle against my chin.

"Kitasa!"

Colleen—

Her voice was joined by a growling roar that had haunted my dreams.

I squeezed the trigger because I knew *he* wasn't here—it didn't matter that I felt a familiar warmth roll across my frozen skin in that very moment.

"A fucking trick."

Now. Had to do it—

Silver slashed through the air. And the gun was just gone.

"*No!*" I screamed.

No...no...*no*...I had to get away, damn it. I had to.

I jammed my hands against my temple and then I lifted my head and stared at the chasm. It was deep. If I was lucky, it would kill me. I backed up a few steps and ran. Leaped.

For one lovely, wonderful moment, I was free.

But then something caught my waist.

Struggling and fighting, kicking, I tore at it. And I gave voice to the years worth of screams that I'd kept trapped inside.

CHAPTER SEVENTEEN

"Kit!"

I slammed my fist outward and broke free. But I didn't even make it two feet before something took me down. Heat blasted me. *Heat—*

It had been so long since I'd felt warm.

Against me, I felt soft, warm fur…and a hard body. As massive, clawed hands closed around my wrists, panic slammed into me and the animal Jude had tried to make me into finally broke free. I clawed, I bit, I fought with everything I had in me…but I couldn't get free.

"*—not helping, damn it—let—*"

Voices rose.

Fell.

There was raging. I heard the voices, in some deep part of me, and I waited for the pain. I hadn't gotten free. I'd be back in that cell again and the beatings would come, the rapes—

I screamed and huddled in on myself.

And then I was free.

The hands that had pinned me down were gone and I huddled alone in the snow.

"Kit."

I flinched away from the sound of her voice.

It wasn't her.

I'd hoped maybe she'd care enough, but Colleen wasn't a fighter and she'd never come—

"Oh, Kit…I hate having to do this, but we can't stay here like this…"

Hands caught me by the hair and tugged my head back and I found myself staring at an illusion. Colleen crouched in front of me, Justin kneeling at her side.

"Don't," I begged, hating the tears that rolled down my face. He'd broken me, damn it. That son of a bitch had broken me, but I just couldn't do this. "Please don't do this anymore. I'll…I'll stop. I'm done. I give up."

I couldn't take it to see the rest of my hopes smashed so brutally.

Colleen's face—no—not *her*—the fake Colleen—her face crumpled and she looked down.

"Move over, Coll," the not-Justin said.

I tried to pull away but I couldn't. The hands holding me were just too strong. Whining low in my throat, I shrank in on myself as he laid a hand on my forehead, the other on my chest. "Kit…look at me—"

Magic slammed into me. *Hot* magic. *Familiar* magic—

It burned through me, clearing away the determined fog that had driven me the past few days. *Survive the pain. Hold on. Survive the pain.* At some point, *Escape* had replaced *Survive the pain* and *hold on.*

All of that muffling fog disappeared, and even the fear faded enough for me to see past it.

See the man in front of me. Familiar green eyes, set in a face all but ravaged with grief and rage. A stocking cap covered his dreads and snowflakes clung to the dense, dark hair.

Justin—

Words rose in my throat, but I was almost afraid to let them out. Reaching up with a hand that shook, I brushed one of the snowflakes off. Against my fingers, I felt the familiar, nubby texture of his hair. *Justin…*

239

Somewhere off to the side, I heard a low, ragged growl, one that made me shudder, but I couldn't look. I didn't dare. Focusing on Justin's green eyes, I poked at his dreads again, this time tugging on one. Real. He felt *real*.

"Justin," I whispered thinly. "You...are you *here*?"

"Yeah, Kitty-kitty." His hand shifted away from my breastbone to touch my cheek. He shot for a teasing smile, but it fell flat. I grabbed at his wrist, desperate. "Did you ever doubt it?"

"You're here." What strength I had left drained out of me, and I sagged to the ground. Justin crouched down with me, staying on eye level as I muttered again, "You're here... you're really here."

"Yeah." He reached out and caught my hands. "I have to ask one you thing, and you have to answer. Flat-out. It's brutally important, Kitty-kitty."

"You're here," I whispered again as I started to shiver. "You're here."

"Kit!" His voice was a slap in the air and I flinched.

Staring at him, dazed, I nodded. "Answer. Important."

Behind me, *just* behind me, I heard a broken, ragged growl. Instinct drove me away from that sound, toward Justin. Gentle hands caught me and he murmured, "Shhh....shhhh. It's okay." The look in his eyes said anything *but* okay, though and he shot a look past my shoulder that scared me even more.

I flinched and pressed even closer to him. His arm came around me and he sighed. "It's okay, Kit. I swear. You hear me?" He shrugged out of the black jacket he wore, wrapping it around my shoulders. "But I need that answer and I need it now. Did you *willingly* leave Florida and travel *anywhere* with Jude Whittier?"

Terror choked me. I wanted to cry. Scream. Beg. But Justin had come.

Vaguely, I realized there were people gathered around us. A lot of them. I wanted to hide between Colleen and him, these two friends who I'd wanted so desperately to count

240

on...but I hadn't let myself. Justin was counting on me now. "Answer," I whispered, pressing my head against his shoulder as I tried to think. I was so damn cold. So damn cold. "Important."

"It is."

I nodded jerkily. "No. Was outside my office." Fear slammed into me as I made myself think. "Had packed up...went to grab some weapons. I called—"

Justin touched my shoulder. "It's okay, Kit. He can't hurt you now. Did he call you about a job or something?"

I shook my head. "No. Called..." my voice broke. "Called the Lair. They wouldn't..." I plucked at my borrowed jacket as shame flooded me. It was done. Over. Done—and if I thought of anything else, I'd break. Just the answer. I could only think of the answer right now. "I called the Lair. I looked down...Dart in my chest...couldn't move...Xavier...freelance witch. Everything went black and I woke up here."

"And you didn't come willingly?"

Hadn't I just said that? Lifting my head, I stared at Justin and tried to figure out what he needed.

"No," I whispered.

A hand touched my shoulder.

From the corner of my eye, I saw it. And flinched. Skin a warm golden brown. Strong, beautiful hands—

Desperate, I bolted.

Behind me, I heard a low, furious roar and I tried to block it from my mind. I had to get away.

I made it five feet before I crashed into a mountain.

This mountain was big, living and had hands that were gentle and soothing as he picked me up. "Easy there, Kitty," Goliath said. "No reason to run now. You're safe."

I heard Damon snarling again.

Goliath, big, gentle Goliath growled, deep in his chest and then he turned away. "Come on, little Kitty. You need to get warm. Don't know how long those stupid Banner boys are going to be, but you don't need to be here for this."

"Wolf," Damon snarled.

Goliath covered one of my ears with his hand while I huddled against his chest and the thud of his heart beat against my other ear. Between that, and the thundering of my own heart, the roaring of blood crashing inside my head, I barely heard anything more than a rumble at first.

The words barely connected, anyway. At first.

Don't you get it, cat? You're scaring the hell out of her and she's already scared enough.

Goliath was wrong.

Oh, I was scared.

But I couldn't face Damon now.

I couldn't face him…I couldn't face myself.

I didn't know if I could face anything, ever again.

* * * * *

Silver lights flashed.

I strained my head to see no matter how hard Goliath tried to keep me from looking. Part of me had to know it was done.

I don't know how much time passed as he tried to protect me from it and I tried to see around him.

Finally, he looked down at me and asked, "You have to know, don't you?"

"Yes."

He sighed and carried me back to the fringe of the trees. "We waited here for hours, trying to get a lock on where you were," he said softly.

Something made a weird *thnk* sound down by our feet and after about sixty seconds of rabid fear, I made myself look.

The tiger looked terribly vibrant against the snow. I flinched at the sight of him, but Goliath rubbed his cheek against my hair. "Doyle's a tracker, Kitty. Almost as good as you. Never seen the like of it. He didn't track you by scent. It was…" He shrugged. "It was amazing. I ain't never seen anything like it."

"Doyle," I whispered. Closing my eyes, I turned that over in my head. "Doyle found me?"

"Yes." He crouched down in the snow by the tiger and I had no choice by to stare at his face. Golden eyes stared back at me. "Everybody else was scouring Orlando. Nobody would listen to the kid and he showed up in Wolf Haven, roaring like a big, dumb….well, tiger. I go out there and he shifted, stared at me. Asked if I was the one who'd raised you." He settled me on his legs and then reached over, stroked Doyle's head. "Told him that he'd need TJ for that…that's close, isn't it, little Kitty? We were all looking, but he says everybody was looking wrong. So I say we were friends, sure, and he tells me he can find you but nobody is helping him. I tell him if he's wrong, I'm gonna have me a tiger-skin rug."

My gut twisted. "How…" The tiger sighed and stretched his weight out in the snow.

"He doesn't know how, Kit. He just knew." Goliath settled in the snow, unfazed by the cold, but it was starting to kill me. Shuddering, shaking, I huddled inside Justin's jacket and tried to get warm, but it just wasn't possible.

Doyle inched closer, pressed his torso against my exposed legs and feet. The relief was almost painful as pins and needles replaced the numb sensation.

Trapped—

"Tiger might as well do something useful," Goliath said, his voice lazy and quiet. "Keep your feet warm better than I can right now. Once Justin is finished, we'll find you something to wear, but for now…"

I latched onto the sane, simple presence that was Goliath. He'd pulled me through a lot. I could trust him. Shivering, I rested my head on his shoulder and stared at the house. "What are they doing?"

"Well…if we're lucky, they'll burn Jude's ass into ashes," Goliath said, a nasty growl edging into his voice. Then he shrugged. "We probably won't get lucky. Jude's an opportunistic son of a bitch and he knows all about survival. He knows he's fucked and he won't give them a reason to kill him."

"What will happen now?"

I heard a branch crack behind us. The sound of it had me ready to bolt off Goliath's lap. He let me and I would have tripped over Doyle, but the tiger shifted his long body, bracing me with his weight instead.

Three bodies—I counted them by their feet.

Two males. One of them, I couldn't look at. Ever. I hunched my shoulders and focused on the pain in my frozen feet. I could handle the cold, but this was getting to be too much.

"Jude violated one of the major laws of the charter," Colleen said softly. "He's going to trial and if he wasn't one of the older ones, if he wasn't one of the Speakers, he'd probably be a dead man walking. In more ways than one."

I looked at her. She was safe to look at. Very safe.

Her eyes were dark, troubled. So sad. "As it is, he's looking at confined jail-time. Decades of it, at least."

"He's going in a box," I whispered.

A pleased smile curled her lips as she swung a pack off her shoulder. "If we're lucky, he may very well leave in one." She pulled a blanket out and approached me, moving slowly. "You need some clothes. I've got some if you want them...?"

I swallowed, jerking my gaze around. Where could I get dressed—?

Seemed a foolish thing to worry about considering I'd spent more than half of the past two weeks naked. They'd taken my clothes. My weapons. Their loss was an empty, jagged hole in me and I couldn't even explain it.

My sword—it was a jagged, raw wound inside of me and I wanted to cry. Wanted to sob. Instead, I focused on the clothes that Colleen held.

Jerking my head, I whispered, "Yes."

Goliath got up. "I think if Miss Colleen holds the blanket by this tree and I stand just here..." He turned his back.

"Between the tree, my big self and the blanket, you practically have a dressing room, Kitty."

I nodded again, took one stumbling step away from Doyle's sturdy presence. I almost fell and those booted feet—they belonged to a man I couldn't look at—moved in my direction. I backed away and sank my hands into Doyle's fur.

"Doyle, why don't you help Kit over here?" Colleen said quietly. "I think the cold's making her legs stiff."

Doyle started to walk.

I heard another low snarl.

Colleen snapped, "Shut the *fuck* up before I turn you into a toad."

I flinched. From the corner of my eye, I saw him moving and I lunged for the solid presence of Goliath. Tucked away behind him, I sagged against the tree. *Hide...I could hide here.*

* * * * *

The problem with hiding behind a big, living mountain...the living mountain eventually decided to move.

I had clothes on. For the first time in too long. Colleen was a few inches taller than me and a lot curvier, but they were warm and clean and there was something terribly comforting about the scent of her herbs and magic wrapping around me.

I had barely finished shoving my feet into the spare boots before Goliath moved. And he moved fast, hard, and low.

"Not *now*," he snarled as he caught Damon around the waist.

"Get the *fuck* away," Damon growled.

I fell backward against the tree, arms wrapped around myself, staring at them.

His eyes cut to me and I sank to the ground, feeling like a cornered animal.

Hide...have to hide...

"Not *now!*" Goliath roared and he slammed a massive

245

hand down on Damon's head, shoving him into the ground.

Doyle rose and paced between us, that striped body cutting off my view.

"Kit. Come with me now," Colleen said, reaching down and grabbing my arm.

I just huddled there. I couldn't move. Couldn't breathe.

His eyes. I could still feel the weight of his eyes cutting in me.

Had he seen—?

I plucked at the high neck of the sweater, holding it up over my throat as I looked around, staring out into the night. At anywhere but here. The sweater. I needed something with a higher collar, something to hide what Jude had done. Needed it higher, had to keep the marks on my neck covered. He'd chewed me up, marked me well and good and I needed to hide it—

"Kitasa, *come with me*," Colleen said again, dragging me upright and walking.

The men on the rocky forest floor were still struggling but despite Goliath's massive size, Damon was getting the better of him. *Come...yes. Colleen. Go with Colleen. That sounded good—*

"*Kit!*" Damon rasped out. And his voice sounded broken. "Baby girl..."

I sobbed and nearly fell.

A hand caught me and I froze.

"I'm sorry, Kit, I just..."

Chang. I looked up and saw him staring at me. Just like all of them. Everybody. Staring.

Staring at broken, ruined Kit.

Carefully, I backed away from him, shaking my head. "Colleen. Get me away from here," I whispered. "I can't..."

Her arm came around my waist.

"I know, Kitasa. I know."

* * * * *

246

Silence reigned in my head.

Colleen found us a sheltered spot in the trees and she cast a fire.

It didn't burn from wood.

It hovered above the ground, spinning out of her magic and warming at least my body, even if it couldn't touch anything else.

Her hands hovered over my ribs, my arms, my belly, careful not to touch any part of my skin as she checked the injuries she'd managed to coax out of me. "His healer is decent," she said reluctantly. "There's no lingering damage, no scars except..."

I twisted away from her and hunched up my shoulder, pulling the collar of the sweater higher to block them from view. In a broken, stilted voice, I whispered, "Can you get them off?"

"No," she said softly. "They've already healed. The only thing that might remove them would be surgery and that's not always an easy option with us."

Us. Witches and aneira, others with bodies that were more than human but not quite something else. Our bodies didn't take well to non-natural forms of healing. Sometimes it worked just fine. I knew one witch had attempted to have scars from an attack removed, and she'd arrested on the table.

She'd died because she wanted her scars removed.

I thought it might be worth it.

Colleen touched my hand. "Warriors learn to carry scars."

The silence in my head had never seemed so terribly loud. "I'm not a warrior anymore," I murmured. *I'm nothing.* My hand seemed to so terribly empty and I so terribly needed my blade.

"You *are*," Colleen said, her eyes flashing in the firelight.

No. I wasn't. And the emptiness of my hand was just more proof of that. I twisted my wrist, popped it, longed for that reassuring weight, but it was just...*gone.* And in the back of my head, the music that had always comforted me was so painfully silent.

I'd never felt more alone, more empty in my entire life.

Unable to think about that, I shifted my gaze back to Doyle.

The tiger was pacing ever closer, like he was trying to work up the courage to come up to the fire, but not sure he was ready to do it yet.

"How long are we going to be here?" I stared at the house where hell had held me trapped. Where it had broken me.

"Until they convince Jude to leave without a fight." She drew her knees to her chest and rested her chin on them. "We can start to head out. Anytime you're ready. We'll have to walk, but we can do it. Quickest way out is by helicopter, but we didn't want to make the noise, so we hiked in."

I shuddered. Walking through there didn't bother me. But I was very much bothered by the idea of walking away from here without knowing that he was locked away.

Colleen shifted her foot over and nudged me with her toe. Just that light touch made me want to cringe and I think she knew it. I also think that was why she did it. To show me she could touch me and that I wouldn't break.

But she was wrong. I was already broken.

"If you have to see him in the box, then you have to see it. It won't take any more than a few hours at best. Banner doesn't have the kind of patience for prolonged...debates," she said the word slowly and with relish. "If he fights too much, Justin will just issue the kill order."

Banner.

"How is Banner involved?"

"Kit..." She stared at me. "Sweetheart, almost everybody got involved. Once we knew what had happened..." She shrugged. "The Assembly, in general, wouldn't come after him, but they took a clear step back when we told them we were coming after you. Es told them that Whittier House might be ended when we were done and if any of the vampire clutches had a problem, they could take it up with the whole of the Order of Witches."

I pressed my face to my knees.

They'd come for me.

"Justin knew something was wrong first," she said.

Branches crunched.

I tensed, but managed not to flinch as I lifted my head and watched as she came to sit down next to me. "He went looking for you after you didn't call him back," she said quietly. "He found your car. Your phone. It was only the next day. I..."

A taut silence fell before she finally said, "Kit, I'm so sorry. He told me that you'd mentioned something about Damon and...he said you'd fought." She swallowed.

I could feel the pain in her, but just hearing his name was a bitter strike inside me. "It's over," I said woodenly.

Her hand caught mine as another one of those roars ripped through the night. I started to shudder and she tugged me close. "Shhh. Come on, Kit. Anyway, I told him that maybe you'd taken off for a few days. Gone to Wolf Haven and he told me to get bent. You don't disappear without your phone, your car. So we started looking. Called Goliath. TJ. They hadn't heard from you, so they start looking. You know TJ and she won't leave, but she's tearing up the internet and Goliath is tearing up central Florida. He's the one who went to Damon."

"He didn't need to bother." I turned my face into her neck. "No point in him pestering the Alpha with this—"

"Kit—"

Colleen's voice hissed out my name and she shoved me behind her.

It didn't last for very long, the scant protection of her body. Colleen yelped as she went skidding across the ground and I found myself just a breath away from Damon. On his hands and knees in front of me, the look on his face something I couldn't even understand.

"That big fuck didn't need to *bother* me?" he growled. "No point in pestering the fucking Alpha?"

I inched away, dropping my gaze to my knees.

*Hide…have to hide…*I eased backward, slowly bit by bit, only to freeze when he roared and slammed a fist into the frozen earth.

"Damn it, Kit." Something that might have been tears glimmered in his eyes. "Did you really think I wasn't coming for you?"

The scars at my neck throbbed. Burned. *Marked…ruined…*

It's over, baby girl…

The words sounded in my head and something that might have been the first flickers of anger tried to rise, but under the grief, under the fear, the shame, those embers only flickered, then they died.

Staring into Damon's eyes, I shook my head and forced the words out. I needed him to get away from me. *Now.* "There was no reason for you to come. It was over, remember?"

"Baby girl…" He reached out a hand to touch me.

The sight of that hand made me flinch. Strong, beautiful hands…and even the thought of being touched by him, by *anybody* now filled me with fear.

Broken. Ruined.

Bitterness well inside me and I surged upward. He moved with me and I was trapped. Trapped between the warmth of his body and the trees at my back and everybody gathered around us. "I can say it now." Now that nothing stopped me, the words came spilling out of me like poison. "The job's done. Nothing binding me or tying my throat into a knot if I try to speak the words I'd wanted to say from the beginning. I was trying to save *you*."

A muscle jerked in his jaw. "I know. Kit, I'm sorry—"

"You're *sorry?*" I stared at him, shaking my head. "You're *fucking sorry?* I had a couple of days at the most and if I didn't find them some justification, Banner was going to put an execution order out on you. And I couldn't *say* anything because I'd been bound. I couldn't say a word. My lungs froze up and it was pain on end just to *think* about saying any of the words burning inside me…but oh, okay…*you're sorry.*"

His lids drooped low, shielding his eyes. "Kit—"

"Shut *up!*" I shrieked. The sound of it startled me, echoing all around us. Staring at him, I shook my head again, backing away as much as I could. "You wanted me to talk to you then, and I *couldn't*. I can do it now so just *shut up*. Do you have any idea what that was like for me? I had that job weighing down on me and the only things I knew for *certain*…I couldn't tell *anybody* so no way to ask for help in clearing you and if I screwed it up, you were dead."

Spinning away, I shoved my hands into my hair, cradling my head. I felt like I was going to come apart into ten thousand pieces. "I couldn't say *anything*," I whispered again. "The *one* time I tried to give a warning was to Chang, after you'd walked away. I wanted to make sure you'd stay in the Lair until Justin told me it was all done and I had to stab myself in the fucking leg just to get the vaguest warning out."

Somebody out in the circle of bodies muttered something. It might have been Chang. I didn't know.

I heard somebody move and the sound of it sent fear scurrying through me. Spinning back around, I tried to find the source of the sound, but saw nothing. Great…just great. I'm back to jumping at shadows. Cringing at the smallest bump in the night.

"I did it for you." I stared at him. "I tried to protect *you* the way you're always trying to protect *me*. And you walked away."

Damon just stood there and his eyes locked on my face.

"But I still tried to call," I whispered as the agony ripped loose. "I still had the phone in my hand from calling the Lair when I realized I had a dart in my chest. All I wanted to do was tell you I was sorry…" I reached for the neck of the sweater, the scars feeling scratchy and raw.

"Kit, please….would you just…"

I had to make myself do this. He needed to stop. For the past few hours, while Justin did whatever he had to do inside that house, I had been hiding and cringing away while Damon stalked my steps. Maybe he needed to understand. Maybe he needed to see. *I* knew what had been done to me. *I* knew how broken I was.

"You were smart to end it when you did, Damon. Maybe it was sheer dumb luck on your part, but it's best for you." I tugged at the neck of the sweater. "I understand that you feel guilty, or angry, or upset. But it's not going to be enough to help you see past what he made me into."

"You're still *you*," Damon said. One big hand closed into a fist and his eyes glittered as he stared at me.

"No. I'm not." Tugging the neck of the sweater down, I craned my neck to the side. On the other side, I had the marks Damon had given me. Jude had been careful not to touch those. I think he took some sort of perverse pride in marking up the other side, and mark it, he had. A map of scars marred my neck and there was nothing neat about them. "Two weeks as a vamp's bloodwhore, Damon. His *thing*...his *toy*. I'm so far from me, I don't think I'll ever find my way back."

"*I'll* find your way," he rasped.

"You can't...and what's more, *I* don't want you around me right now." I swallowed the lump in my throat and tried to breathe around it.

Damon took another step. "Kit, for fuck's sake...*please.*"

"No." I backed away, stumbling this time. Yet again, Doyle was there. I sank my hand into his fur and knelt beside him. Anything to avoid looking at the man still hovering too close to me.

Doyle bumped his head against my chest, once, twice. After he did it a third time, I slowly wrapped an arm around his neck. "Thank you," I whispered against the warmth of his body. "I don't know why you came after me, kid, but thank you."

He wrapped himself around me and when somebody moved toward me, he growled.

"Don't," I whispered. I stroked a hand down his back.

"You need to go to your Alpha, okay, kid? Just leave me alone with Colleen, okay? I need to be alone."

He just twined himself tighter around me and continued to stare past me. And he wasn't leaving.

Gradually, I realized the others had.

Gradually, I realized it was just us.

Me, Colleen, and a boy who'd shapeshifted into a tiger...a boy who'd somehow managed to track me across a continent.

Colleen settled against my back, her head on my shoulder.

"You're still you, Kit," she whispered.

"No, I'm not."

I really wished everybody would quit telling me that.

* * * * *

"They're moving him."

Goliath appeared out of the snowy night.

Doyle nudged my chest again and I pushed my hand against him. "You need to go back to your clan," I said quietly. In the past hour, I'd made myself look away from the protective circle of Colleen, Goliath and Doyle and I realized there were nearly twenty cats there, not including Doyle.

How *could* I include Doyle, when he'd all but glued himself to my side?

Goliath nudged the tiger with his foot. "He's picked his place for the time being, Kit. You aren't moving him, so don't bother." Then he patted my shoulder with a hand the size of a fist. "Come on. They're moving him, I said. I heard the ruckus. A couple of his more stupid servants tried to fight and I think Justin was kicking ass."

Moving him—

My heart shrank up, shriveled with fear.

The muscles in my legs knotted and I wanted to run.

"You don't have to see, Kit," Colleen whispered.

"Yes." Goliath gripped my arm. "She does."

He started to haul me across the frozen ground and I tensed up, started to jerk.

"You big bastard, let her decide," Colleen said, her voice slicing through the air.

"She already did, before she started to panic," he said, his voice implacable.

I clawed at his hand, popping my wrist but the heat wasn't there. The music was gone. And I started to sob. She was *gone*—

A massive cat barreled our way.

Goliath hefted me in his arms, glaring at the leopard in front of us. "You need to move," he said quietly. "She needs to see she's safe."

The leopard opened his mouth, screamed defiantly.

Goliath's lip curled back in a sneer. "If I didn't currently hate your guts, that might impress me," he said. "But she's going to have nightmares."

I struggled against him even as his voice stabbed into me.

"She's going to remember this, every second of it for months, probably years. And if she can't think back and remember *seeing* the box that hauled him away, part of her is going to wonder if he's after her."

Now Goliath looked at me and his eyes were gentle. "You'll have those nightmares anyway. You probably know that. But it will be a little easier, I think, if you can tell yourself you know he's locked away."

Silver lights flashed out of the corner of my eyes and I heard a raised voice, distorted by magic. The charges being read against Jude.

They were bringing him out.

"You need to see this, Kit," Goliath said quietly.

Some of that awful panic inside me eased as I looked into his pale blue eyes and I made myself breathe. "Yes." I nodded. I shoved away from him. "I need to see it...and I need to walk."

My legs were stiff and awkward, locking beneath me with

each step as I started toward that house. I wanted to see it razed to the ground. Wanted to know nothing but rubble remained and then I wanted to burn the rubble until it melted away into molten rock.

Instead, I walked across snow-swept grounds, Goliath at one side and a massive tiger at the other side.

Whispers echoed and shivered around me, bodies creeping out of the night. I glanced behind me and saw just how many had hidden in the darkness. Twenty-four cats, I realized. Some of them had hidden so well, I hadn't seen them, hadn't sensed them.

Chang stood beside the leopard and when I glanced at him, staring just over his shoulder, his eyes shifted to the ground. None of them looked at me now.

And Damon was nowhere to be found.

Good. That was good. One less heartbreak to worry about. He could deal with his guilt and whatever he felt away from me.

Pushing thoughts of him out of my head, I focused on others as I walked on.

I knew some of them. Some of TJ's wolves and they stood apart from the cats, watching me solemnly. Unflinchingly.

And the others...witches of the Green Road. Colleen was the only healer among them. The rest were their warriors—five of them. They'd sent five of their warriors after me. A veritable army.

"Come on, Kitty," Goliath said.

I froze when I saw a massive shadow up ahead. Working through the dark night like it belonged to it. My heart jumped into my throat as we rounded the corner and that shadow bled away into the night. What was he doing—?

Then I couldn't think about anything, because now I was standing in front of the house.

And there was Jude.

A mass of people huddled in front, his slaves, all guarded by a long line of guards dressed in the distinctive uniform of the Banner cops. I was stunned to realize how many of the Banner cops were familiar.

One of the slaves was the healer Yasmine. Her gaze cut toward me and then moved back to the front of the house. One of the Banner cops, a slender black woman who stood nearly as tall as Goliath was still reading through the charges.

And Jude stood on the top step.

Impassive.

The woman from Banner wrapped it up and said, "You'll be transported back to face trial with the Assembly. Do you wish to deny these charges?"

Jude's eyes shifted and my heart stopped as he sought me out in the crowd. "I'd like a moment with my property," he said lazily.

"Unless you want to kiss your house good-bye, there's no fucking need," Justin said as he came striding through the door. "People are not considered chattel under the charter and in case you didn't figure it out, Whittier, you just majorly fucked up."

Jude smiled.

Justin stopped long enough to stare at him and shake his head. "You know…part of me is really hoping you'll fight when we go to lock you in the box," he said, heaving out a sigh. "But you're not that stupid, are you?"

"I always seek to comply with the trappings of law," Jude said mildly.

Justin grunted and turned on his heel, striding toward me as the Banner cops started to herd Jude toward a long black box. The magic coming off of it stung my skin, my eyes to even look at it. Somebody opened the lid and I saw the silver lining.

Jude approached it without pause.

Goliath said, "Come on…be a pussy for once and fight."

Jude slid a look in our direction, that queer little smile on his face and started down the steps, a guard at his front and at his back.

A scream, high-pitched, almost deafening, split the night

and that shadow I'd glimpsed separated itself from the rest. It blurred, blended into the night. But only for a moment, and then that shadow became death.

Damon had shifted to his full cat form—a leopard nearly as tall at the shoulder as Doyle, and quicker than any other creature there. It happened so fast, my eyes were still processing it as he powered the guards out of the way and then hamstringed Jude with one massive paw.

Blood splattered out, an arcing spray. The stink of it flooded the air and Jude spun away, even as voices rose in the night.

Damon struck again.

Jude said something, but his words were lost in the roar of voices and magic. The magic, it built so thick, so hard and so fast, it all but choked me.

A leopard's scream tore through the air, defiant and furious even as magic tried to wrest everything under control.

I saw Damon's paw lift, slash down—more blood splattered.

I heard another growl, although how I could hear *anything* over the pounding of my heart, I don't know. Those roars, the fury of them, echoed straight through me.

And Jude…somehow, I could even hear his mocking laughter as he shoved his way to his knees.

My brain finally caught up with what was happening, just as Damon took Jude down, one more time. A giant leopard, crouched atop the creature of my nightmares.

Jude struggling, but the silver bonds on him had his hands restrained. He rolled to the left, trying to dislodge Damon. The harsh, odd stink of vampire blood flooded the air as Damon managed to sink his teeth into part of Jude's throat. But not close enough.

Power screamed through the night and something cut through them. Damon went flying back. Jude…he just lay there.

Still.

Unmoving.

But damn him, he wasn't dead.

I flexed my hand…so desperately wished for the sound of the music.

* * * * *

"Alpha Damon Lee."

The sound of Damon's name came cutting through the courtyard like a blade.

I still stood there, unable to move.

Unable to breathe.

Damon was pinned, trapped by magic.

And Jude was bleeding, oozing black and bitter blood.

If only he'd bleed to death.

But at the sound of Damon's name, in a familiar voice, I forced myself to look up.

Justin.

He stood just outside the puddles of blood and magic crackled around him.

His eyes glowed green and his gaze cut into Damon like a blade. "You will stand down, Alpha."

Damon snarled, his scream building in his throat.

Justin lifted a hand and silver sparked in the air. The scream went silent. Cut-off, I knew. By magic.

Around us, Damon's cats screamed in the night.

But here, in this place, magic outnumbered the clan. "You'll stand down…or you'll fall." A sharp smile split his face. "Trust me, it makes no difference to me."

Then Justin looked to me.

That look packed a punch and I all but fell away as I saw what he held. Mesmerized, I watched as he slowly closed the distance, one step at a time. Yards separated us, but it wasn't enough. Suddenly, I wanted to flee. *Needed* to flee, as he came toward me.

I managed to take one pitiful, paltry step backward before he came to a stop in front of me, his green eyes locked on my face.

"Kit…"

I swallowed.

Mine…they are mine…

He held two things in his hands.

My blade.

My bow.

"Why were they still inside the house, Kit?" Justin whispered softly. He was one of few who understood. One of the few who knew what those weapons were, what my connection to them was.

And he'd know what it meant when I said the next words.

"He broke it, Justin. He found a way to break it." Lifting a shaking hand, I touched the blade and although she felt warm under my hand, although she buzzed with a warm magic, it didn't feel like *mine*. Tears burned my eyes. "They aren't mine, anymore."

I let my hand fall away, but he caught my wrist. "No." He tucked the sword into my hands. "No. They are yours. *She* is yours. We'll find out what he did and we'll fix it."

I stared into his eyes, wondered if he could possibly be right. But I didn't know.

I looked around, keenly aware of what was spread out around me.

Jude, still bleeding, although now two Banner witches were hauling him to his feet.

Damon, nude, shoving upright, and staring at me with eyes that burned.

And everybody, staring at me. Everybody staring at broken, ruined Kit.

Even Jude, the bastard, as he was forced toward that silver box. He watched me with that knowing, taunting smirk. I flinched as I heard the top of it slam shut behind him.

Safe…I'm safe…aren't I?

No. I didn't know if I'd ever feel safe again.

Clutching the sword to my chest, I turned to Goliath and whispered, "I want to go home."

He nodded. "We can start back now. I'll let TJ know I'll stay with you a while, if you want company."

"No." I shook my head and moved forward, leaning my head against his arm. "Take me to Wolf Haven, Goliath."

I had to feel safe again.

He paused and then reached up, hugged me gently. "Wolf Haven is always home to you, Kitty. Come on, then."

It was agony to walk away.

Not because I didn't want to leave the house of my nightmares.

But because I heard a cat's ragged snarl, echoing through the trees with every step we took. Almost as though my walking away from him was painful. Maybe it was.

Each step added to the scars on me, it seemed.

If there was a part of me left unscarred by this, it would be a miracle.

Read on for a snippet from Broken Blade...coming in 2014.

BROKEN BLADE

"Oh, somebody had fun with you..."

I looked up and found myself staring into red, red eyes.

That fear tried to scream at me again, but I screamed back at this time. Flexing my hand, painfully aware of the absence of song in my head, I studied the vampire. Somewhere in the back of the room, a were snarled.

I blocked the sound out. The weight of the Desert Eagle strapped to my thigh was the only thing that mattered right then. Like most modern weapons, the Eagle hadn't ever sang in the back of my head and sometimes I thought that made it easier. I didn't miss the music and it wasn't so painful now as I stared into those fiery eyes.

I missed my sword...I could see myself spinning, striking—

As those red eyes glowed, I forced myself to think past that. He was staring at my neck and that popped the bubble of terror as it tried to swell out of my control.

I realized I was furious.

Vampire. Young. Dead maybe as long as I'd been alive and that wasn't very long. He had some strength, but he wouldn't be much to deal with until he'd seen a century or more.

The gun's weight at my thigh settled me even more and I

realized I could smile.

"Not used to having vamps in here," I said levelly. "We've only got some cheap blood whiskey on hand."

Blood whiskey was the vampire's poison of choice when it came to bars. The older one smiled, a closed-lip smile that didn't show a hint of fang. "That will be fine."

I nodded and went to pull it up. TJ kept it on hand just in case, but it wasn't used often, a synthetic blood blend, mixed with alcohol. It was cut-rate whiskey, I could tell from the smell of it as I poured it, but TJ wasn't going to waste her good stuff on blood suckers. I poured their drinks into the heated glasses and carried them back to the bar, set them down, but before I could I could move away, the older leech reached out, brushing my hair aside. "He was careless."

I backed away, popping my wrist again. "No. He took great care, trust me. He did exactly as he wanted to do. Please don't touch me again."

The vampire inclined his head, nodded slowly.

His companion snickered. "He had a lot of fun, I think. You were all but ripe with fear a minute ago."

My gut clenched and although the magic that connected me to my sword was gone, my hand started to itch and heat pooled there. It hadn't done that in…months. The need to draw the gun was strong. The need to *hurt* something was strong.

I could control it, as long as he didn't make a move, bu—

"I can show you it's not always bad," he whispered, flashing fangs at me.

I drew the Eagle and leveled it at his head before the last word had even left his lips.

The red in his eyes burned hotter, brighter.

"You can't kill me with that," he whispered and cold crashed through the room.

"Want to bet?" I cocked my head and studied him. "You're no more than thirty, thirty-five at the most. That's just a baby. If I bury enough silver in your brain, you're dead, and I mean for-real dead."

He swayed, the moves oddly snake-like but I kept my focus. "You'd never be fast enough."

His partner laid a hand on his arm. "Benjamin. You've upset her. Perhaps we should—"

The younger one leaped.

Vaguely, I was aware that the older one misted away. Benjamin, though...he came at me in a rush. I aimed, squeezed.

His head disappeared in an explosion of blood, brain and bone.

As his lifeless body dropped to the floor, I lowered my gun.

Nobody ever thought I was fast enough.

I guess that's not a bad thing.

ABOUT THE AUTHOR

J.C. Daniels is the pen name of author Shiloh Walker. Shiloh/J.C has been writing since she was a kid. She fell in love with vampires with the book Bunnicula and has worked her way up to the more…ah…serious works of fiction. She loves reading and writing just about every kind of romance. Once upon a time she worked as a nurse, but now she writes full time and lives with her family in the Midwest. She writes urban fantasy and erotic under the pen name J.C. Daniels and romantic suspense and contemporary romance as Shiloh Walker.

Read more about Shiloh & J.C. at www.shilohwalker.com

CPSIA information can be obtained at www.ICGtesting.com
Printed in the USA
LVOW11s2251240714

395882LV00004B/377/P